PRAISE f

"Kept my interest from beginning to end . . . Really looking forward to reading more in Ms. Harper's Grim world, and I definitely recommend Storm Warned if you're in the mood for some Fae."

—Literary Addiction

"Wonder touches Spokane Valley, Wash., and the life of veterinarian Morgan Edwards in Harper's beautifully narrated foray into Celtic myth and legend . . . Harper provides excellent texture and depth with a touch of sincere empathy for animals, rounding out an already excellent novel."

—Publishers Weekly

"Harper skillfully builds characters and situations that evoke empathy for the good citizens of both the human and shapeshifter species . . ."

—Romantic Times Book Reviews

"Storm Warned is captivating! The characters are great and the world the author has built is strongly reminiscent of the original dark faery tales."

—Bibliophilic

"A delicious and elegant read, filled with humor, beauty, friendship, hotness, and a little horror (as things with the fae often are). I think Dani Harper is a MUST READ!"

—Fangs, Wands, and Fairy Dust

"Harper has created touching stories about love and loyalty with an added bonus of humor."

—I Smell Sheep

"Harper's changelings are among the best in the genre."

—RT Book Reviews

"Not your everyday werewolf story line. Changeling Dawn has romance, kidnapping, and murder . . . along with some mystery and intrigue."

—Dee's Musings

"Dani Harper's Changeling Moon is one of those rare stories that literally catches you with the first paragraph and never lets go."

—Author Kate Douglas, author

"Dani Harper breathes life into her characters."

—Coffee Time Romance

THE
HOLIDAY
SPIRIT

Book One of the Haunted Holiday Series

DANI HARPER

THE HOLIDAY SPIRIT

Text Copyright © **Dani Harper 2015**

Published by Dani Harper, September 2015

Walla Walla, Washington, USA

Cover Design by Fiona Jayde Media

Interior Design by Dani Harper

ISBN-13: 978-1517247317

ISBN-10: 1517247314

THE
HOLIDAY
SPIRIT

Dani Harper

For my husband, Ron Silvester,

the best gift I've ever received.

Millions of spiritual creatures walk the earth

Unseen, both when we wake and when we sleep.

~ John Milton

PROLOGUE

Humans milled about the transit station, this way and that, both purposeful and directionless. Their comings and goings reminded him of foolish ducks. And truly, they were little more than livestock to such as him. *Less.* Even livestock would not have been so blind to a predator in their midst. With their light-dependent eyes, the mortals perceived nothing more than another body, an obstacle to be dodged, a being so unremarkable as to be faceless and nameless.

He was none of those things. And his prey's lack of reaction changed in a hurry if he touched them, even if he only brushed against them in passing. A vestige of primal instinct flicked on then, a warning spark that filled them with fear. Some backed up, some excused themselves in a silly attempt to disengage politely, some became angry and aggressive, and others—perhaps the wisest and therefore most deserving to be called *sapiens*—simply started running.

Once he hadn't needed to touch humans at all to get what he needed. Pulling his hands from the pockets of his long dark coat, he let his arms hang loosely at his sides but splayed his fingers (claws retracted of course) and directed his palms outwards—

A moment later, energy began slowly trickling into him. It wasn't nearly enough to nourish and strengthen him, yet he relished its cool and soothing sensation as a desert dweller appreciated water. Humans had many names for it, countless names in numberless languages: *chaitanya* and *prana, ch'i* and *qi, pneuma* and *ruach, napistum* and *ka,* and the one he'd

9

learned first, from the Sumerians: *shi.* All the words meant roughly the same things: *Life force. Essence. Spirit. That which animates the body.* That which animated creatures such as himself as well, though he was insubstantial by nature. In fact, his kind took physical form only to feed.

If anything could be found to feed upon.

He'd left the shadowy domain that birthed him almost immediately, wandering from one dark realm to another, hunting for sustenance. It was a frustrating quest. The absence of light harbored few beings with sufficient *shi* to keep him from fading. There was never enough to satisfy, and certainly not enough to give him the strength he knew could be his, and the power he craved. His needs urged him to bolder action, until finally he'd pushed his way into this over-bright dimension. His reward had been greater than he could have hoped. He, Nah'mindhe, the Unspoken One, had become all but immortal, assured of unceasing existence as long as two-legged creatures filled with *shi* roamed this world. For millennia he'd taken advantage of the easy prey, and dared to believe that there were no boundaries to his strength and power—

Until Time dared to increase *its* demands.

Only a thousand years ago he could walk through a throng such as this and snatch up bits of essence here and there, little extractions that left mortals puzzled by their sudden fatigue but yet living. An hour or two spent amid a crowded dusty marketplace, or a stone arena packed with spectators, would sustain Nah'mindhe for months, sometimes years. The *shi* had simply flowed into him like a river then—and he had drunk long and greedily.

What he could draw into himself now was a mere smattering of rain by comparison.

Humans had not changed over the centuries; they didn't possess any less *shi*. In fact, the swarm in the transit station was fairly glowing with it. No, something had happened to *him*. Perhaps it was his advanced age. He would not give in, however. He would not be satisfied with a pathetic crumb on his tongue in the presence of a feast.

Nah'mindhe put his hands back into his coat pockets. While it was entertaining, merely sipping at the energies of humans as a moth sips at flowers in passing was never going to be enough. *Moths have short lives.* He had even begun to weaken at one point and, like the moth, was forced to spend every moment of his awareness seeking nourishment.

The problem lay in the fact that he had to assume a corporeal shape before he could take in energy. That hadn't been a concern during the first few millennia in this plane of existence. Gradually, however, becoming tangible, physical, required more and more of the precious *shi*. For years, he'd been forced to conserve his energy, hopelessly caught in a paradox of requiring more yet having to spend it in order to obtain it.

Desperate, Nah'mindhe began singling out individuals and draining them of every bit of their life essence at once. It renewed his strength immediately of course, but the practice brought its own set of annoying complications. For one thing, he was designed to absorb *shi* gradually. Draining his prey completely necessitated that he hide away and rest like some bloated python until he'd assimilated all of it. Plus, it was increasingly difficult to move about in this world unseen— especially when both living and electronic witnesses had to be avoided, and bodies needed to be disposed of. He'd quickly learned that if he left lifeless humans strewn about, it panicked the rest of the herd, and eventually he had to leave to find easier prey.

No more.

After years of trial and error, a marriage between magics from antiquity and medical practices of the present day provided him with an elegant solution. Nah'mindhe could now go wherever he pleased, *and all the energy came to him.* Even now, as he stood passively in the Plaza, energy was being channeled into him. None of it came from the humans waiting for their buses. No, this originated from his private collection, many life essences directed into an invisible conduit like small tributaries feeding into a river. Wherever he was, the *shi* flowed to him, into him.

All he required was a steady supply of the young and the strong—

Blue, green and white buses arrived and departed. People boarded, disembarked, boarded again. One woman in the crowd caught his attention as she crossed the sidewalk and entered the Plaza. Her aura was bright, and her life force shone in her eyes. She was smiling, happy, radiant. *Her* shi *must be exceptional.*

Nah'mindhe, the Unspoken One, smiled too. And followed her.

ONE

The handles of her heavy shopping bags were probably leaving marks on her arms right through her coat sleeves, yet Kerri Tollbrook was transfixed by the giant screen in the window of Northtown Mall's electronics store. The most awesome video game in the world (according to her nephew, Drew) was being demo'ed: *Siege of Tiannon*. Kerri watched every high-resolution detail with a horrified fascination usually reserved for witnesses of slow-motion train wrecks and car accidents. A hulking forest troll battled a dragon. Blood shot everywhere as the dragon bit off the troll's arm, then the troll split the dragon's skull with an axe. Dragon brains, dragon scales and even one of the reptile's large golden eyes appeared to splatter the front of the screen and slide down it. When the bloody mess cleared, a large contingent of heavily armed soldiers appeared, climbed the dead dragon and sliced at its destroyer with their swords. More blood spurted and pooled as they somehow managed to decapitate each other instead of the troll. The realistic graphics left absolutely nothing to the imagination—

She jumped a little as a sudden deep voice spoke right next to her.

"You probably don't want this game in your living room."

A dark gray hoodie hid most of the tall man's face, but Kerri could feel the color rise in her own. Good grief, was she actually *embarrassed* to be caught watching this? Darned if her gaze didn't snap right back to the screen, though.

The troll was still standing, despite his wounds—until a flock of gryphons suddenly swooped down. Half-lion and half-eagle, they used their beaks and claws to blind, then disembowel, the hapless monster. Kerri had a fairly strong stomach but ... *eeyew!* The gryphons proceeded to feast messily on both troll and dragon carcasses, while a pack of were-rats left the forest shadows to devour the fallen soldiers.

"From the ratings, I was expecting some kind of heroic quest, not a bloodbath," she muttered. "What the heck is the point of this game?"

"Probably to make your wallet lighter."

"My eight-year-old nephew thinks he *really* wants it."

"Of course he does. He's eight. But if he gets it, it's just going to end up in the nearest donation bin as soon as his parents get a good look at these graphics. Besides, where's the warm fuzzy feeling in wrapping up all this gore as a Christmas present?"

She nodded. Her gaze was still riveted to the screen, but other parts of her were starting to notice that the man beside her had a great voice. Deep, melodic, with just a slight rumble...the kind of voice that begged her to lay her head on his chest and listen to its vibrations. The kind of voice that aroused extremely pleasant vibrations within her, too. "Christmas is supposed to be a magical time of year," she said aloud.

"Supposed to be," he said, so softly she could barely make out the words. "Not always."

The sudden sadness in the words jolted her into turning away from the window, and she finally took her first good look at the guy beside her. Kerri's eyes widened, and the video game was completely forgotten. Not because he was broad-shouldered and powerfully built, and the hooded sweatshirt simply added to his *fresh from the gym* look. Not because his ruggedly handsome features matched his sexy voice. Not even because his eyes were an arresting shade of golden brown. And not even because he was only wearing socks, not shoes. *But because she could see right through him, all the way to the nineteen-foot Christmas tree on the other end of the brightly-lit mall.*

"You're a ghost!"

He looked shocked. "You can see me?"

"What's the big surprise? You didn't react when I could hear you."

"It's not the same. Lots of people hear me, but usually they just chalk it up to their own thoughts. I talk, and they think they just had a great idea. Or they think they've overhead someone else's conversation."

"But I talked *back* to you!"

"Not that much of a novelty. More people talk to themselves than you can imagine. I even read a blog about how it's a way of focusing your thoughts." He pointed at her. "But nobody *sees* me. Why aren't you running away, screaming?"

Kerri shrugged. "I see the dead all the time. It's what I do."

"It's what you—wait a minute, I'm not dead!"

Instinctively, she glanced around. A couple seated on a bench near the food court watched her and whispered to each other. *Great. I look like I'm talking to myself again.* At least the incessant Christmas music from the sound system had likely drowned out what she'd been saying. She turned her face back to the game display, lowering her voice just in case. "Look, how 'bout we continue this without an audience? Besides, I have *got* to put this stuff in the car before my arms get longer."

Too bad she couldn't ask the guy to carry her bags. He looked like he could portage a piano without breaking a sweat. Ah well, big and strong didn't count for a lot once someone had died. It certainly didn't help them accept their new reality and move on. The Universe must have led the guy to her for help. Kerri's tired feet protested, but she walked briskly through the mall, anxious to get to the parking lot. The crowds of trudging shoppers yielded to her determination and made way for her.

"I'm not dead you know," he said frequently. She didn't dare answer until they'd passed the mall security guard and left through one of the double doors.

"Yes, you are!" she whispered fiercely.

"I'm not. Believe me, I'd know if I was."

"Really? Is that why you're walking through the snow with no shoes on?"

"That's not my fault!"

"Listen, bud, you're a disembodied spirit in denial." She wasn't usually so blunt, but she was tired, and the guy wasn't budging on his story. "You're going to make this so much harder for yourself." *And me.*

"Make what?"

"Crossing over. Moving on. It's probably what you need to do."

Exasperation showed on his face. "What I *need* is your help, lady."

"No question about that." She juggled her purchases around until she could just reach her purse. Before she could make up her mind whether to put the bags in the snow or dig for her keys with her teeth a man ran past, neatly grabbing the purse and all the bags from her left hand.

Kerri didn't hesitate, but ran after him. "Hey! Stop!" She was in good shape but the thief was faster, dodging back and forth through the maze of snow-covered cars until she slipped and went down—

And someone caught her arm before she hit. Her long hair fell across her face as she was eased to the ground, and the helping hand was gone before she could see who it was. What she did see was a sudden furious blast of wind that whipped up snow and ice and gravel from the pavement to form a small whirlwind in front of the fleeing thief. She watched in amazement as the icy vortex pelted the man until he was forced to a stop with his arms over his face—and dropped his ill-gotten prizes.

What the hell? A few other shoppers in the lot were staring at the localized phenomena as well. But she wanted her stuff, dammit, so she scrambled to her feet and plunged forward. She was just four car-lengths away when the twister evaporated, and the thief scrubbed his eyes clear, swearing. He saw her then and dropped down to gather up the loot—

"Don't you dare!" she yelled, trying to go faster without wiping out again.

Suddenly her newfound spirit friend appeared beside the purse-snatcher and whispered something in his ear. The thief shrieked as if the bags had suddenly become snakes. Crab-walking backwards, he finally flailed to his feet and ran away, stumbling and falling several times as he went.

The ghost stood beside her packages as she approached. His arms were folded, and he looked pissed. "What the hell did you think you were doing?"

She stopped. "What?"

Whatever he might have said was drowned out by the rapid approach of several fellow shoppers, who gathered her bags for her, oblivious to the ghost standing among them. Every one of them asked her if she was all right, and one older lady kept patting her arm. Kerri was surprised to see a teenager running towards her with an honest-to-god policeman in tow! As it turned out, the officer had been parked in front of the mall on another call.

Quickly Kerri gave a description of the would-be-thief, which was corroborated by three other witnesses.

"Glad you're okay, ma'am. If you find anything missing from your bags, let us know," said Officer Hughes, putting his pad away and handing her a card. "Or call if you remember anything else about the guy who did this. I'm sorry to say there's a lot of it going on at this time of year, and you can be sure he's going to try to rip off somebody else."

"I promise I'll phone you," said Kerri, although she doubted that the terrorized thief would be committing a crime for quite a while. She thanked the bystanders who had come to her aid. Three of them helped carry her bags and walked her to her little red Ford Focus, where she put the packages in the trunk and made a show of locking the lid with a key. Once inside the driver's seat, Kerri gave them all a thumbs-up as she locked the doors and switched on the ignition. Satisfied, they waved and left. *What would they say if they knew there's a ghost sitting right next to me?*

As the last Good Samaritan disappeared, she turned to look at the guy in the passenger seat. His golden-brown eyes still gave off a helluva glare. "What on earth are you so upset about?" she asked.

"*You* chasing that perp! For the love of God, he could have had a gun or a knife or he could have just beaten the daylights out of you. What the hell were you thinking?"

Actually, she'd been thinking of a spell she could use.... "Maybe I thought I could handle it."

"What if you were wrong?"

Protective much? "Thanks for your concern, and for your help," she said, striving for patience. "It would have been horrible to lose all those gifts—even if I could afford it, I don't think I could brave another trip to the mall so close to Christmas. The crowds will be even worse next week."

"You're taking this way too lightly."

"Not really. I'll get wobbly-kneed later when I allow myself to think about it. And maybe you're taking this too seriously. As in, you're kind of a hall monitor. What's up with that?"

Surprise crossed his face, then he sighed. "Brody says the same thing on a weekly basis. Calls me *Mr. Responsible* when we're not on scene. I'm a—well, I *was* a firefighter for about eight years."

"I'll bet you were in charge too."

"Incident commander usually. I hoped to make chief one day."

There was nothing in his expression to give him away, but Kerri's instincts detected a subtle note of disappointment in his voice. Her heart went out to him at once. It was the toughest part of her calling, hearing about goals and dreams that could no longer be achieved. Sure, she tried to point her clients into moving on, and most eventually did. But disappointment *hurt*, dammit, and she couldn't help but hurt with them. Suddenly changing the subject seemed like a great idea. "So, what's your name?"

"Galen. Galen McAllister."

"Kerri Tollbrook. And hey, what you did was pretty awesome, you know. Most ghosts can't manifest as well as you can."

"That's because I'm not a ghost."

Aaand we're back to this. "Many of the newly departed have a hard time adjusting. It's totally normal."

"There's nothing normal about it."

"Death is pretty normal, actually."

"I'm *not* dead," he said through clenched teeth. "I just need your help."

She folded her arms and surveyed him. "If you really want help from me, then you're going to have to take the first step."

"What's that?"

"Admitting that you're dead."

"For God's sake, haven't you been listening? *I'm not dead!*" he shouted.

Kerri put her hands up in a show of surrender. "All right, all right, maybe the *d* word is too traumatic for you right now. We'll slow down and start from scratch, okay? When did you, um, *notice a change in your state?*"

"Day after Christmas, last year. I woke up and found that I was separated from my body."

A whole *year* of denial? "We have a word for that."

"Look, I can show you my body. It's in Sacred Family Hospital. In a bed. Being tended to like a houseplant. Because I'm not dead."

She stared at him then. "Omigod, are you in a coma?"

"No. And hey, your teeth are chattering," he said.

"It's nothing. J...Just takes a while for the car to warm up." She was hugging herself and shivering. In the mall, her coat had been far too warm, but it wasn't helping much now. She was feeling the aftereffects of the attack, not the winter weather. It had shaken her more than she first thought, but still she tried to make light of it. "I swear, it's c...c...colder inside this t...t...tin box than st...standing outside."

Suddenly the car was filled with warmth. Kerri found herself drawing balmy air into her lungs and felt her body immediately relax. She touched the steering wheel, then the seat. Both were warm to the touch. The windows cleared as if by magic. "*You* did this?"

Galen shrugged. "Seemed like a good idea. Since you were, uh, *cold*." He made quotation marks in the air with his fingers, and she knew he saw right through her bravado as surely as she'd seen through his image at the mall.

"Thanks," she said quietly. "You know, I've never met a spirit with your abilities."

"You meet them all the time?"

"Ever since I was little."

"Don't take this the wrong way, but isn't that kind of creepy? You sound like that movie with the kid and the psychiatrist."

Kerri shook her head. "Those ghosts were depicted as gory and scary. It's really not like that."

"What *is* it like?"

It wasn't often—okay, make that practically *never*—that she got the chance to talk to someone new about this part of her life. Usually, the dead were pre-occupied with their own issues, and the living were seldom receptive to this kind of information. She took deep breath. "All the women in our family, as far back as anyone can remember, can see ghosts. In my lifetime, that means my grandmother, my mom, my aunt, my cousins. I grew up with this. I was taught not to be afraid of them, that ghosts are just people. And I learned to listen to them and find out what they want."

"And what is it that ghosts want?"

"Some just want a little attention. Some have unfinished business that they need to work through, emotions they have to process. Some want to get a message to a loved one. A few—" she looked pointedly at Galen. "—don't understand they're dead. You can see why I might jump to conclusions about you."

Without warning, her car shifted into gear, backing out of the stall on its own then began wending its way towards the street. "Hey! Stop that!"

"We're going to the hospital. So you can jump to some different conclusions."

"You can't just... *Fine*, I'll go, but let me drive my own damn car!"

"Why? I'm a good driver."

"Galen!"

"Oh, all right. Have it your way."

The engine died, and the car came to an abrupt stop near the end of the vast parking lot. Muttering angrily about *pushy ghosts*, Kerri put her seatbelt on and restarted the vehicle. Out on the street, she threaded her way through traffic, grateful that Spokane's rush hour was long over, and headed for Sacred Family Hospital.

* * * * *

Room 440 was exactly as Galen had left it. Nothing ever changed, yet it was still a punch in the gut every time he saw his body lying so still and silent, with white tubing and pale blue connectors everywhere. The bed was surrounded by machines with incomprehensible knobs and dials, and little red and green lights that were anything but festive. The noise was the worst—god in heaven, how he *hated* the Darth Vader sound of the ventilator. Yet when he regarded his body, an aching sadness threatened to envelope him, almost like the homesickness that had overwhelmed his ten-year-old self that first time at summer camp... Galen pushed the melancholy away as he always did, and focused on the unusual woman beside him. Her rich auburn hair was trying to escape from its ponytail, and another reddish curl broke free as he watched. It looked soft. Probably smelled good too, but he wasn't in any condition to check it out.

"Okay, Galen, I'm saying it. I was wrong. You're definitely not a ghost. I'm really sorry I didn't believe you sooner."

To his surprise Kerri walked over and sat in a chair next to his bed, took hold of a big pale hand (was it really his?) with both of hers. He tried to imagine the sensation of her fingers against his skin. He was so completely divorced from his body that he could no longer feel what it felt. Dammit, some days he missed *touch* more than anything...

"So, you really get that many people in denial?" he asked.

"A lot of people think death is nothingness, that somehow they'll stop existing. They're pretty surprised to find themselves still aware, thinking, seeing. Feeling emotions. Things they associate with life. So, they're often confused. Other people have so much fear built up around the idea of death that it's too scary to contemplate, even after they've passed on."

"What, they just ignore the evidence?"

"You'd be surprised what people can make themselves believe."

She was rubbing his hand now, his arm. Although it was hard to think of them as his own. After all, *he* was over here, awake and aware, standing near the door. Near enough that the night nurse, a tall black man with gray hair, passed within inches of him. Fred Granville, right on time as always. *This should be interesting.*

Fred stopped short when he saw Kerri. "Sorry, ma'am—didn't know you were here. Visiting hours ended a few minutes ago, but you take all the time you want." He appeared to shake off his surprise, and went about his business like the professional he was, checking the monitors, adjusting this and that, and writing on his clipboard, but he eyed Kerri with curiosity all the while. "Nice to see Mr. McAllister get a visitor for a change," he said at last. "You family?"

"Just a friend. I've—I've only just heard about Galen. I can't believe what happened to him."

"Damn shame is what it is. Young and strong and *bam*—he ends up like this and no one knows what's wrong with him."

"Really? But he was always so healthy," said Kerri. "He worked out, you know. He was a fireman."

"I'd heard that. Well, he's still healthy. Just not awake."

"When do you think he'll wake up?"

"That's the million-dollar question. Five minutes, five weeks, five—well it could be a while, ma'am. Patients like this have their own timetable. You gonna visit again?"

She nodded. "You bet I am."

"Glad to hear it. Because what Mr. McAllister needs is someone to talk to him, read to him. I try to do a little of that in my spare time, but patients like this need a lot more. Gives them a connection to the world. Sometimes even gives them a reason to wake up."

"I'll bring a book next time."

"There you go. Music's good too, if you know what he likes. My name's Fred by the way. I'm on most nights."

She shook his hand. "I'm Kerri. I'll see you next time, Fred."

The nurse gave her a mock salute as he left the room.

Galen nodded approvingly. "You sure won over old Fred. That's not easy, you know. He's a real good guy, but he's also damn smart and an ex-Marine. Served in Vietnam and should have retired long ago, but I've heard him tell people he'd *rather wear out than rust out*." He paused for a long moment. "Fred doesn't even know me, but he comes in every day on his breaks and reads the newspaper to me. To my body, I mean. I—uh—I usually make sure I'm here then just so he's not reading for nothing."

"Does he see you?"

"Nope. He doesn't hear me either. But somehow, he usually knows where I am. When he talks to me, he's not directing his words towards my body on the bed, but always to wherever I'm standing. Doesn't matter where that is in the room, he almost always gets it right." As he often did, Galen breathed a prayer of thanks for the nurse. The guys from the station had come by frequently at first. They'd tried hard, telling Galen the latest jokes and work-related stories. But as time rolled by and he still hadn't responded, the visits naturally become fewer and fewer until hardly anyone but Brody came by anymore—and then only for a few minutes. Galen didn't blame them in the least, any of them. But it had been steady, dependable Fred who had kept him sane as those first few terrible weeks stretched into months....

Kerri's voice brought Galen back into the present. "A lot of people are sensitive that way. Most don't even know it."

"Speaking of things you don't know, what about those things you told Fred? Were you just making stuff up, so you'd sound like you knew me?"

"I admit I was fishing for a little information, but you'd told me yourself you were a firefighter. So is my cousin, Keith. He works out and so do most of his friends. Looking at your arms, it doesn't take a detective to guess that you hit the gym regularly."

He was pleased that she'd noticed. "I miss it. I miss a lot of things. You held my hand and I miss being able to feel that." Galen hadn't planned to say that out loud. The novelty of being able to talk to another human being—especially a pretty red-haired woman—must have loosened his tongue. "We should go," he said. "It's late, and the guy in the bed is a lousy conversationalist anyway."

Rising, Kerri leaned over and kissed his body's pale forehead. "See you later," she whispered in an ear. For one brief instant he allowed himself to imagine the press of those soft lips on his skin, the tickle of warm breath in his ear. Then shoved those thoughts away and headed for the elevator, leaving Kerri to follow.

In the hospital lobby, a group of pink-shirted volunteers were hanging Christmas swags and garlands. A two-foot tree had been set up on the security guard's counter by the door. Kerri scooped up an ornament from the floor and placed it back on the little tree as she walked by, waved at the volunteers and told them how nice the decorations looked. Galen followed her silently out to the car, wondering at her. She was appealing, sure, especially with those big hazel eyes, but she was also something much rarer. She was naturally, unthinkingly kind. Why hadn't he met her when he was, well, *himself*? And would he ever get the chance to be himself again?

"So, do you think you can help me?" he asked as she started the vehicle. She left it in park and turned towards him as much as the seatbelt would allow.

"I could, if you were dead, but a coma? I honestly don't know how to help. I mean, I'll make sure I come by and visit as often as I can, but…"

"It's not a coma."

She raised her eyebrows.

"I know what it looks like. The doctors are just calling it a coma for lack of a better word, because even they admit the symptoms don't match up. And they can't find a reason for it either." He sighed. "Look, will you just take my word on this one? I was right about not being dead, wasn't I?"

Kerri laughed. "Okay, okay, let's say it's not a coma. Then what is it?"

"It's like—like being locked out of my house and I can't find the keys."

"You can't get into your body at all?"

He shook his head.

"That's awful—and really strange. You said you couldn't feel my hands?"

"Not a thing. It's like my body's been stolen. Or maybe *hacked into* and somebody changed the password."

"So, you weren't in an accident? No injuries, no illnesses? Bug bites? Food poisoning? Inhalation of smoke or gas?"

"None of the above. Well, a small amount of smoke, but nothing serious—it's the first thing they check out in Emerg when a firefighter comes in. I read my records." Actually, he read them frequently, looking for some little note from one of the doctors, some indication that something had changed, however small, or that they were going to try something new to coax his body into waking up. There'd been no encouraging entries for a long time except the same general assessment of his condition, which was pretty damn low on the neurological scale. *It's a wonder someone hasn't yanked the frickin' plug on me by now.*

He knew the answer to that of course. Physically, his body remained as healthy as ever. His muscles were still strong and sound, and his organs worked just fine—to a point. *Why can't I breathe on my own? Why is my body unresponsive? What goddamn switch got turned off?* Those same questions fascinated both his own doctors and the new ones who came from other centers just to see him. They all concluded that Galen's condition wasn't a true coma. But what it *was*, no one knew. And at this point, no one had any new ideas to check out either.

Kerri's voice shook him out of his dismal thoughts. "What's the last thing you remember doing?"

"Everything should have been routine that last day. Go to a fire, put it out, go back to the station. Except I didn't go back to the station. There was only one weird thing, a guy who ran back into the building after we got the blaze under control. I went after him..." Galen spread his hands. "And then nothing. I don't remember a goddamn thing until I woke up standing next to my body in that hospital room." *Why can't I remember more?* He'd asked Kerri for help, but just what had he expected when he had so little information to offer her? He tried to brace for the inevitable *I'm sorry, there's nothing I can do* speech.

"You know, I'm not as sensitive to it as some members of my family, but I could swear I felt an undercurrent of magic in your room. I wonder if it's a spell."

Okay, he wasn't expecting *that*. In fact, there was a time when he'd have laughed at such a notion. He didn't believe in magic. He wasn't too sure he believed in ghosts although Kerri obviously did. But magic? Of course, he'd loved reading fantasy stories as a kid. But surely that's all they were, just stories. And yet, what other explanation could there be? "I really don't know much about that kind of stuff."

"I'm still learning, myself. But my Aunt Elizabeth—actually, I call her Aunt Libby—is well-grounded in magic. I think we should ask her what she thinks."

"'Well-grounded in magic.' That almost sounds like an oxymoron. I've always pictured magic as kind of ethereal, wispy, airy-fairy, you know? Imaginary."

She gave him a look. "This from a man who's gotten locked out of his own body? Trust me, there's nothing *airy-fairy*—or imaginary—about it. Magic is actually very earthy, especially the type that Aunt Libby practices. She's a wonderful healer you know." Kerri checked the time on her phone. "Right now, she's giving a lecture and slideshow on her latest dig, but I can text her."

"*Dig?*"

"She's a history professor but she's also a respected archeologist. That's what she loves best, really. Calls it 'hands-on history.' She's gone out on digs every summer as long as I can remember. I even got to go with her a couple of times." Kerri thumbed the tiny keypad with practiced speed before shoving it in her purse, then proceeded to back out of the parking spot.

"So, your aunt is Indiana Jones *and* she uses magic. You both talk to ghosts. Sounds like your family is pretty interesting."

She laughed. "You don't know the half of it."

"I also don't know where we're going," he said.

"To my place. I'm tired, I'm hungry and I've got a ton of Christmas gifts to wrap."

"Really?" God, how long had it been since he'd been invited into a home… "You're sure you don't mind me hanging around."

"That depends. Are you going to make a nuisance of yourself?"

"Hell, no. I could even give you a hand with those gifts." He hoped he didn't sound desperate then laughed at himself. *Dude, you* are *desperate.* It was late, and under normal circumstances he might have said goodnight. After all, he'd only just met her. He would have thanked her, made a date (*definitely* made a date) to meet up the next day, and let her go home to her life. But these weren't normal circumstances at all. For the first time in a long, lonely, scary-ass year, he'd found someone he could talk to, someone who could hear him and respond. Someone who even seemed to care.

It might be selfish, but he wasn't ready to let go of her, not even for a few hours.

"Really, you can wrap? That would be great. I'm all thumbs, and Waldo isn't very good at that kind of thing either."

Oh God, she had a boyfriend. Maybe even a husband. Why hadn't he thought of that? The sudden flare of disappointment pissed him off, knowing he had no right to *be* disappointed, even as he choked out a reply. "Sorry, I thought you lived alone. I don't want to be in the way."

"You won't be in the way at all. Waldo loves company."

"He'll be able to see me too?"

"Most animals can. Some are upset by it, but Waldo is used to it. In fact, there are a couple of ghosts that come by regularly just to visit *him*."

"Waldo is a—"

"Dog."

TWO

Kerri couldn't say what perverse impulse caused her to tease the guy like that. But the way his face lit up when he found out Waldo wasn't human gave her pause. She liked Galen. A lot. Although she didn't know him well, he had, as Aunt Libby would say, "good energy." But energy was all he *was* at the moment. It was one thing to come to terms with being deceased. She could usually help the spirits she met find some resolution and move on. She could do nothing of the sort for Galen. How could there be any resolution, any peace, for him when he was still living? Basically, he was a prisoner, caught between two worlds and belonging to neither. She glanced at the clock on the dashboard, noted it would be another hour or even two until her aunt was finished with her class. And prayed that Dr. Elizabeth Watson—noted historian and archeologist, experienced shaman and talented witch—would know how to help Galen reconnect with his body.

"Thank heavens they finally plowed my road today." Kerri swung onto a long tree-lined cul-de-sac in an older section of town and parked in front of a Victorian two-story house.

Galen surveyed the ornate but dignified building with its soft greens and cream-colored trim, then eyed its unusual neighbors on each side. "Please tell me this one is yours. I don't think I can go into a purple house."

"It's lavender. We have a lot of artists in this little neighborhood. I kind of like the vermilion one with the tangerine trim."

"In *guy colors*, I'm guessing that's the orange one across the street?"

She smiled and gathered up her packages from the trunk.

"I could help you with those."

"You sure can if you're telling the truth about being able to wrap."

"I am. But I meant I can also carry them for you."

What? "Why didn't you help me with them at the mall?"

"Possibly because you were in such a frickin' hurry to get to the car, and arguing with me about being one of the life-challenged. Here, stand still a minute."

She watched him poke at the packages here and there. She couldn't feel him as he settled in close behind her, but suddenly the entire collection of bags became weightless! "Wow, that's a whole lot better."

"If you don't walk too fast, I should be able to pull this off without alarming your neighbors. I'm sure they don't need to see this stuff floating in the air."

"They probably wouldn't think anything of it. Urban legend says the yellow house at the end of the cul-de-sac is haunted—although between you and me, it's not. And we just had a couple hundred zombie runners divert their race through here last week."

He looked skeptical. "No pun intended, but it's a *dead end*."

"Only for vehicles. There's a jogging trail that runs between that blue house and the coral and white house over there." She pointed. "It links up with a park on the other side. Anyway, hardly anyone batted an eye. Not when Elsie Greenlough frequently walks out to her mailbox without a stitch. But she's ninety, so I guess you can do what you want when you're that age."

"Dementia?"

"Nope, she's as sharp as ever. Nice lady. Just doesn't like to wear clothes."

Galen didn't ask her any more questions—perhaps he didn't dare—until they made it onto the porch. "Can you reach your keys?"

"Don't need them." She leaned close to the door and whispered a word. The latch depressed instantly, and the door swung open.

"Cool. Voice recognition security?"

"You could say that." She decided to explain it later. After she explained a few other things. "Thanks for helping me with the bags. We can—" There was no need for directions. The moment the door closed behind her, all her packages flew from her arms and lined up in a neat row on the dining room table. "Nice flourish, Galen. You must have practiced a lot."

"I don't sleep so I have an awful lot of time on my hands. Might as well learn a few new skills and besides, I like to be busy."

Excited wheezes and gasping snorts sounded above them, and a stocky tan-colored pug raced down the stairs like a small beer keg on legs. After ten years, Kerri still didn't know how Waldo managed not to tumble headfirst.

"What the heck is that?" asked Galen as he caught sight of the pug's enormous eyes, black mask, and jack-o'-lantern grin. "You said you had a dog, not a goblin."

"Hey, be nice. This is Waldo. Waldo say hello to—" There was no need. The little dog had already trotted directly over to her insubstantial companion, hindquarters wagging.

Galen looked stunned. "He can see me!" He dropped to one knee and ran his hands carefully over the dog's thick coat. Kerri saw the fur move a scant second after the hands passed, and wondered again at the man's skill. Meanwhile, Waldo seemed to be in heaven, turning every which way to garner more rubs. Finally, the pug flopped onto his back with his feet in the air, his wrinkly face and bulging eyes looking rather crazed from the odd angle. Galen laughed again and rubbed the well-fed belly.

Kerri hadn't heard him laugh before. For a few moments he looked carefree, just a regular guy having fun with a dog. Ordinary, everyday, and yet more... Suddenly she realized she could get used to this man being part of her own ordinary, everyday life. Of course, her life wouldn't look normal in the least to Galen, even considering his present condition. *And why am I even thinking about such things when I just met him?* "I'll leave you guys to your male bonding while I put some things away."

Two of her shopping bags contained food and she carried them to the kitchen, still wondering at herself. She had a good life, didn't she? Her writing career hadn't put her on any bestseller lists, but it had been successful enough that she'd been able to buy a house she loved. And she found a great deal of fulfillment in her work with spirits. She adored her family, although of course she'd like to see them more—thank goodness for Aunt Libby still living nearby. And she was well-loved by them in return.

But it would be silly to pretend that she didn't sometimes wish for something more…

* * * * *

Galen waved at Kerri without looking, his attention all on Waldo. *This is awesome.* How long since he'd played around with a goofy dog? Could all dogs see him? Funny that he hadn't noticed before. He'd be sure to put it near the top of his mental list of *things to check out.* "Let's go find a toy, buddy. You got a ball or something?"

Waldo's toenails clicked along on the hardwood floor behind Galen as he scouted the living room. On the coffee table sat a trio of boxes with Christmas decorations spilling out. There was no tree yet, but a space had been cleared for one by the window. A bright red and green throw was draped on the couch, and nestled in its folds was—*Bingo!* Galen used his energy to pull the braided rope toy to him. "Hey, bud, how about some tug o' war?" But the pug was watching the doorway, its tight-curled tail doing its best to wag. Galen glanced up expecting to see Kerri and was startled to see an old man instead. A tall thin old man in a plaid flannel shirt.

With an upraised baseball bat.

"Hey—"

"Who are you? How the hell did you get in here?" he demanded, and took a solid swing at Galen. The bat passed harmlessly through him, naturally, but the old man didn't seem to notice anything strange. Instead he readied the bat for a second blow.

Pure instinct caused Galen to throw the rope toy—only to see it fly through the stranger like he wasn't there! He stared at the figure in front of him, unsure if he wanted to accept what his mind was telling him.

With the bat still cocked, the man paused too, glaring until Kerri appeared between them.

"Galen, I'm sorry, this is Everett."

"He's a…" He couldn't make himself say it.

"Yes, he's a ghost. A real one. He used to live here, and now he's my roommate and my friend. Everett, this is Galen. He's a good guy—in fact, he's a firefighter. I invited him here."

The baseball bat lowered to the floor immediately, and the man stuck out an enormous hand. "Sorry. Can't be too careful you know."

Galen gingerly extended his hand. For once he was relieved to feel nothing when the big fingers closed around his own—and kept going. The man was no more substantial than he was.

"Shit, dontcha just hate that?" snorted Everett, retracting his arm and brushing his palm on his shirt in disgust. "Can't even shake hands like a man anymore."

Galen nodded slowly. "Yeah. Yeah, it really sucks." What was it Kerri had said about ghosts? *They're just people.* In fact, Everett sort of reminded him of his Great Uncle Roy.

"Of course, I don't miss the arthritis a bit and my hip doesn't bother me none. So, it ain't all bad," said the ghost. "Mind you, you don't ever get to change your clothes, if that's important to you. I remember my oldest sister used to say she 'didn't want to be caught dead' wearing such and such—and by golly, she was right. Lucky for her that she passed wearing her favorite dress. Only one shoe though. Guess you can't have everything." He stopped and looked Galen up and down. "Though I see *you've* got no shoes at all. Thought Kerri said you're a firefighter. Where's your uniform?"

He'd noticed his shoes were missing, but until now, Galen had never given a thought to his gear. "I honestly don't know. I guess the EMTs must have got my boots and turnout gear off me before I became whatever I am now. Still got the clothes on that I was wearing underneath, though." He indicated the hood of his sweatshirt. "It was a damn cold day, so I had this on under my helmet, trying to protect my ears."

"Well now, that makes more sense. I thought you looked a little old to be one of them skateboard kids." Everett turned his attention to Kerri, who seemed to be trying to hide a smile behind her hand. "Things were pretty quiet while you were out shopping. Don't have a single message for you, just a couple more clients making appointments."

"Thanks Everett," she managed. "I don't know what I'd do without you."

"Probably hire yourself a secretary." He ambled out of the room.

Galen stared after him. "He answers your phone for you?"

"No, not at all, he—well, never mind," she said, then snorted with laughter. "You *do* look a little old to be a skater."

"Thanks a bunch. FYI, this is the stationhouse logo." He pointed at the small red and gold emblem embroidered on the upper right of the dark gray sweatshirt. "Not many teenagers have one of these."

She quelled her mirth. Mostly. Her eyes still danced with amusement. "Look, I'm so sorry Everett took you by surprise. I should have thought to warn you. He's been really overprotective since we had an intruder last year. Are you okay?"

"As okay as anybody can be after meeting their first ghost. Don't get me wrong, I like him all right. Just trying to wrap my head around the whole concept."

"You know, you've probably seen lots of ghosts and not realized it."

His eyes widened. "That's a real comforting thought. *Not!*"

"Let's get your mind off it, shall we?" She checked her watch. "Everett's gone back upstairs to watch the news. We can wrap presents for a while until Aunt Libby gets here. That is, if you're any good at it."

"Ten bucks says I'm very good at it."

"You're on."

* * * * *

Kerri lost the bet, but she didn't mind. It was amazing to watch Galen use his energy to wrap the gifts on the kitchen table. She had to look closely to even notice that his hand movements and his intended actions were slightly out of sync. It reminded her of voice dubs in some foreign movies—lips moved, and the words followed a beat later.

"I admit it, you're doing a great job," she said as she took another finished package and added a cluster of bows and a tag.

"Flattery won't get you out of owing me ten bucks."

"Hey, I had to try. But really, I've never met a guy who does gift wrap, never mind one who does it so precisely. What's your secret?"

"My mother was an architect. She had a thing about straight lines and angles, and so wrapping presents was a chance to teach me about them. Believe me, I got great marks in geometry." He stopped and looked down at himself. "Wonder what she'd say about this?"

Kerri knew he meant his strange altered state. She ventured to ask. "Where's your mom?"

"She's been gone for a few years now. She had cancer, fought it for a long time. Made it to my college grad, though the doctors said she wouldn't. In fact, Mom made it all the way to the end of my first year as a firefighter with the Spokane Department before she passed."

"I'm sorry."

He shook his head. "She'd say there was no need. Towards the end, she said that although her life wasn't going to be a long one, it had been very full. I think it was. She really enjoyed everything, was always laughing about something, loved deeply, and that's more than a lot of people can say."

"I'll bet you miss her," she said gently.

"Yeah, I still do. Mom was one great lady. You'd have liked her." He flourished his fingers over a scrap of paper, turned it into an origami crane. "She'd have liked you too."

"Thanks," smiled Kerri. "Any brothers and sisters?"

"Nope, just me. No dad either. He left before I was born."

"His loss," she declared.

"Yeah. My mom said something like that too."

Kerri wondered what her life would be like without her parents, her three older brothers and their families. They all lived far away now—Ryan even had a job in China at present—and couldn't always get together for the holidays anymore. But a week wouldn't go by without two or three phone calls and virtual buckets of email. At least her irrepressible aunt was always close by. "So, is Christmas a hard time for you?"

"Not at all. My mother would kick my ass if I ever became one of those people who humbugged Christmas. It's the best time of the whole year. Me and the guys, we decorate the station, put up a tree, the whole nine yards— presents, food and friends. The guys who are single take the holiday shifts so the guys with families can be at home, but we have a good time." He snorted. "Sometimes we even have some excitement. My best bud, Brody, barbecued a turkey out back about three years ago. Managed to set it on fire and we had to turn the extinguishers on it."

"You had a *fire* at the fire station?" Kerri was incredulous.

"The deputy chief had a fit. We've all been razzing Brody ever since, and the brass sentenced him to indefinite PR. He's been in charge of every outdoor cooking safety presentation in the community—Fourth of July, Thanksgiving, you name it. In fact, I just watched him give his spiel to the Lions Club. I have to say, the guy's getting pretty good at it."

Kerri wondered what Brody would have thought if he'd known that his best friend had been evaluating his performance.

Galen snapped his fingers then, although they made no sound. "Damn, I almost forgot," he said. "Becker's sister, Samantha, promised she would bring in a Cajun turkey with a dirty-rice stuffing this Christmas. I was supposed to come up with a New Orleans theme for the tree."

He looked genuinely disappointed, and Kerri wished she could grasp his hand. Instead she asked, "You really do love Christmas, don't you?"

"Every minute of it. Don't you?"

"Sure I do. I guess I just haven't met many guys with so much holiday spirit. In fact," she chuckled, unable to resist, "you *are* a holiday spirit!"

He groaned loudly just as the doorbell rang, a deep Westminster chime that suited the old house perfectly.

"Got it," Everett's voice boomed out from the front hallway.

"He answers the door for you too?" asked Galen.

"Not exactly. He can't open the door, he just looks through it and tells me who it is. He does greet some people after they come in if he's downstairs."

"Right. With a baseball bat."

"Only strangers," she said, then lowered her voice. "Besides, there's a bit of a secret about the bat. It's not real, not in the sense of anyone being able to see it or touch it."

Galen's eyebrows went up. "No frickin' way. You are *so* not going to tell me that's a ghost bat."

"It's one hundred percent incorporeal. The real bat was interred in Everett's casket twenty-five years ago."

"What? Who the hell gets buried with a *baseball bat*?"

"Shhhh—not so loud. It's not just any bat. Look at it closely next time. When he was ten years old, that bat was signed for him by Babe Ruth and all the Yankees except three, right after they won the 1923 World Series. It was Everett's most prized possession during his lifetime. He didn't have any kids to pass it on to, so he put it in his will that the bat went with him." She shrugged. "He figured maybe he could get the rest of the team's signatures on it in the afterlife."

The ghost in question stuck his head into the living room. "Just the UPS man, the careful one. Package is on the doormat."

"Thanks, Everett. I'll get it right away."

The old man nodded and a moment later, the theme song of a game show could be heard from upstairs.

"I'll be damned," said Galen. "So that's why—"

"Why he can't open the door, but he can pick up the bat?"

He nodded. "But didn't I hear him say that he had messages for you?"

"They're not phone messages, Galen." She held her hand up as he started to ask another question. "Nuh-uh! Trust me, that's probably all you want to know for now."

"Okay, we'll put a pin in that. But at least tell me why the dude's still here if you help people 'move on'."

"Because I can't make people move on if they don't want to, you know. Everett fully accepts that he's dead, but he prefers to stay right here. He lived in this house for sixty years, and another twenty-five or so since he died. It's his home, his neighborhood. So, I can understand his feelings. And besides, he likes Waldo a lot. He seems to like me too."

"It's easy to see why."

Suddenly Galen was close, very close. His golden-brown eyes had darkened, deepened to the color of aged whiskey. As his hand appeared to brush the hair from her face, she could feel his energy. It vibrated subtly along her skin, cool and sweet…and answering energy leapt within her in response. "You don't know how badly I want to kiss you," he said.

Kerri was surprised at just how much she liked the idea. At how much she liked *him*. And that was a big-time problem. She frowned, and Galen took a couple steps back.

"I'm sorry. I had no right to say something dumb like that."

"I wouldn't call it dumb, just a little *premature*. For one thing, we only just met." She hated to discourage him but somebody in this room had to be sensible, didn't they? Although part of her demanded to know why she was volunteering for the job... "More importantly, you might not be dead but we're not exactly on the same plane of existence. That's a bit of an issue for me."

Nodding, Galen walked back to the couch and flopped down beside a snoring Waldo. He must have been distracted because he misjudged the distance, ending up sitting about four inches above the cushion. Which simply served to underscore Kerri's point.

"You're right," he said at last. "I got carried away. I mean, yeah, it's been a long year and you're the first person I've been able to talk to and all that stuff. But I gotta tell ya—" He looked up and met her gaze. "If this had never happened to me, and I'd just met you in the mall? You'd better believe I'd be asking you out. And I'd still want to kiss you, and I can't apologize for that. I've never met anyone like you."

She'd never met anyone like Galen either. And wondered if she was already in trouble. *Because if we can't get you back together with your body, a relationship with you is going to break both our hearts.*

* * * * *

The night sky was moonless. Only streetlights illuminated the snow, and at this time of night the glow was concentrated along the laneways and parking garages of Sacred Heart. The hospital grounds, with their many ornamental trees and bushes, were layered in shadow, dark upon dark. The cold air was still—yet one of the shadows moved. Shapeless and silent, it glided slowly along the ground, unhurried but with purpose, a steady encroachment of oily blackness that only paused to merge with the surroundings when a vehicle passed by. Each time, like a new cell breaking free of its twin, the thing pulled away from the darkness that sheltered it and continued its winding course. Finally, it veered away from the brightly lit emergency center and flowed directly to the building that housed the hospital's neurology department.

Nah'mindhe, the Unspoken One, had been there many times...

Locked doors provided no barriers. Less substantial than air, he slid effortlessly through the seams, then hugged the walls within like the stain of long-ago floodwaters. The elevators sat idle, but he didn't require them. Instead, he simply entered the nearest and rose upwards through the shaft, as slow as the final exhale of the dying.

Like the last breath of the young woman at another hospital.

The Unspoken One made his way to Room 440, slipped under the door, and assumed a physical form at the foot of the bed. A delicious satisfaction rose in his heartless breast as he surveyed the body of Galen McAllister. Still strong, still healthy. *For now.* To a human's limited view, the man was attached by tubes and wires to a number of machines, but to Nah'mindhe, there was much more to the picture. Long thin conduits of purest energy, *shi*, sprang from the body's various chakra points. The essences merged into one silvery channel—and that channel led directly to *him*.

It was a brilliant system. Through experimentation, he'd perfected both his spells and his methods. Now, dozens of hapless humans were in his thrall at any given time. They were scattered all over the country, yet intimately connected to him, sustaining him with their *shi*. The result was that he now enjoyed a level of power nearly equal to that which he'd commanded millennia ago—and he needed to spend very little of that energy in obtaining more. Other mortals tended to the donors, believing them to be ill and caring for their needs as they lingered in *La'atzu*, between the planes of existence.

Nah'mindhe didn't need to bother with them further, yet he soon developed an interest in viewing his private collection regularly. Humans tended to gloat as they amassed their useless treasures. He was *evaluating his assets*. He wanted to know when a body was all but drained, because there was one last delight to be savored...

The *shi* left the dying body not as a pitiful stream, but in a final concentrated rush, the *Ezebu Shi*. Though it was smaller, the burst of energy and light was not unlike the nova of a dying star, and being in close proximity to the event afforded him pleasure like no other, a perfect satisfaction that bordered on bliss. He drank deeply then, devouring all the precious essence, and in that brief but exquisite moment felt more alive, more powerful, more like the immortal being that he was. *More like a god.*

Later, he would carefully select a replacement: young, healthy, with *shi* that was vivid and strong.

The Unspoken One considered the body on the bed, and the glowing umbilical of energy that connected him with it. He could feel the subtlest of changes in it, a barely discernable lessening of its flow. "Of all my subjects, Mr. McAllister, you have lasted the longest, and I believe I shall miss you most of all. Not for your personality, of course." He smiled at his own joke. "But for your *shi*. It has been quite exceptional."

The fireman would last a month more perhaps, as humans measured time. No more than that, despite the mortal's undeniable strength. *Perhaps even less.* Nah'mindhe would make a point of lingering in the area for a time. He would take no chances on missing Mr. McAllister's moment of *Ezebu Shi.*

It would surely be impressive.

THREE

Thanks to hours of practice on countless electronics department TVs, Galen didn't require a remote to surf channels on the living room screen over the fireplace. Kerri had said she had "work to do" and retreated to her office in what was once a sunroom at the back of the house. It was on his mental to-do list to ask her what she did for a living, but it didn't take a rocket scientist to understand that right now she wanted some space between them. He'd been honest about his feelings, sure, but there was a time and place for honesty, and it had been too soon. So here he was, flipping back and forth between old holiday movies, *A Christmas Story*— Ralphie's quest for a Red Rider rifle reminded him of a pellet gun he'd desperately wanted for his ninth birthday—and *National Lampoon's Christmas Vacation*. Someday he'd like to cover a house in 25,000 twinkling lights, just for the sheer hell of it…

Shit.

There was that weird feeling again, like something had just crawled out from under a rock and slithered through his brain. If he was still in his physical body, he'd probably have broken out in gooseflesh, maybe even shivered. Brody, who had more damn superstitions than a Vegas gambler, would have said it was "somebody walking over your grave." *Nice mental picture there. Not!*

The doorbell chimed again.

"Elizabeth's here!" Everett called from the hallway, and Galen was surprised the old guy had gotten to the door so fast. *I guess he was right—there* are *a few advantages to being a ghost.*

Kerri's voice was muffled from behind her door. "Coming!"

A moment later, Galen saw her sprint for the entry, and he followed at a discreet distance. She flung open the door to reveal Everett already out on the porch, chatting with a smartly-dressed older woman who was resting her hands on a slim black cane with a silver handle. She looked anything but formal, however. Her hair was busy escaping from a loose twist, the pale strawberry blonde curls every bit as untamable as Kerri's auburn ones. Her eyes weren't the same color as Kerri's, light blue rather than rich hazel, but they were no less bright with intelligence and fun. Even without the old ghost's shouted introduction, Galen would have known who she was.

"Get in here quick before you freeze!" insisted Kerri.

"Everett was just telling me about your guest." The woman allowed herself to be hurried inside by her niece, and surrendered her long woolen coat to the antique hall tree by the door.

Kerri hugged her fiercely. "Omigosh, just *feel* how cold you are! Why didn't you use your key?"

"Because I left it in my other purse, that's why. I got your text and came straight here from my classroom." The woman turned to regard Galen, who was standing back in the archway to the living room. "Your young man doesn't look very much like a ghost to me, hon."

"Aunt Libby, this is Galen McAllister." Kerri reached towards Galen to pull him closer, then seemed to realize that it wouldn't work. *Sorry* she mouthed as she retracted her hand and jammed it in the pocket of her jeans. "This is my aunt, Dr. Elizabeth Watson. She's a professor of history at the university."

"Glad to meet you, Dr. Watson," said Galen.

She snorted. "You're too old to be one of my students, hon. Call me Libby."

"Okay. Libby then. What kind of history do you specialize in?"

She didn't answer. Instead, she walked around him carefully, tapping her cane on the oak floor as she went, studying, pondering, considering. Finally, she unshouldered her enormous handbag and from its depths produced a fist-sized chunk of what looked like raw quartz. Thick crystals speared from it in all directions, and Galen wondered why the prickly thing hadn't stabbed its way right through the purse. Kerri's aunt balanced the exquisite formation on her upraised palm—then proceeded to pass it back and forth right through him!

He looked at Kerri for an explanation, but she had her fingers pressed to her mouth, probably to keep from laughing. She had to know he was biting his tongue to keep from asking questions.

The older woman returned the rock to her purse. "Milk," she declared. "I do believe we need a little milk magic."

"Beg your pardon?" asked Galen, but Dr. Watson—*Libby*, he reminded himself—simply motioned them all to follow her into the kitchen. *What the heck is milk magic?* That sounded like he was seven years old again and messily mixing chocolate syrup into a tall glass of the white stuff. Or possibly a little later, after he and his grade-school buddy Dave perfected the art of grossing out girls by drinking lunch milk through a straw and shooting it out through their noses… Galen again glanced at Kerri for a clue, but she just shrugged and dutifully took a half-gallon carton from the refrigerator as her aunt selected a bright blue mixing bowl off a shelf and set it on the table.

"I hope this'll be enough," said Kerri.

"Are we making pudding, or sharing a communal bowl of Fruity Pebbles?" asked Galen. "Enough milk for *what*?"

Libby simply laughed. "I'm sorry, hon—this probably looks insane to you! Although you manifest far more powerfully than any ghost, I still need some help in order to discern details. Half the time I'm looking right through you, you know. My niece has a much stronger gift than I do in that regard." She poured the entire contents of the carton into the bowl, then bent over it to whisper a few words:

"Element of water mixed with nurture's essence white,

Reflect the luster in this room, reveal him to my sight!"

She straightened. "Now Galen," she said. "Please humor an eccentric old lady and place one of your hands in the bowl."

"You're not old!" he blurted.

"And believe me, that's wonderful to hear. However, Kerri's dad is the baby of our family, and what my mother called *the door prize*. I'm twenty-two years older than he is, so I'm pretty certain I qualify as a senior, and Social Security happens to agree."

He had no reply for that. Galen did the math in his head twice, but *no frickin' way* did the woman look to be in her seventies.

"The bowl," Libby reminded him, tapping it with her finger. "Put your hand into it."

Kerri gave him an encouraging nod, enabling him to comply with the weird request without further questions. Slowly Galen immersed his insubstantial right hand…and abruptly the milk began bubbling. Every bubble then reformed into a tiny bead of liquid that *traveled up his arm*. Soon the bowl was empty, and strings of tiny white droplets clung to each of his arms and hands, and even his face. At a word from Aunt Libby, the droplets simply sank into his spectral shape—then merged. They quickly coated the inside of his image as if they were filling a mold.

"You're painting me!"

"Exactly," she said.

He couldn't feel the milk. It might have been steaming hot, ready to froth a latte, or cold enough to make ice cream for all he could sense—but Galen could feel *something*. A vibration maybe? Energy? Whatever it was, it wasn't unpleasant, and he reveled in the novelty.

Meanwhile, Kerri's aunt peered at his head, his face, his eyes. Then she turned her attention to his hands. She didn't touch them but asked him to hold them straight out in front of him, palm up. As she inspected them, his mouth quirked. It was like trying to prove to his mom that he'd washed up before supper. *I never did manage to fool her…*

"Young man, your astral state is remarkable," declared Libby, bringing him back to the here and now. "And your lifelines are quite long by the way."

"My what?"

"In your hands. I can see them clearly now. *Here*. And *here*." She traced her finger over both of his palms. "More importantly, you have a unique energy," she said. "Bright and strong, plus a powerful aura as well. That's the good news. Let's put the milk back where it belongs now, and we'll talk."

Not yet. He turned to Kerri, unsure of what he wanted to do or express except that he simply had to touch her, had to make some kind of connection however fleeting. The possibility that he might actually feel something was too great a temptation. Libby was shouting something in the background that sounded like *wait*, but he had already raised his bright white hand to Kerri's face, smiling as he softly stroked her cheek—

Kablammo.

The milk lost its structural integrity just as his fingertips made contact with Kerri, and every bit of the liquid transferred itself to her as surely, and as instantly, as if he'd dumped a bucket over her head. She gasped for air, snorting milk out of her nose better than he or Dave ever had. Streamers of it ran from her hair and soaked her blouse to the skin, clearly revealing beautifully rounded breasts tucked into a dark lace bra. For a stunned moment Galen could only stammer out apologies. He should have been able to manipulate the milk and remove it from her—he'd driven her damn *car* for heaven's sakes—but surprise had ruined his concentration completely.

Fortunately, Aunt Libby was more on the ball. She tossed a handful of dish towels to her niece from a nearby drawer.

"Are you okay?" he managed to ask as Kerri gratefully wiped her eyes.

She snorted. "My doctor told me I needed more calcium in my diet," she said wryly. "But I'm not sure if I can absorb it through my skin. Excuse me." Blotting her hair and face, she left the kitchen, leaving a wet trail on the hardwood floor.

Libby shook her head and followed her niece. At least Waldo was happy—the stout pug's tightly curled tail waggled back and forth as he lapped up milk from the floor as fast as he could.

Sighing, Galen turned to search for a mop or something, but he'd completely forgotten about Everett in the corner of the room. The old man burst out laughing and slapped his knee. "Did you *see* Kerri-girl's face? That was better'n anything I seen on the TV in *years!*"

"Glad you liked it," he said without enthusiasm.

"Aw, now, son, it ain't that bad. It was just milk. And hey, at least she didn't cry over it!"

After a moment, Galen grinned too. "No. No, she didn't. So, you think she'll still talk to me?"

"She's not the kind to hold a grudge. Unless of course you're planning to leave her kitchen like this?"

"Hell, *no.*" Cleaning up the mess was the least he could do. He glanced into the deep linen drawer and was surprised to find a few neatly folded dish towels still in it. As a bachelor, he'd owned maybe three in his apartment, and two were usually in the laundry. Shrugging, he concentrated on wiping down every inch of the counter, the cupboards and— much to Waldo's disappointment—the floor.

Everett looked on with something like longing. "Nice job. Watched you wrap those presents like a pro too, but I sure can't figure out how you did it. You think you could give an old fart a tip or something? I don't need to know any fancy tricks. Just that it'd make things a whole lot easier if I could change the channel on the damn TV myself."

"I'd be happy to try," said Galen. "But I don't know if what I do will work for a—for a real—well, you know."

"*Ghost.* You can say the word, son. I ain't sensitive about it." Everett nodded to the door. "The gals are in the living room now. We'd best make an appearance."

Kerri was wearing a thick plaid shirt that hung almost to her knees, and Galen was both relieved and disappointed that it effectively hid most of her appealing shape. Fortunately, her reddish hair drew his gaze away from temptation. Freed from its ponytail, it seemed to have taken on a life of its own, its bright tendrils coiling into tiny spirals.

I'd love to pull one of those curls just to see it bounce back... Galen resisted the impulse to smile as he took a chance and sat beside Kerri on the couch. "Can you stand to hear another 'I'm sorry'?"

"Oh, it's all right." Her smile made him believe it. "I know darn well you didn't mean it. Besides, it was only milk, not tar, and I'm totally washable."

And didn't *that* put a picture in his head he didn't need?

Thankfully, Kerri's aunt began speaking. "Let's get down to business. As I said before, Galen, your energy is bright and strong. But there's also a darkness around you that isn't your own." She exchanged a look with her niece. "Thanks to the milk, I could see a very complex pattern in place, similar to a binding spell, yet it's not anything I'm familiar with. Nasty for certain, though. Maybe even vindictive."

"Do you have any enemies, Galen?" asked Kerri. "Any rivals or competitors? An old lover with a grudge, maybe?"

"It doesn't have to be recent, either," added Libby. "Was there anyone who didn't like you as a child? Or perhaps was jealous of you as a teenager?"

"No. At least, not that I remember." He searched his brain anyway but came up blank. The closest thing he'd ever had to an actual enemy was Amy Braithwaite, who had tripped him on purpose when he was walking back to his desk after sharpening a pencil. *We were only six years old, so I'm guessing that's not grounds for a magical vendetta. Besides, I was the one who banged my head on a desk and needed stitches!* "My mother didn't raise me to mistreat people, and that makes it kind of tough to accumulate real enemies."

"No one obvious then. Well, we're going to need a great deal more information, and quickly," said Libby. "Where is Galen's physical body?"

"At Sacred Family Hospital," said Kerri. "Visiting hours end at eight, though, and it's past ten."

"Good. I'd much rather go after hours. There'll be far fewer people around. But—" The older woman pulled a phone from her pocket and checked the screen. "I have an early morning class. Tomorrow night would be much better for me—we could meet there about eight-thirty, I think. And that gives me some time to do a little research beforehand." She rose and headed for the entryway. "Will you walk me to my car, hon?"

"Absolutely."

Kerri helped her with her coat, and was just about to usher her onto the porch when the door shut in front of them. "What the—?" Recognition dawned in her eyes when her own coat suddenly leapt from the hall tree and wrapped itself around her. "*Galen!*"

"I'll just be waiting on the porch," Libby said tactfully, and winked in his direction as she slipped outside.

"I can dress myself, thank you!" Kerri chided, fumbling with the buttons.

"I'm sure you can," he said. "But your hair's still wet and I don't want you to catch cold on my account." He stood firmly in front of the door—although he wasn't overly sure he could stop her, he could certainly slow her down—and handed her a hat and scarf. "Besides, you're not really dressed for the occasion. We don't want the neighbors to talk."

Kerri snorted. "Are you kidding me? With Elsie Greenlough living down the street?"

"She probably wouldn't appreciate the competition."

"Fine." She jammed the knitted hat over her unruly hair, and he opened the door for her.

As she passed, he whispered. "You know, I like your aunt's direct approach, but even close relatives can get turned away by security that late at night. Ten bucks says they're not going to let you in tomorrow."

"*They* don't know Aunt Libby. And I'd love to win my ten bucks back. You're on."

As her aunt's old Lincoln Continental disappeared down the street, Kerri made her way carefully up the icy flagstone pathway to the front porch. The temperature had dropped further, but Galen had her arm, and as insubstantial as he might be, she was confident he'd find a way to catch her if she fell. A tiny voice in her head piped up: *Who's going to catch you if you fall in love with him?*

She sighed inwardly. Aunt Libby had pointed out that Galen was safer staying with one of them. Both their homes were strongly warded to defend against any number of things—*except renegade milk!*—and it was obvious that whoever had separated Galen from his body had malevolent purpose. Kerri could have sent Galen to stay with her aunt, knew darn well it would have been a more sensible choice, but she felt better being able to keep an eye on him right here. *You just didn't want the guy to leave*, said that annoying voice. *You like him.*

True enough, but she wasn't completely crazy. There were damn well going to be some ground rules.

Kerri stopped in front of the door and put her hand up before Galen could open it for her. "We need to talk about boundaries," she said. "This is my home. It's my place of business as well as my sanctuary. I have work to do and clients to see, plus I need uninterrupted sleep and a healthy dose of privacy just to stay sane."

"You think I'd invade your space?" He frowned. "Besides, you don't exactly live alone. What about Everett?"

While she could see her own breath in the cold, there was no mist when Galen spoke. It strengthened her resolve. "Everett and I have an understanding. He likes *his* own space too. That's why he has a TV in his room, and his favorite chair, and almost all the things that are important to him. I never go in there, except when he invites me or asks me to change the channel."

"So, you're saying that you guys have carved out some kind of peaceful co-existence. I don't intend to cause trouble or get in the way, you know. And don't forget that I asked you if you'd prefer that I went with your Aunt Libby."

"Believe me, it's a big point in your favor. Don't get me wrong, I'm happy to have you here. I don't want you to feel unwelcome in any way. But I need to show you something. Stand right here while I go in and close the door. Then see if you can follow me."

"Is this a game?" He waited on the porch as asked, however.

As she crossed the threshold, she quickly made a sign with her hand that activated the ward to the entry. Closing the door, she waited.

There was a muffled *thump*. And several more thumps, followed by a few choice words, the ineffective rattling of the heavy brass knob, and then, finally, a tremendous *bang*. The thick century-old door didn't so much as quiver. She took her time taking off her coat, her hat and scarf, and hanging them on the oak hall tree. Out of the corner of her eye, however, Kerri saw Galen's face appear first at one window, then another. She grinned as she heard him try the knob on the kitchen door, then the upper balcony door over the dining room. Nothing yielded to his efforts—*of course.*

There was some banging on the roof then, followed by Galen's voice echoing down the long brick chimney into the empty fireplace. "I hope you know that Santa's not bringing you anything this year!" It had no effect. Not even a particle of soot was dislodged.

Finally, there was a quiet knocking at the front door where she stood. Kerri opened the door and looked up at Galen with a smile. "What can I do for you?"

"Very funny. You made your point. I don't know why but I can't get in."

"Unless I invite you," said Kerri, and gestured for him to come inside.

"What, like I'm a vampire?"

She laughed. "Same principle, except it works with everything. Ghosts, mortals, spells, energies—and you."

"Whatever I am," he said. "I'm guessing this is where you tell me that invitations can also be revoked if I don't behave. Am I right?"

"You got it. But I'm pretty sure that won't be necessary. The basics are simple: when I'm sleeping, I'm sleeping, and when I'm working, I'm working. Just don't bother me during those times, and we'll get along great."

His hood was shadowing his face again and she could only catch a glimpse of his frown. *He's not mad. He's worried.* So was she. Worried, concerned and afraid for him. Kerri locked the door behind him, and this time she deliberately made the sign to activate the ward in front of Galen.

He just shook his head. "I guessed it had to be magic. I've never *not* been able to get into a place. But now I gotta ask: you're not just feeling sorry for me, are you? I don't want to be like a stray cat or something."

"Trust me, I want you to be here," she said, and led the way to the living room.

"I want to be here too. I'm wondering if it's such a great idea for you, though. It's pretty tough to have a relationship with a ghost."

"I can be *friends* with anyone I want," she said lightly as she flopped on the couch. "And besides, you're not really a ghost." She knew darn well what he meant, however, and she was *so* not going anywhere near the R word. *Too soon.* Too soon even if he was a nice, normal wrapped-in-a-physical-body kind of guy. *We just met, for Pete's sake!* So why did it sound like she was trying to convince herself?

Because I already care about him way more than I should, that's why. And this can't possibly end well unless the spell is unmade.

FOUR

Waldo the pug came rollicking down the stairs and raced for Kerri's lap. She braced herself for the impact, but he landed like a furry cannonball just the same. "You're such a little lead-butt," she crooned to him as she rubbed his velvety ears.

Everett arrived in the room a moment later. "You've got six clients lined up for tomorrow, Kerri-girl."

"Thanks, Everett. How early?"

"I figured ten was soon enough."

"That's perfect. I'll be able to get in a couple hours of writing before anyone comes. Thank you so much for setting that up."

"Hey, I know what works around here and what doesn't. See you in the morning, folks." He waved and left. After all, the late night classic movie would be starting any minute.

That was usually her cue to go to bed, but Kerri pushed her stocky pug off her lap and headed for the kitchen instead. She was positively *starving*. Small wonder too. Had she had anything since that latte at the mall? *Dumb, very dumb. My blood sugar is probably too low to even register right now.* No way would she be able to sleep well without some nutrition, especially protein. She was finishing off a small container of peach yogurt while checking out the low-fat dinners in the freezer when Galen came in, followed by an enthusiastic Waldo. *Somebody's had a good belly rub.*

"You said something about writing, but you also said you see clients. I never asked you what you do for a living," said Galen.

Kerri decided to go with the easy part first. "I write quite a few things actually. Magazine articles about the paranormal, a weekly blog for Otherworld News, plus I try to get two novels out a year. Urban fantasy mostly."

"*Urban* fantasy… So not swords and sorcerers but more like werewolves and vamps and things that go bump in the night? Surely you get enough *strange* in your life just by being able to see ghosts."

"One person's strange is another person's normal," she laughed. "Besides, the novels are purely for entertainment, both mine and the reader's. Fiction, you know? I watched every single episode of *Buffy the Vampire Slayer* as a teen and my family claims it's influenced me for life. They could be right."

He nodded then. "My mom really loved that show too. She was always trying to get me to watch it with her, but I just wasn't into it. Too busy with sports and Xbox, I guess. Hey, can I see one of your books? I could use some reading in the middle of the night."

"You'll find them on the bookshelf by the fireplace." Kerri popped a dinner into the microwave and pressed buttons. "All twelve of them," she added. She wasn't trying to impress him. She was just hoping for a distraction, that curiosity would compel Galen to head out to the living room right away to check out her work…

No such luck. Instead, with smooth movements that looked easy and natural, he pulled out a kitchen chair and sat down at the table. Obviously he'd gotten his focus back, and she braced herself for the questions she knew were coming.

"How about telling me the big secret now? Only you and your family can see or hear Everett, and we already established that he can't open the door or pick up the phone. So how the heck does he manage to take messages and make appointments for you?"

The microwave pinged as if punctuating his question. Kerri opened the door and checked her meal for doneness. It was ready, but was she? There was no point in delaying her answer however. If Galen was staying here, he was going to find out the truth for himself at ten the next morning. *He's handled everything else so far...* She carried her steaming food to the table and sat across from him. "My clients," she said carefully, "can see and hear Everett just fine."

Kerri watched his face as he made the connection. Clearly it wasn't the answer he'd anticipated.

"You—you're scheduling *ghosts*?" he managed.

"Why should that be a surprise? You already know that I see them and talk to them. You just *met* one for heaven's sake."

"Yeah, but I'm having trouble wrapping my head around the fact that you're fitting them into time slots. Seeing ghosts is one thing, but organizing them?"

"Well, it's pretty hard to have a life if they're popping in and out all the time."

He stared at her for a long moment, but finally seemed to shake himself free of the initial surprise. "I guess it would. You must see a lot more ghosts than I first imagined. I figured a few, maybe a handful…" He waved a hand. "I have no idea where to start guessing now. A dozen? *Two* dozen?"

She might as well spill it all. "Since I started setting appointments a few years ago, I've been visited by nine thousand, six hundred and thirty-three individuals," she said.

"Holy shit!" Galen's eyes were wide now, but she saw no panic, no rejection, just honest amazement. "I'm sorry, I just had no clue. That's—that's beyond incredible. Hell, Ebenezer Scrooge only had to deal with three."

"Four, actually." She drank deep from her cup and bliss crossed her features. "I don't keep a running count of my clients, but Everett does. He's amazing with stats. I think it comes from decades of watching baseball."

"So, nine thousand-and-something ghosts. All different?"

Kerri nodded. "That's the number of first-time visitors. I do have a few that come by regularly *just because*. Most spirits are content after one or two visits, thank goodness, or I'd never fit in as many as I do."

"Are you helping all of these ghosts to move on? Telling them how to *walk towards the light* or something?"

She shook her head. "Of course not, only the ones that truly need it and want it. Like I told you when we first met: ghosts are just people. They can get lonely. Ghosts can see and talk to each other if they want to. Like making appointments with Everett. But to be acknowledged by the still-living after being literally invisible to the world you knew for a long, long time?"

"Priceless," finished Galen, nodding. "Believe me, I have a little bit of experience in that department."

A line from one of her own novels sprang to mind: *People, people all around, and not a soul to see me...* What was it like to be Galen McAllister? Knowing that he wasn't dead and helpless to do anything about it. Trapped in a bizarre limbo for nearly a year and, for all he knew, it was never going to end. Ghosts could communicate with each other if they wanted to—but he had never realized he had that option. Only the strongest of souls could withstand that kind of isolation, could stand up to the ongoing fear and uncertainty. *I'd be terrified,* she thought. *Completely and totally terrified.* Her eyes teared up at the thought and her hand slid across the table towards his. Kerri wanted so much to connect with him in some tangible way, but whether it was to comfort him or to comfort herself in that moment, she couldn't say. It wasn't possible of course. Or so she thought until he pushed his hand forward, palm down, so that his fingertips met hers—

Warmth flooded through her hand, like soft rays from the early morning sun in her summer garden, sweet and gentle. The sensation traveled partway up her arm before gradually receding until only her fingertips were warm where they appeared to touch Galen's.

She smiled and left them there.

"So why do you do it?" he asked. "Why visit with ghosts? I can't imagine that life-coaching the dead pays very well."

"It's not a job, silly," she said. "It's called respecting the gift I've been given. They need my help, and I have a responsibility to do what I can. That's what I learned from my family, and I believe it. You know how everyone talks about *following your passion*? Well, I feel strongly about the work that I do with spirits—it's very rewarding—and I also love writing. How many people get to have *two* passions they can follow at the same time?"

Galen nodded, but she could tell by the thoughtful furrow in his brow (as best as she could see it under his hood) that he wasn't finished asking questions.

"If you feel so strongly, why were you hesitant to tell me about being a ghost consultant?"

"A *ghost consultant*." Kerri laughed a little. "I like that. I'll have to put it on my business cards."

"Jesus, you have business cards for this too?"

"Of course not, I'm just teasing you. I do have cards, but only for my career as a writer. Ghosts hardly need business cards. They have a grapevine that makes the Internet look like a cave painting. That's how they find me."

"Okay, back to my question: why didn't you want to tell me? You talked about ghosts when you first met me, but then you put me off twice when I asked about Everett's secretarial duties."

Kerri sighed. "I talked to you quite freely about ghosts because I thought you *were* one! For Pete's sake, I don't go around advertising my ability. Honestly, would you have believed me before this happened to you?"

"No, not at first. But I'd like to think I'd have tried. I know I would at least have respected that *you* believed it. By the way, your dinner is getting cold."

She poked a fork into her food and discovered he was right, but resolved to eat it anyway. She just didn't have the energy to get out of the chair and ferry the *Chicken Broccoli Alfredo* back to the microwave. But Galen scooped up the dish and did it for her. She watched as he pressed buttons and a half beat later, the numbers appeared, and the microwave started. How much had he practiced to perfect his unique abilities?

"Thank you," she said. "I have to admit that I'm really tired. And I should have asked if it would bother you if I eat in front of you."

"It would bother me more if you didn't eat, especially after I just slaved over a hot microwave for thirty seconds." He winked at her. "Don't worry about me. I can't smell the food, so it's a lot like looking at a television commercial."

"I don't know. Those things sure make *me* hungry. Especially the ads that come on late at night."

"Fast food joints know that your resistance is down after dark. Everything looks more appealing then."

Maybe I need to keep that in mind, she thought. Because Galen certainly looked appealing, in more ways than one.

"Eat," he reminded her, and waited until she'd taken a few bites. "If you've always had this ability, I'm guessing things might have been a little rough at school."

She nodded. "It wasn't easy. I can't remember a time when I couldn't see ghosts, and the more I talked to them, the more came to visit me. I didn't think anything of it until age five when the little girl next door, Jennifer Rossi, told her mother that she didn't want to play with me anymore. Jenn said I had 'too many imaginary friends.'"

"Let me guess. Her mom talked to yours?"

"You bet she did. Mrs. Rossi was a nice lady, but really concerned that I lived in a fantasy world. I didn't, of course.

So that's when my family sat me down and we had a talk about setting boundaries." She laughed. "Actually, it was the first of many, many talks on that subject."

"And that's why you had that little chat with me on the porch. I wasn't all that sure you were going to let me back in, you know."

"Of course I was! But I have a lot more protections in place than what you experienced. For instance, no spirits are allowed in the house between six p.m. and eight a.m.— except for Everett, of course—unless they have a specific invitation. I'm very strict about that now. Aunt Libby worked the spell for me."

"You set business hours? For ghosts?"

"Well, hey, a girl's gotta get some sleep some time." She laughed a little. "Of course, I had to learn that the hard way."

"On one level, it's all very common sense. But on another, it still seems a little surreal!"

She shrugged. "For me, it's just normal life. I have my work and I have my family. And Waldo of course." She reached down to rub the furry head that was presently leaning against her leg and snoring loudly.

Galen paused for a minute as if trying to decide how to phrase his next question, but Kerri could guess what he was going to ask—and decided she would share. There was no denying that she felt more comfortable with Galen than with almost anyone she'd ever met, as relaxed as she was with her family. In fact, she felt like she'd always known him. That annoying little voice in her head chimed in: *And you'd like to know him a whole lot better.* "I don't have a significant other, or anyone campaigning for the position either. I've certainly gone on more dates than I did in high school, but they tend to fizzle after two or three. There were a couple of relationships too that didn't last too long."

His brows rose at that, and Kerri explained: "It's not that hard to understand. First of all, it's never easy hanging out with a writer. We tend to keep to ourselves a lot, spend long hours over a keyboard, drink too much coffee, constantly stress over deadlines, and run off to jot down an idea at any given moment of the day or night."

"Right, you're such a difficult person to be around," he grinned. "I don't know how I can stand to be in the same room with you."

She rolled her eyes. "Seriously. But even if the guys could handle the writer aspect—and I admit, some of them found it kind of cool—they drew the line at ghosts. Then, instead of being an interesting *creative-though-slightly-eccentric* author, I was just plain crazy."

"Couldn't you show them? I would have tried to prove it to them."

"I only did that once. Most ghosts don't manifest well enough to have an effect on the human world. But I knew one that could, and before she crossed over, I asked her to please demonstrate her presence to my boyfriend." Kerri shook her head. "Never again. I learned that it's not fair to force things on people that they really *really* don't want to know. He left the next day, after some pretty hard words."

"That sucks. No wonder you didn't want to talk about what you do." Warmth pulsed in her fingertips as he again brought his hand to hers. "But for the record, *I'm* not running away."

"I am, I'm afraid." She got up and took her dishes to the sink. "I have to run off to bed. I'm too tired to keep my eyes open anymore."

"Sorry. I didn't mean to keep you up. But I gotta tell you, it's been the best day of the whole year for me, and I have you to thank for it. Have I mentioned that I've never met anyone like you?"

"You might have. For the record, I've never met anyone like you either." She decided to take a chance and say what she was thinking out loud. "You know, if we were dating, I'd definitely want to see you again."

"Yeah?" He looked pleased.

"Yeah. Ghosts, magic, spells—it's a lot to take in, but you're dealing. I like that in a man."

They left the kitchen laughing. Connection pulsed between them, then flared strong and clear as they paused at the bottom of the stairs. Without thinking, she put her hands up, as if she could slide her arms around Galen's neck and pull his lips to hers. Just as she realized her mistake, however, he suddenly winked at her. His big hands circled her upraised ones, and she felt that same warm, sweet energy that had teased her fingertips now lightly bracelet her wrists. Galen bent his head and pressed his lips first to one palm, then the other. It didn't feel like a kiss, exactly, but more like tiny circles of mild electricity that tingled pleasantly in her palms. An answering vibration tugged deep within her as he smiled and released her.

You're in so much trouble, her little voice said to her.

Shut up, she told it, and headed up the stairs where Waldo was already waiting on the landing for her.

* * * * *

Galen looked up from his book as Kerri came downstairs in her pajamas. The amazing auburn jungle of her hair looked even redder against the rich blue bathrobe she'd thrown on and left untied. The robe's belt clung by a single loop and trailed behind her like a tail. Without looking left or right, she headed straight for the kitchen.

I think I'll just wait a couple of minutes before saying good morning...

The fast-paced novel—*Romancing the Wolf* by Kerri J. Tollbrook—pulled him back in immediately however. When he looked up again, he found its author sitting in a velvet wing chair across from him, where the morning sun transformed the dark reds in her hair to an autumn blaze. Her hazel eyes had taken their color from her blue robe, the smile on her face could melt a snowman at fifty paces, and she was cradling a large mug in her hands as reverently as if it were the Holy Grail. One of her slippers had fallen off and her socks didn't match. Right then and there he decided that he liked this image much better than the beautiful-but-totally-professional photo on the back flap of the book.

"You made coffee for me," she said. "Thanks."

"Just trying to earn my keep."

"Yeah, well, keep this up and you can definitely stay. Your coffee is way better than mine, believe me." She nodded at the book in his hands. "I'm sure to write better today with such high-quality fuel."

"Not sure you need to get much better. I opened this up to read a sample and now I'm on page two hundred and seventy-eight. Can't wait to find out what happens to Mitch and Martina."

She beamed. "And now you've just made my day."

"Well, I'm at the part where the vampire captured the hero. Can't leave him there, you know." He eyed her with mock sternness. "But Mitch does get away, right? Because Martina just turned into a werewolf, and she could really use a shoulder to howl on."

"You'll get no spoilers from me." Kerri glanced up at the mantel clock and slid out of the chair. "Gotta go. I have to write for a while before my clients start arriving. I just turned in a manuscript, but I'm trying to finish a synopsis for the next story before my edits arrive."

"Before you leave, I gotta ask—will I be able to see your clients like I see Everett?" Galen didn't know what answer he really wanted. From a practical standpoint, it was probably better to be able to see what—or who—was walking around the house.

"Of course you will!"

"Why 'of course'? Am I'm starting to see ghosts because I'm near you?"

"Like my abilities are contagious?" she snorted. "*Not.* I told you, I think you've seen lots of spirits since you've been out-of-body. You just haven't recognized them. Didn't you think Everett was an ordinary guy at first?"

"An ordinary guy with a baseball bat."

"Okay, but that's a different issue. Look, when *I* see a ghost, he isn't a hundred percent substantial. For instance, I can see through you if really try, or if I look longer than a few seconds. It's different for Aunt Libby. To her, spirits are nearly transparent, as if they're made of glass. But in your case, I'm thinking that ghosts probably appear as corporeal to you as the living because you're in both planes of existence right now."

"English?"

"You have a foot in two worlds. Both look completely normal to you."

He thought a minute. "Okay, I'll buy that."

"Don't worry about it. Besides, Everett usually comes downstairs to direct traffic so it's not like you'll have to deal with anybody." She paused in the doorway. "I was too tired to think about it last night, but I really felt guilty this morning about just leaving you alone like that. Are you awake all the time? Every minute? You don't rest, or close your eyes, or take a break?"

"Believe me, my body's getting more than enough rest for both of us."

"I guess it is. But don't you get bored? Everett watches TV all night."

"So I heard. I didn't think *Matlock* was still on the air."

She laughed. "What can I say? There's a network that shows nothing but vintage programs and movies, so I turn it to that channel for him in the evening. But you haven't answered my question. I don't want you to be bored while I'm working today, so is there anything you need or want?"

Actually, he thought of something he'd like a whole lot, and it was wrapped in a blue robe... Galen shook himself free of that thought—mostly—and held up the book instead. "No worries. I have Mitch and Martina to keep me company. And I can turn on the TV all by myself."

"Great. See you later."

Temptation vanished as the office door closed a few moments later, and he wished he could smack himself in the head. Funny how he hadn't thought about sex overly much since he'd gotten booted out of his body. Of course he'd continued to look at pretty girls—hey, he was a guy after all—but it was almost out of habit. And now? The intensity of his feelings for a woman he just met had surprised him. The powerful physical desire that came with it was a shock.

I think I just proved that guys don't think with their penis. After all, he'd been reduced to visiting rights only when it came to his own...

FIVE

Kerri had suggested that he might want to remain in the living room while she saw her clients. But after Everett ushered the very first ghost from the entryway to her office, Galen couldn't contain his curiosity. The spirit was a short round man with a thick pair of glasses. Hunched over, he bowed his balding head as he wrung his stubby hands. The gesture touched Galen deeply, putting him in mind of some fire scenes where the shell-shocked survivors stood on the sidewalk, praying, pleading with deities, the EMTs, the cops, the firemen, and the universe in general. Everett was surprisingly comforting, patting the guy on the shoulder (although his hand didn't connect), and telling him things would get better.

Sure enough, the man stood a little straighter and the hand-wringing had disappeared when he was escorted back to the front door. That piqued Galen's interest too—the fact that the clients used a door at all. He'd truly expected them to pop in, well, anywhere they liked. *Kerri really* does *have this organized.*

The second ghost was female, maybe sixteen, maybe even younger. Hard to tell under the generous black eyeliner and even thicker layer of pure *attitude*. A large hockey jersey (the Seattle Thunderbirds) gaped loosely over her narrow shoulders, revealing the thin straps of her lime-green bra. The long shirt knotted at one hip showed off jeans so tight they could have been painted on, and cutouts where the back pockets should have been. Had she been older, Galen might have enjoyed the view. Instead, he averted his eyes until she disappeared into the office, wondering if her parents knew she was wearing pants like those in public—

That's when Kerri's words came back to him full force: "You've probably seen lots of ghosts and not realized it."

Well I'll be damned. If he hadn't known in advance that these people were dead, he wouldn't have noticed a thing. They appeared to be as substantial as any other person on the street. No transparency, no fading in or out. Certainly nothing like the movies. Kerri had been right, the ghosts looked perfectly normal to him. *So does Everett, come to think of it. I wonder why I didn't question that before.* But then, why would he when the man seemed so completely ordinary?

Galen left his book on the couch and ventured to the threshold between the living room and the long hall, in hopes of catching a glimpse of the next client. But the formal entryway was empty. Did Everett meet them outside? Galen could have walked through the door himself to find out, of course, but he preferred to maintain an *unofficial observer status* and zipped back into the living room to a window. Sure enough, the front porch served as a virtual waiting room. The short man and the young girl were gone now, but there were four more people—four *ghosts*, he corrected himself—awaiting their turns. Everett was having an animated conversation with one old guy in a fishing vest as if they'd been friends for years. Maybe they had been.

Things got even more interesting when the mail carrier came into view. Without hesitation, the uniformed woman walked up the flagstone pathway and mounted the steps…and passed right through the little gathering to deposit a fistful of letters through the slot in the door. Galen's brow furrowed as she re-crossed the porch to leave. He couldn't see one single lick of difference between her and any of the ghosts. One was as solid in appearance as the other.

He saw Everett check his watch, then head through the door. When he reappeared, the girl in the Thunderbird shirt accompanied him, minus a little of her attitude. Galen wondered what her story was as she walked down the sidewalk and vanished from sight.

Meanwhile, the old man was already escorting the next client—a dedicated *Goth* dressed in black—to his appointment. Galen continued watching through the window, fully expecting Everett to return to the front porch.

"Boo!" The gravelly voice behind him made him jump.

"Shit, Everett!" If he'd had a physical heart, it would be hammering out of his chest. And who'd have guessed that he could still be startled out of his skin when he didn't even have any? "I never heard a damn thing."

"Well, us ghosts are *supposed* to be sneaky. I gotta stay in practice, you know." Chuckling, Everett headed up the stairs and motioned Galen to follow him.

* * * * *

"You really don't mind being dead?" Kerri surveyed the young man in her office and pegged him for somewhere between eighteen and twenty. Matt Evan's mohawk was dyed as black as his clothes, his lips and nails likewise the color of night. Piercings ringed his ears and tattoos covered half his face, while his t-shirt boasted a white skull with a small gray dragon wound around it.

"Fuck, *no*. That truck mighta done me a solid because the concerts are just too fucking awesome! I can go anywhere." He spread his arms wide. "*Anywhere* a band is playing, you know? I can follow their whole fucking tour if I want to. Don't have to pay for a ticket or rush for a good seat. I get to check out the band backstage, even ride in their fucking tour bus! Did you know the bass player for Nirvana brings his iguana with him? His name is Boris."

"The bass player?"

"Naw, the lizard. Big-ass reptile, about five feet long but really laid back. He's like their good luck charm, got the band logo painted on his side!" He leaned forward and whispered, "Non-toxic, natch—they take really good care of the scaly guy."

Kerri couldn't help but smile. It wouldn't be the first time a fierce exterior hid a kind heart. "I'm glad. But if you're having so much fun, why come to see me?"

Matt's face sobered at once. "It's my sister. I been gone about a year now, and Mel's still really down. She doesn't know I'm *okay*, ya feel? How come even Boris can see me and hear me, but my own baby sister can't?"

"Animals just seem to have an extra sense," said Kerri, and waved a hand at Waldo. The pug was sitting at Matt's feet, looking up at him.

"Yeah. Yeah, I guess," he said at last, and waggled his ring-clad fingers at the dog, who favored him with a wide panting grin. "But it's not fucking fair."

"Doesn't seem so, does it?" she agreed. "Would you like me to try to get a message to Mel? It sounds like your sister needs to feel some peace."

"Hell yeah, that'd be awesome, but there's more, see? There's this blonde bitch in our neighborhood been offering her meth, says it'll *help her with her pain.*" His fingers made air quotes around the words even as he shook his head. "Mel can't go down that road, you feel me? She's a good kid, got good grades. Hell, she's up for a fucking scholarship. All she ever wanted was to be an animal doctor, used to bandage up our old dog all the time." Matt's voice caught, and he slumped back in the chair, hovering halfway through it. "I tried to scare off that drug-shovin' skank. Nothing works. Not a fucking thing I do."

"Mel's still in danger as long as she's around."

He nodded miserably.

I think this is gonna be one of those times I really *love my job.* "You know where this dealer is, where to find some solid evidence that the courts can use to put her away?"

"Fuck, yeah, I know her whole ring. I even know where they cook the stuff."

Kerri picked up a pen and a pad of paper. "Then why don't we give the police a few anonymous tips?" Matt's face brightened as he unleashed a veritable torrent of information—names, addresses, and more. She had to write fast to keep up, and it wouldn't be the first time she wished that otherworldly voices could be captured on the little digital recorder she used to save new story ideas.

When they were finished, and Everett escorted a much-relieved Matt to the front door, Kerri surveyed the stack of scribbled paper in her hand and made a mental note as well. She'd find a way to visit with Mel of course, but she'd also speak with Waldo's veterinarian, Morgan Edwards, in Spokane Valley. Maybe a little mentoring plus some hands-on with animal patients could help Matt's sister move forward with her life and her dreams.

* * * * *

"You do this appointment thing every day?" asked Galen, catching up to the old man.

"Four, five days a week, 'cept for holidays and vacation. Lots more ghosts this time of year, though. From now through January, Kerri'll probably be booked solid. Normally she'd take a break, but her family won't be home for the holidays this year."

"I still can't believe how structured this is."

Everett snorted. "It is *now*. Son, you shoulda seen it when Kerri first came. Ghosts bothering her at all times of the day and night. She ran herself ragged—couldn't sleep more'n a couple hours at a time. I chased off a lot of 'em but more would always come."

Galen had a mental picture of the guy swinging that baseball bat like a knight with a sword. "She's lucky to have you for a friend."

"Yeah, well, I'm pretty lucky too. Can't tell you how glad I am that she bought my house six years ago. Had a couple other owners before her that bugged the bejeebers out of me. Kerri-girl, now, she's different. Darn good company, that's for sure, but real thoughtful too. Come on in and see for yourself." He passed through the third door on the second floor.

Galen followed—and found himself in another era. From blond furniture to aqua wallpaper to brocade curtains to black and white photos, everything in the big room was straight out of the nineteen-fifties. Everything, that is, except the big flat-screen TV on the opposite end of the room. The modern television's silvery remote sat on a small Formica table next to what was clearly the oldest piece of furniture in the entire collection: a faded overstuffed chair in which Everett sat.

Or rather, *most of him* sat. One leg protruded right through the cushioned arm, while the rest of him appeared to be sunk halfway into the turquoise upholstery. Galen had to remind himself that the old ghost's skills were limited when it came to interacting with the physical world. He'd likely just aimed for the general direction of his favorite seat.

"This used to be my den, once upon a time." Everett motioned for Galen to take a chair across from him. "Of course, by the time Kerri came along, I didn't even *have* a room anymore. I usually hung out in the attic with what was left of my stuff. Anyway, I saw this red-haired gal walk in with the real estate agent, and she didn't get any farther than the living room before she asked him if she could go through the house on her own. Said she needed to get the feel of the place."

"Did he let her?"

"What do *you* think?" snorted Everett. "Would you have said *no* to that smile? Anyway, the house itself was as empty as an old icebox, nothing in the basement or attic worth stealing. Naturally the agent told her to take her time, and went out to his car to make some calls."

It wasn't hard to guess what happened next. "Kerri knew you were here, didn't she?"

"She sure did. The minute she was alone, she came straight up to the attic to talk to me," said Everett. "Can't tell you what it meant to be spoken to by a living person after such a long time."

Galen had a pretty good idea after nearly a year of being invisible. But Everett had been *life-challenged* for twenty-five times as long. *Jesus, how do ghosts stay sane?*

"The long and short of it is, she not only asked my permission to buy the house, but invited me to share the place with her." The old man swiped at his eye. "She has a big heart, that girl. Got her brothers to drag my old furniture down from the attic, and what I didn't have anymore, she found for me at flea markets. Even brought in an extra television *just for me*. Imagine that! I'm like the star boarder here, but she just calls me her friend." He sighed. "That Kerri's somethin' special, you know."

Galen *did* know, and he knew it more surely by the hour. "What about all the other ghosts who come here?"

"Holy Moley, it was like bees to honey. They're attracted to her gift, so it didn't take long for word to get around. One or two spirits a day soon became ten or twenty. I kept telling her she shouldn't spread herself so thin, but all she could see was the *need*." He waved a hand in the air. "She can't help herself—cares too much if you ask me. Good thing Libby finally sat her down and made her see sense. Kerri agreed to let her ward the house, and then the three of us came up with the appointment idea. Been doin' it ever since. That's why I'm glad you came along when you did."

"Me? Why?"

"Because that girl deserves something for herself—some*one*. I've seen the way she watches you—and don't give me that look, you been doing plenty of watchin' yourself, son. You're both downright moony over each other, and it does my heart good to see it. Does it even more good to know what kind of man you are, and that you *might* almost be good enough for her."

"I'm not sure about that," said Galen. "She deserves a man who lives in the same world she does. In case you haven't noticed, I don't exactly have a physical body. That's a big drawback where I come from."

"Pffft. Things have a way of sorting themselves out. Kerri and Libby will come up with something, that's certain."

"I sure hope you're right. Hey, a while back you said there were a lot more ghosts around right now. Why would there be more of them at Christmas?"

"This ain't Dickens, son. It's not Christmas that brings them out. It's the Solstice."

"Um…I'm going to need more details."

Everett laughed. "I guess I've kinda gotten used to all this stuff after hanging around with Kerri and her aunt. I forget some things are brand new to you." He thought for a long moment, head bent, hands on his bony hips. "Well it's like this. Everyone thinks the Winter Solstice is just an interesting day on the calendar, but it's a whole lot more than that. It's a season all its own, really."

"A season for what?" Galen vaguely recalled mentions of old Celtic celebrations and pagan festivals from some long-ago history class, but surely none of it applied to the here and now—did it?

"For when the veil between worlds thins out, of course," said Everett, matter-of-factly. He waited a beat for Galen to catch on. When it didn't happen, he continued. "Look, there's a couple times a year when spirits can cross back and forth easy-like. Kerri says that other things do it too, like faeries and—hey now, don't go staring at me like that, son! I'm a ghost, and you're a—you're an *I-don't-know-what*, so why the big surprise that other critters might exist too?"

"Sorry. Just not used to it yet. You're right."

"Course I am." Everett motioned him to a window and pointed out. "See that big old rhododendron at the far corner of the yard?"

Galen looked. An enormous bush with aspirations of being a shade tree hid half the garden shed. "Yeah, so?"

"*So*, Waldo just went out the dog door. Watch what he does."

The stocky little pug ambled through the yard, sniffing intently here and there. As Galen watched, Waldo appeared to inspect every inch of the landscape, and at extremely close range since the pug's big round eyes were nearly even with his flattened nose. The dog paused frequently to mark his territory with gusto. "What is it I'm looking for?" he asked at last. "He hasn't gone anywhere near that end of the yard."

"Exactly!" said Everett. "See, that tree just happens to be Waldo's favorite spot to take a leak. I mean, that dog *never* misses a chance to water it. But during the Solstice, he keeps his distance. Once in a while, he'll even start barking at the tree, but believe you me, it's from the far side of the yard. Now around February, when the Solstice magic loses its strength, Waldo goes right back to pissing on that rhododendron like nothing was ever wrong."

Galen put his hands up in surrender. "Okay, I'm definitely missing something here. What on earth does a pug's peeing habits have to do with Solstice and magic?"

"Simple. The rhododendron is a crossing place. Kind of like a doorway of sorts. Libby says there's a whole lot of them scattered around, and we just can't see them. But Waldo's a dog, and a dog has senses that we don't, right? He knows when the doorway is there and when it's not."

Okaaay. "And where does this so-called *doorway* lead?"

Everett shrugged. "Dunno. Neither does Libby or Kerri. Every now and then I see a ghost go through it. But nobody ever seems to come back. I figure Waldo has the right idea by leaving it strictly alone. You might want to keep your distance too."

No kidding. If he had his body, Galen was certain he'd be sitting down at this point. His brain was spinning like a hamster in a wire wheel. "Let me get this straight. You have some kind of interdimensional portal in your goddamn *yard*? Why isn't there a ten-foot fence around it with armed guards?"

The old man looked surprised. "Well, 'cause it doesn't work unless it's a special occasion like the Solstice, or else Beltane—that's in May, by the way. The rest of the time it's a damn fine tree. Besides, Libby says you can't walk through it by accident, or there'd be people disappearing into thin air every day of the week." Everett leaned over and peered closely at Galen. "You all right there, son?"

"Yeah," he nodded. "At least I think so. It's just that the world is a much stranger place than I thought."

"Ha! Wait'll you get to be my age. Believe me, this old dog has had to learn a lot of new tricks—speaking of which, how about a lesson on moving stuff around? You could probably use a change of subject anyway."

"Don't you have to ride herd on the clients?"

Everett glanced at the vintage clock on the wall. "Lemme go change 'em over. Be right back."

SIX

Everett vanished, but not for long. Galen had barely begun examining the photos on the walls when the old man reappeared in his chair.

"We got us some time now," he announced. "Ed Murray's up next. He's one of our regulars, and he'll talk to Kerri till the cows came home if we let him."

"That fisherman guy?"

"Yeah, he was always real fond of steelhead trout. Ed used to live down the street, so I know him pretty good." He pointed. "In fact, that's him and me in that third picture on the left, down at Moses Lake."

Galen peered at it. Both men—much younger than they appeared to be now—were holding up strings of fish. "Kerri won't mind being left with him, will she?"

"Naw. Says she consider Ed's visits a treat. He's full of great stories. And he really tries to be helpful too—he gets messages out to the other ghosts for us. Like when she's going to be out of town and stuff." Everett eyed Galen with speculation. "I figure *I* could be a helluva lot more help to Kerri if I could do a few little things around here. Maybe keep the place tidy or something. I saw you making coffee for her."

Galen grinned. "Coffee seems to be pretty essential around here. But for a first lesson, let's start with something less messy."

"Well, what about the TV controller?"

"The remote? Um, yeah, that could work." In reality, he was thinking more along the lines of moving a simple piece of paper, but Everett was clearly enthused about his choice of object. All Galen had to do was find a way to explain *how* to affect that object...he'd never analyzed his methods before. "I'll just warn you in advance that I'm a firefighter, not a teacher, so I hope you're patient. And this could take a while too."

"I got twenty-five years of patience banked up. Take your time, son."

Okay then, here goes Lesson One. "You need a power source. To move something, you've got to gain and control some kind of energy. Luckily, it seems to be all around us, so you just need to connect with it."

"Makes sense so far. How?"

He struggled to find the right words. "It's like—like *pulling a string.* You reach out with your senses and feel around for a tiny little thread, then grab hold and pull it to you. Before you know it, the whole sweater is in your hand. Or in this case, the energy."

"Grabbing a string, huh?" Everett looked dubious, but the old ghost proved to be one determined pupil. Galen demonstrated picking up the remote and Everett doggedly tried to copy him. There was frustration and increasingly frequent cussing...

Until at last the remote control slid a few inches across the table!

Galen shot both fists in the air as if the old man had scored a touchdown. "Booyah!"

"Holy Moley. I did it." Everett stared at his fingers as if they belonged to someone else, his expression a mixture of wonder and delight. "I honest-to-damn-well *did it*." Without thinking, he reached out and grasped Galen's hand—

And *connected* solidly.

For a long moment, both men sat there, mouths open, staring at their joined hands. Then slowly Everett lifted his up and down in an approximation of a shake. *It worked.*

"Well, I'll be double-*dog* damned," he said. Slowly, the connection faded, and Galen's hand once again fell through the old man's phantom grip just as it had when they first met. But they were both grinning like idiots.

"Energy," announced Galen when he finally could find his voice. "That's what it is. You must have had some residual energy in your fingers from working with the remote."

"I never woulda thought of it." Everett shook his head in amazement. "Don't know how to begin to thank you, son."

"You did it all on your own. I just gave you a little direction, that's all." Galen didn't know much about teaching, but instinct told him it was important to end on a high note. "Why don't we leave the lesson there for now? We'll practice on the remote again later tonight."

"Yeah, sure, that'll work fine." Everett still looked a little bit stunned as he checked the time. "I gotta go swap out Kerri's clients again anyway. Wouldn't want to lose my job, you know."

At three in the afternoon, the last client of the day had finally departed. Everett had retreated to his room to practice his newfound skill. And Galen was relieved to discover that *Romancing the Wolf* concluded with a happily-ever-after for Mitch and Martina. Things had been touch and go for the characters throughout the book. And what a plot twist! He'd never seen it coming.

Come to think of it, there was another thing he hadn't seen: the author of the book eating lunch. Kerri had emerged from her office exactly three times that he knew of—and only to refill her coffee cup. Sure, he'd been busy with Everett for an hour, but a quick scan of the kitchen showed no sign of food prep, though it was nearly two in the afternoon. She hadn't left her office when the clients were gone either. Was she writing again? He didn't want to disturb her, especially when she'd warned him not to. *When I'm sleeping, I'm sleeping, and when I'm working, I'm working...*

But it just didn't seem right to let her live on air.

In the end, Galen made another pot of coffee, and rounded up enough ingredients to create a respectable sandwich. He tapped on the office door before entering, a steaming mug and a laden plate floating along behind him—

And found Kerri sleeping soundly at an old oak desk. Her head was no longer pillowed on her arms but resting on her keyboard. It was the incredibly loud snoring, however, that surprised him. Shuddering snuffles, buzz saw rumbles, and gasping wheezes seemed to reverberate off the very walls. *Wow, you must really be tired*, he thought...and then thought again. Being careful not to wake her, he drew back the unruly curls that had fallen in a curtain across her face. Her perfect mouth was closed, her breathing soft and even.

Yet the ungodly buzz saw sound carried on. *Where the hell is that coming from?*

There were plenty of options. Having once been the sun room of the old house, the office was enormous. An assortment of mismatched bookcases lined two walls, a mammoth cork board lined another wall, and the entire space was punctuated by filing cabinets big and small. Two comfortable chairs made a pleasant reading area in one corner, amid piles of books and bins of papers. *Maybe one of Kerri's clients is still hanging around...like that Ed character.* He definitely looked like the snoring type. *But ghosts don't sleep, do they?* He'd have to check with Everett on that.

Galen searched the office but saw nothing, until a hunch made him take a second look beneath the dinosaur-sized desk. Far at the back, between the wall and an ornate heating vent in the floor, was a plump well-worn pillow. And an even plumper pug lay sprawled on his back across it! His broad pink tongue hung out of the side of his mouth like rumpled linen from an open drawer, and the thunderous sounds that escaped his throat were being amplified by both the open space beneath the desk and the metal heating duct beneath the grating.

Well at least Waldo is comfortable. Galen couldn't say the same for Kerri. Not only was she leaning on her computer keys, but the angle of her neck and back made him wince.

Only one way to handle a situation like this...

* * * * *

The bedroom was dark when she awakened, and it took a long moment for Kerri to sort out that it was six in the afternoon and not six in the morning. Switching on the light revealed a bigger surprise—a large sandwich on a cellophane-covered plate. Immediately her stomach growled. She wasn't sure how the sandwich had ended up on her nightstand of all places, but she recognized the sliced turkey and the sourdough bread from her own kitchen. *Aunt Libby must have stopped by. I'll just have a couple bites and take the rest with me…*

Her body had other ideas, however. It demanded that she stay put until she'd eaten all of the deli-worthy creation, and topped it off with the cup of cold sweet coffee that accompanied it.

"I guess I really needed that," she said to her reflection in the mirror as she fixed her makeup. There was no denying that she felt a great deal better. The nap had refreshed her, but the food had steadied her and cleared her head. Kerri ran her fingers through her uncontrollable hair, then gave up and simply tied it back before heading downstairs.

Galen was at the kitchen table, looking over a spread of solitaire, but he smiled and rose when she came in. "You look like you got some rest."

"I guess I needed it." She shrugged, then peered at the cards. "Hey, that's Everett's hula dancer deck! He must really like you to lend you those."

"I've been trying to teach him to hold them. We worked with the cards for a while after I carried you upstairs. He *almost* got one, but then he said one of his shows were on and left. I think that's his way of saying he's frustrated and needs a—

"Wait, you carried me? *That's* how I got to bed?" Most women would find that endearing, romantic, even exciting— and she might too *if Galen was inside his big strong physical body*. Given his current state, however, Kerri found herself more appalled than anything.

Galen seemed unaware of any problem. "I didn't want to leave you sleeping at your desk. Well, technically, you were sleeping on your keyboard. What kind of man would I be if I let you wake up with square marks on your face?"

"You. Carried. Me. All the way up the stairs?"

His brow furrowed in puzzlement. "Yeah, well, *firefighter* here."

"Yeah, well, you didn't exactly use your firefighter *muscles* to do it. I'd have some faith in those! For heaven's sake, didn't Everett say something? He must have seen you carrying me."

"Sure he did. He warned me not to bang your head on the newel post at the top of the landing."

"Don't bang my head? That's all?" She was stunned. Her friend and roommate was not just protective but often overly so. *What the hell?*

"You have to admit it was pretty good advice. And I did get you to your room without a hitch."

"Why didn't you just put me on the couch?" That much she could probably have handled.

"I thought of that. But you were so tired, I figured you'd rest better in your own bed. And it worked, right?"

She put the heel of her hand to her forehead, searching for words. "You're so not getting this. Not a happy camper, here. I'm really uncomfortable with the idea of being levitated in my sleep!"

"I would never let you fall," he said solemnly.

Kerri believed him, but he was missing the point. "This is about *boundaries*, mister." She pointed her finger at him. "Do. Not. Levitate. Me. I know you meant well, but if I'm asleep on a bed of goddamn *nails*, just leave me there. Okay?"

"You're not afraid of heights, are you?"

She stared at him for several long seconds, then mentally threw up her hands and headed to the kitchen without another word. It took two cups of coffee before her brain cleared and she felt like a functional human being. She was contemplating a third when Galen appeared at last. To his credit, he looked somewhat contrite.

"I'm sorry," he said. "I get where you're coming from now. Honest, I didn't even think about boundaries and shit, but I should have. From now on, I promise not to levitate you without prior written permission."

She studied his face, but there was no trace of humor in his expression. In fact, he looked, well, *kind of adorable really*, as he tried to apologize. She'd have to be made of stone to resist those golden-brown eyes...even if her inner voice was making fun of her for being such a softy. "Well, I guess I *get* where you're coming from too," she said at last. "You were just trying to make me more comfortable." It was easy to picture any one of her older brothers doing the same. In fact, wasn't that a *guy thing*, to simply see a need and fix it without worrying about all the little social nuances involved? "I'm sorry if it seems like I'm overreacting. But how I feel is how I feel."

He nodded. "So we're good?"

"Yeah, we're good. Especially after that incredible sandwich," she said, and grinned as his face lit up. "I admit I ate the whole darn thing before I came downstairs. You're a pretty good cook. And there's *this* too." She raised her empty cup.

"Aha, my clever master plan to become indispensable is working. You *have* to forgive me or you won't get any more of my coffee!" he teased.

Kerri fired a potholder at his head, hitting him right between the eyes—

Except that the potholder sailed on through until it landed on the other side of the kitchen. Galen blinked in surprise, and Kerri began to laugh. After a moment, he joined her. And there it was again, that strong sweet connection that throbbed with a heartbeat all its own. The space between them evaporated and it seemed the most natural of things to find her face close to his. He smiled, and stroked a finger over her temple, drawing away a wild curl. The connection created that odd little electrical tingle she'd felt before, and suddenly she wanted to feel that on her lips. She tipped up her face just as Everett stuck his head into the doorway.

"Your aunt just drove up!" he announced, and she practically jumped away from Galen like a guilty teenager. The old ghost gave no sign of noticing anything. "Oh, and

Waldo is scratching at the door to the office. Got himself shut in again."

The man beside her smacked his forehead. "Damn, I forgot him. He was sound asleep."

"He's usually sound asleep. It's his natural state," said Kerri, straightening her clothes as if she really had been wrapped in Galen's arms. Her pulse was hammering behind her ribs and her heartbeat pulsed in her ears. *Holy cow, if I can get this wound up just wanting to kiss him, what will it be like if I really do?* She ignored her inner voice that insisted she had no business thinking—or doing—any such thing, but she also ignored the hot ache inside that wanted to pick up right where they left off...and keep going.

"You go get Waldo," she said to Galen, as casually as she could manage. "And I'll open the door for Aunt Libby."

SEVEN

Galen had expected the women to try to sneak in somehow. Instead, they walked through the front door of the hospital without hesitation, and right by the security kiosk. The guard didn't even look up from his magazine. A pair of nurses passed the women at the elevators without a glance. Wherever Kerri and her aunt went, no one looked in their direction. They seemed to be as invisible as he was. When they reached his floor without incident, he was relieved but baffled. Had Aunt Libby done something to—what exactly? Shield them? Cloak them? *But that's not possible. Is it?*

The hospital was a very different place at night. The only bright lights came from the nurses' stations. The intercom was silent, the clatter of carts was absent. Rooms were darkened, and even his own room had been dimmed. As for his body, it didn't look any different to him at all. *Doesn't even look asleep.* Save for the slow rise and fall of the chest, it was completely inanimate. Soundless, but for the unrelenting sound of the goddamn ventilator. *Might as well be one of the rubber CPR dummies at the station*—except, thankfully, the hair wasn't painted on.

Libby stopped dead as soon as she entered the room, and her niece nearly ran into her. "Something's been in here. Something nasty."

"I feel it too," said Kerri. "But it certainly wasn't here yesterday. I don't recognize it, do you?"

"Not at all." Her aunt appeared to gather herself. She tossed her coat over a chair, leaned her cane against it and focused instead on her enormous purse. The standard issue hospital bed-table was sitting idle against the foot of the bed, and Libby rested the handbag on it while drawing out several items. "Our first item of business is cleansing this room as best we can."

"I don't understand. Does it smell bad or something? Housekeeping comes by every day," said Galen. He frowned at his body. *You better not have farted, buddy.*

"Not that kind of cleansing. She means we need to get rid of the negative energy," said Kerri. "Whatever was here left an awful taint. It's pretty creepy, actually."

He almost didn't say anything, but wasn't *creeped out* exactly what he'd felt earlier? Maybe it was important. "Okay, this probably sounds crazy, but maybe I know when that happened. I felt something in my mind while Kerri was working in her office yesterday evening. It was just before you arrived, maybe around nine-thirty."

Libby stopped what she was doing to look at him. "Felt what?"

"Just like she said, something creepy. It wasn't physical." Hell, *nothing* could be physical for him. "But it was weird, and it was real. I've felt it maybe five or six times before."

"Nothing at my house caused it," said Kerri. "I do a cleansing ritual every day after I finish with my clients, and you would have noticed immediately if I'd missed anything. But this room? Like I said, I didn't sense anything when Galen and I were here before."

Her aunt looked thoughtful as she pulled two small bottles from her bag. "That's very interesting. I wonder if your attacker drops by to admire his handiwork now and then."

Although Galen wasn't in his body and couldn't have fallen if he tried, he still experienced a powerful impulse to sit down. It was bad enough to think that someone had deliberately stolen his life. It was another thing entirely to imagine the damn perp standing *right here* in this room and gloating over his helpless frame. He was reminded of how arsonists often mingled with the crowd at a fire, eager to witness the chaos they had caused.

Funny that he could feel sick without a physical form...

Kerri leaned in close to him. "Listen, I'm going to perform a cleanse, okay? Why don't you step out into the hall with Aunt Libby? The door has to be open, so you'll be able to watch what I'm doing, and I'm sure you'll have lots of questions." She took the bottles from her aunt—the words *Sage Oil* and *Essence of Rose* were handwritten in flowing letters on the tiny labels—and moved to the farthest corner of the room to uncork them.

"That's our cue, Galen," said Libby, pushing the door wide and pressing down the doorstop with the toe of her shoe. She took up a position, not in front of the door, but off to one side. "She'll be sending the negative energy out the door and you don't want to stand in its way," she explained.

Sure, whatever. He stood where she directed him, but decided to ask his questions later, if at all. Outside of taking a crash course in Magic 101, he doubted he would understand a fraction of what was going on anyway. For now, he would just watch.

Like a priest tossing holy water on the faithful, Kerri sprinkled droplets from both bottles into the corners of the room, along the tops of the doors and windows, and the tops of light fixtures and shelves. She used the pad of her thumb to smear a near-microscopic amount of the stuff on the upper surfaces of every piece of equipment and over the headboard and the rails of the bed. Every step was carefully placed, almost like a dance, and he realized her choreography was designed to eventually bring her to the open doorway. The entire time she worked, she recited again and again:

"By the power of three times three,

We cleanse this room's impurity.

Let in the light of clarity.

We banish all negativity,

Sending all dark energy

Back to its source, where'er it be."

Galen was surprised. "Why all the poetry?" he whispered to Libby. "You did that too when you were working your milk mojo. I thought maybe that rhyming stuff was just in the movies."

"It focuses the mind," she said. "The words aren't that important. It's your purpose, your intention, that matter the most when you're casting a spell. But rhyming? Believe me, it sharpens your focus like an arrow."

Sounds logical, he decided. He'd been afraid that the ritual might look silly or hokey, or cause his inner skeptic to roll its eyes. Instead, he almost felt like apologizing. It was plain that Kerri was working with something he didn't understand, and her own respect for what she was doing awoke an answering respect within him. She was trying to help him, trying to protect his body from whoever the hell had deliberately damaged it.

And when her shapely thumb gently smeared a drop of oil over his body's pale forehead, it was like the tenderest of benedictions, and it moved him deeply.

A few moments later, Kerri joined them in the hallway and returned the bottles to her aunt. "I've done a pretty thorough sweep. It should be okay to enter now."

She smiled at Galen and he grinned back. "That was really something. Thanks." Normally, he'd hug her or something now—God knew he wanted to. "So, did I hear that right? You sent the bad vibes back to their owner?"

"All that negative energy has to go somewhere. You can't destroy energy, and I can't just turn that dark stuff loose. It's like toxic waste. The safest thing is to return it to the source."

"Makes sense," said Galen. "But pardon me if I hope it gives whoever owns that shit a goddamn headache. Thanks again for getting it out of my room."

"Do something for me?" she asked.

"Anything." And in that moment, he knew he would. He would give absolutely anything, everything, to Kerri Tollbrook...

"Can you pull your hood back for me? You've been wearing it ever since I met you, all Mr. Mysterious n'Cool. Just once, I'd like to see your whole face. Unless you're bald of course..."

He laughed. "Geez, I'm not bald! And for your information, I'm just damn happy I'm not wearing what the guy in the hospital bed has on." Galen swept his hands over his head. They didn't connect with anything of course, but somehow, the action got the job done. "Well?"

"Looking good." She nodded approvingly. "Looking very good. And cool, definitely still cool. Shall we go in?" She crooked her arm and he looped his through it. If he concentrated very hard, he could use his energy to apply a nominal amount of pressure, briefly creating the illusion of an arm she could feel. They walked through the wide door together, and Galen was truly surprised. Although the lights were still dimmed, the room seemed inexplicably brighter. It was as if a thick layer of gray dust had suddenly been removed from every surface. There weren't many colors in the room to start with—whites and beiges and pastel blues—but they were far more vivid now. "Wow, you really *did* clean it."

Libby was already standing by the bed, one hand on the top of his head, the other cradling the large quartz crystals he'd seen earlier. She stood like that with her eyes closed for several moments. Galen followed Kerri's lead and said nothing. But he was at Libby's elbow, supporting her, the moment she opened her eyes.

"Are you okay?" he asked. "Do you want your cane?"

She waved him off. "Thank you, hon, I'm quite fine. And I don't need the cane for support—it has other purposes. I'm just experiencing a momentary tiredness. It takes a lot of energy to make connections, especially when no one is in there. You'll be glad to know your body is quite vacant by the way."

"I know that," said Galen. "I'm out here."

Kerri shook her head. "She means that nobody *else* has set up housekeeping in there."

He goggled. He couldn't help it. "You mean someone—something—could move in? Please say this isn't like *The Exorcist*, because movies like that scared the crap out of me when I was a kid." He'd watched them anyway, of course, but there were times he wished he hadn't. Like right now.

"No, not really. But sometimes unoccupied bodies get unwanted tenants," Kerri explained. "It's not a big crisis, more like an annoyance. Because then we have to evict them."

"It's a nuisance, certainly," agreed Libby. "But I wish that was what we were dealing with, because then the solution would be simple. Instead, I can see plainly that you've been the victim of deliberate, malicious magic."

Magic. Galen shuddered to think what the guys at the station would say if they ever got wind of any of this. But then, none of them had come face to face with an honest-to-God ghost. Or witnessed milk acting on command. They hadn't seen spirits lining up for a chance to talk to someone who could see them. Nor had his friends watched two women walk through a secure building without turning a single head. Most of all, none of them had had some crazy person steal the vitality right out of their body. If magic had created the problem, then it stood to reason that magic was the only thing that could fix it, right? *Anything's worth a try.* Anything to get back into his body and back to his life. "I believe the malicious part. And I think I'm starting to get used to the other *M* word too."

The older woman nodded as she rummaged in her purse. "It always takes a little time to adapt to new realities."

"I didn't get to tell you that he only just met Everett," said Kerri. "And then I had a full slate of clients today."

"Everett is your first ghost?" Libby looked up, clearly surprised.

Galen nodded. She studied him for a long moment, then beamed. "Well then, you are doing *exceptionally* well, hon. Most people would be screaming down the street and you're still here. If you can handle ghosts, you should have no difficulty adjusting to the existence of magic as well. Just think of it as a science you don't understand yet."

Libby pulled a leather pouch from her purse. Inside was a variety of smooth polished stones, and she quickly began arranging them on the pillow around his head. "Would you agree that ghosts are invisible to most people?" she asked Galen.

"Yes."

"But they've never been invisible to my niece. Why do you think that is?"

"I guess because Kerri has some sort of natural ability, a talent for it."

"Exactly right. And because of my own ability, magic is not invisible to me. Magic is energy, Galen. It's the same as the energy you use to move objects and interact with the physical world. And the use of energy always leaves a signature behind." She paused then, staring for several long moments at the pattern she'd made with the stones. He couldn't see anything himself—they didn't move or glow or levitate. How did she read them?

Finally, Libby sighed, and exchanged worried glances with her niece. "If I wasn't certain before, I am now. There's a very dark signature that clearly shows this isn't the work of any principled practitioner."

It was Galen's turn to look at Kerri. "Is this what you call *black magic*?"

"No, nope, not at all. And again, *no*. That's a Hollywood invention." She put her hands out in a calming gesture, her hazel eyes solemn as she explained. "Magic is magic. It isn't good or bad in and of itself. It's the intent that matters, Galen. Ideally, you treat magic as a gift and you use it to influence natural forces to help and to heal. It's a positive act. What Aunt Libby is saying is that whoever performed this spell did it for purely selfish reasons and didn't care if it harmed you."

Her aunt gave a very unladylike snort. "I'd have to say they *intended* to harm you," she said. "Somebody went to an enormous amount of time and trouble to do this to you, and they're certainly well-practiced. The spell woven around you is tremendously complicated."

Galen resisted the knee-jerk impulse to ask *why me*. The why didn't matter, not now. "Bottom line then: can you undo this spell?" He hated the hopeful note in his voice. He was no wuss. If the answer was *no*, then that was that, and he'd find a way to deal—and he'd have to do it without Kerri. It would be damn hard to walk away from someone so amazing. In fact, it would hurt like hell for the rest of his existence. But if he was cursed to remain insubstantial, no way would he curse her too by entangling her in an impossible relationship.

Libby's face was grave. "I don't want to offer any false hope. I *might* find something helpful, *might* figure out the spell. I'll have to do a lot of studying, however. I haven't seen anything like this before—at least, not in modern times."

"It's old then?" asked Kerri.

"The spell appears to be not just old but *ancient*. And that's going to make everything far more difficult." She sighed, and seemed to gather herself. "There is no time to waste, so let us get down to business and do what we can."

Galen nodded slowly. This he understood: it was like battling a fire. It wasn't a time for emotion, it was a time for doing. Emotion came later. "Tell me what you need me to do."

"You must show us everything that happened the day you were separated from your body."

"Okay, sure, it was Christmas Day, like I said. We got a call for an apartment fire, around noon. I—what's wrong?"

Libby was shaking her head. "No, hon, that's *telling*. We need to see for ourselves." In lieu of explanation, she tapped one of the stones she'd placed on the pillow. "We must have every detail we can possibly obtain. These will enhance memory and bring clarity." There were two yellow stones, one on each side of his head near his temples. Several green ones were placed near the crown of his head. As he watched, she placed a dark blue stone, about the size of a quarter, on his brow. He wondered if it felt cool.

"Citrines, calcite and azurite," explained Kerri. "The blue azurite brings insight and releases any blocks to remembering."

Libby placed one last thing on his body directly over the heart.

Galen peered into the deep golden stone. It was transparent, with dark inclusions: fragments of leaves, a tiny twig, and even some kind of bug. "Cool. This must be amber."

Kerri's aunt nodded. "It's a wonderful aid to memory, but since ancient times, it's also been used as a protector against negative energy and even psychic attack. Now I want you to—"

The door suddenly swung open and Fred stood staring at them, newspaper in hand. "*Two* pretty women tonight? I'm going to have to start asking Mr. McAllister for tips."

Kerri recovered first. She grabbed the nurse by the arm and pulled him in, closing the door behind him. "I know visiting hours were over a long time ago, Fred, but we're trying to help Galen. It's very important that we do this right now."

"Hey, I'm real glad the man's got visitors—it's a welcome change. But hospital policy can only be bent so far." Fred checked his watch and looked undecided.

Galen wracked his brain for something to say. "Tell him about the newspaper article. He read the first section of that paper to me yesterday morning when he came on shift, something about polar bears. I know you can make him believe I'm here," he said to Kerri. "Hell, look at all the stuff I believe in just since I met you." He saw her nod, her face brightening.

"Fred, I know that you care about Galen," Kerri said, patting the big man's arm. "And I'll bet you know that while he's not in his body, he *is* in this room with us. I'll bet you're here to read him another section of the paper. He liked that story yesterday about the polar bears."

The man's eyes widened. "You know about that?"

"He told me. You read to him almost every day. He appreciates it, you know. It's meant a lot to him."

"Tell him he should give his niece the red one, the M-300," said Galen.

"The red what?" Kerri asked, glancing at him. Fred followed her gaze, searching but not seeing.

"Just tell him it's the red one she'll want."

She turned back to Fred. "He wants you to give your niece the—"

"—the red one," finished Fred. "I didn't tell anyone else about choosing a bike for my niece. There was a sales flyer in Friday's paper and I got chatting to him about it, reading the features out loud and all." He looked from Kerri to Libby and then glanced around the room, an expression of wonder on his face. As Galen expected, Fred's gaze came to rest where he was standing. "I'll be damned. He's right here, isn't he?"

"Galen is very much here, and he needs us," said Libby. "My niece and I were trying to discover exactly what happened to him. I think you know it doesn't have a thing to do with natural forces."

"Something's sure not right about this," agreed Fred. "He's much too healthy. He's been lying there for darn near a year and his muscles haven't atrophied, his tendons haven't tightened up. Sure, he gets physiotherapy every day, but it's never enough to stave off all the deterioration. It's like the man's in suspended animation or something. And no one knows why."

"He's the victim of a dark spell," Libby declared. "And our only hope of undoing it is to learn as much as we can."

Expecting Fred to call for security right then and there, Galen considered talking to him himself. Kerri had warned about forcing people to believe, but surely this was an emergency? He quickly discarded that idea, though. After all, Fred had never heard him speak so the nurse couldn't know for sure it was him. That left stereotypical haunted house stuff. Turn the lights on and off? Move an object around? What?

To Galen's astonishment, however, none of that was necessary. Fred simply nodded. "Well, I see you've brought along the right stones for the job. Nice piece of amber, by the way. Great for protection." He grinned as the women stared at him. "My Haitian grandfather was a vodoun priest. I don't practice myself, but I have a lot of respect for those who do. Tell me what I can do to help."

"Can you give us some time?" asked Kerri. "I know you're on shift, but can you make sure no one else comes in here for a while?"

"Not a problem. There's only one other nurse on this floor at this time of night. She has her own patients, so no one will come in here but me. I'll go finish my rounds, maybe check in on you later. Take whatever time you need."

"Thanks so much, Fred." Kerri stood on her tiptoes and kissed his stubbled cheek. "Galen really appreciates it too."

"I just hope you can do something for him."

The nurse left the room, and Galen spread his hands. "Does everyone on the goddamn planet know about magic but me?"

Kerri smiled at him. "It's never an accident when the people we need come into our lives. Fred has been drawn here to help you, just like we have."

Libby moved to the side of the bed, taking one of Galen's physical hands in hers. Kerri stood on the opposite side and grasped the other. Both women extended their free hands towards Galen.

"We need you to stand between us, approximately where the amber is positioned," Libby directed. "We will close our hands behind you to complete the circle."

"All right." Galen felt no sensation, but it was still bizarre to wade through the hospital bed, walk right through his physical body and position himself in the middle of his own chest. Although the bed had been raised considerably, he was a tall man: the gleaming amber stone was positioned over his physical heart, but as far as his spirit form was concerned, he figured it had to be somewhere near his navel.

"Focus on the day," Libby instructed. "Think of nothing else."

Sure, he thought, *no problem*. But as the women clasped their hands behind him, he suddenly felt a surge of energy, power, heat, light, *something*. Something when he'd felt nothing for so long. The sensation fountained through him like a geyser at first, then fell away to a cool, steady stream…

EIGHT

Kerri's voice shook him out of his reverie. "Galen, you have to focus, remember? We need you to think of the day."

Right. The day, Christmas Day. It had always been a good day. His mom had made it special when he was growing up and after she was gone, he kept the traditions going. He had a little tree in his apartment, and he'd been the one to set up the big tree at the firehouse for the past eight years. The one who didn't mind untangling the lights and assembling the complicated tree stand, the one who didn't mind unpacking all the ornaments…

Christmas morning at the station meant fresh cinnamon buns from Kelsey's wife and Brody getting teased about the barbecued turkey fiasco. Gag gifts were opened and laughed over. Deputy Chief Summers was off-duty but came by to make his specialty, Mexican omelets, for brunch.

They'd barely finished eating when the klaxon sounded.

Galen scrambled with the rest of the crew, jumping into gear and rolling out within minutes. Somebody probably left food on the stove, or maybe some holiday lights had overheated, perhaps too many decorations plugged into a single outlet. Likely just a small fire with a lot of smoke… As they approached Holyoke and Houston Avenue, however, Galen could see that they had a real blaze to contend with. Why the hell hadn't dispatch warned him?

Heavy smoke and flames were erupting from the top floor of a large three-story walk-up. From the looks of it, he guessed the fire had started on the second floor and spread over the exterior and onto the roof. There had to be a couple dozen apartments in this unit, maybe more. Worse, there were several more housing units surrounding it.

As incident commander, Galen had decisions to make, and fast. Before the truck had stopped rolling, he tapped Brody to call in another engine company, coordinated the positioning of the trucks he had, then divvied up the team. One party searched the building, floor by floor, making sure everyone was out. The rest unrolled hoses and began putting water on the blaze, from inside as well as outside and, most importantly, from above. It was a dance, a choreographed dance, and he was the director. The responsibility sat heavily but well on his shoulders as he stood at *fireground*, the operational area, with a radio to his ear. Every member of the crew was well-trained, each man communicating what he saw and did. They were Galen's eyes and ears, and that information guided his decisions.

Behind him, police halted traffic, established a perimeter, kept the crowd back and helped to account for the residents, all eighty-nine of them. Paramedics treated a few cases of mild smoke inhalation, but no injuries. Galen was grateful for that. He was always grateful for that but especially on Christmas Day. Bad enough that some people would be looking for another place to sleep. But they'd be alive and unhurt, and that was everything.

Three hours, seven units and twenty-eight firefighters later, they finally managed to knock down the main blaze. It had been dicey for a while. He'd been forced to pull his men out of the building and fight the fire from the outside, but persistence and the multi-directional offensive had finally paid off. The south side of the building looked like a total loss—that was likely a given before they'd even arrived on scene—but at long last the fire was completely out, and the surrounding apartment buildings were safe. No injuries, no casualties, civilian or firefighter. It was a good day.

Time for the postcontrol *overhaul*, checking for hotspots and any areas where the fire might rekindle. He had men surveying the roof, others poking around the back of the building. The interior had just been swept a second time, ceilings, walls and partitions checked and sometimes opened up to *double* check. Everyone was looking for smoke escaping from odd places, the presence of heat, smoldering, any sign at all that the fire had spread into the walls, waiting to burst afresh. Galen walked the perimeter, intent on the building and his men. He had no eyes for the crowd, didn't see anyone cross the yellow tape. Until he spotted a lean dark figure heading across the yard towards the stairwell door.

"Hey! Hey *you*, get out of there!" he yelled into the megaphone. Lots of people wore black leather jackets and black ball caps, yet something about the guy looked wrong. Galen would bet money he wasn't a resident. A thrill seeker or a looter, maybe. Worse, he might be an arsonist, back to admire his handiwork. Another warning went unheeded and the shady figure slipped inside the building. *Shit.* Galen glanced around but there were no cops close at hand. His own men were busy. He grabbed for his SCBA, then remembered he'd given the breather to another firefighter whose tank was empty. He ran for the door anyway and flung it open. "Hey! Come back here!" The power was out, and emergency lights shone yellow through a light haze of old smoke. He couldn't see the man, but the echo of footsteps on the stairs above was plain. *Great, just great.* He'd have to chase the jerk down. He couldn't leave the operation center unmanned, however. Still holding the door, he thumbed the radio clipped to his collar. "Brody, take over fireground for a minute, will ya? I've got a damn civilian loose in the building. Send a couple guys in after me when you can, west side door, upstairs. Extra tanks, just in case. And have a couple of cops waiting too—this guy looks fishy as hell."

"Roger that."

The heavy steel door reminded Galen of a somber clock chiming as it closed behind him, but he was already taking the stairs two at a time. The smoke here wasn't too bad, thank god, although he'd likely cough all night just the same. He paused at the first landing, holding the hallway door open a crack, holding his breath as he strained to listen. Nothing. Performed the same check at the second landing. That's when he heard it: amid the constant drip of water, the metallic snick of a deadbolt sounded somewhere towards the far end of the hall where the roof was now open to the winter sky. Galen closed the door behind him and walked slowly, trying to be as quiet as possible although it was damn difficult to be stealthy in his heavy gear. There were chalk marks on all the doors, showing that his crew had checked every apartment on this level, first for residents, then later for hotspots. Oddly, though SOP dictated all entrances should be closed tight at all times, each of the doors was slightly ajar.

Except *one*.

The apartment was the last intact unit before the newly created "skylight" and the charred debris beyond. He tried the knob and swore under his breath. His throat was raw, his eyes stinging, and he just didn't feel like being polite. Galen shouted as he hammered on the door with his fist. When there was no response, he kicked it in, leaving the deadbolt still hanging from the jamb. It was like walking into a cave. Fire and smoke had blackened everything and although the windows hadn't broken, they were so thickly coated with soot that they might as well be walls. He shone a flashlight around, searching for the man but seeing no one. *Just what I need, a frickin' game of hide and seek.* He thumbed his microphone to give Brody a heads up and got only static. Nice to know that Murphy's Law was still in effect. "I know you're in here, mister," he yelled. "You need to come outside, *now.* It's for your own safety. This building hasn't been cleared."

Something white caught his eye and he looked down. There were lines on the charred floor, crisscrossing lines freshly drawn with what looked like poured sand. The coarse grains glittered under the flashlight beam and the hairs on the back of his neck suddenly prickled as he realized there was some kind of pattern. An enormous eight-pointed star, with strange symbols and glyphs spiraling outward from its arms—and he was standing in the very center of it. He didn't know what it meant, only that every instinct he had was telling him to get out, fast.

In the instant he turned to leap away, the man stepped out of the shadows and somehow Galen knew it was already too late...

"I was rather hoping you'd be the one to follow me, Mr. McAllister."

Galen tried to step out of the strange pattern, but his feet seemed glued to the floor. The room had gone blurry, and so had the stranger in front of him. The man's black ball cap was pulled low, hiding all his features except for a thin-lipped smile.

Raise the flashlight. Raise the damn flashlight! Galen's arm wouldn't obey his brain's command, remaining motionless at his side. A primal tingle ran down his spine, as if his subconscious was telling him: *you really* don't *want to see this guy.* "Who the hell are you?" he gritted out.

"A mere detail. What's important is that I know who *you* are. You're the one who spoiled my lovely fire and my carefully laid plans. A little smoke inhalation and I could have had two or three subjects, perhaps even an entire family. Enough to keep me going for quite a while. But no matter. I've learned to be quite flexible over the years."

This is crazy... Suddenly Galen felt even stranger, dizzy and disoriented as if he was lost in a maze of mirrors. *What did I come here for?* "I have to ask you to leave. The building isn't safe."

"Oh, I'll leave. And so will you." The man's smile broadened, his mouth stretching unnaturally wide—and revealing a double row of pointed teeth.

What the hell? Surprise and revulsion slapped Galen's confused brain into clarity, lent adrenaline to his determined struggles. His left foot moved an inch, then two.

"We'll have none of that." A black gloved finger pointed at the floor for an instant and Galen's feet were again frozen in place. "Although I admit I'm impressed by your strength of will. Perhaps it's serendipitous that I've had to change my plans. You're going to do very nicely for a while." Slowly the man removed his gloves.

And long claws sprang from his fingertips.

I'm hallucinating. It's gas. Modern buildings were filled with synthetic materials that released all kinds of toxins when burned.

"I assure you, it's not gas," said the creature, as if Galen had spoken aloud. "It's all me. And I can tell you that because you won't remember a thing." The thing was suddenly closer, though its feet hadn't appeared to move, and Galen found himself staring into feral eyes that glittered black from corner to corner. Their depths glowed red, like banked coals waiting to erupt into flame. "In fact, you won't even be awake," the monster continued. "You certainly won't recall *this*." Galen's upper arm was seized with an unbelievable grip. He struggled, trying to shake the creature off, but it was as if his body wasn't his. *What the hell?* He tried to shout for the others. Brody would have sent someone in after him by now. But no sound escaped his throat.

"Might as well get used to that, Mr. McAllister. You're going to be experiencing a great deal of it very soon. Just as soon as I gather one more little ingredient for my recipe." The thing raised its other hand, splaying the claws like talons, and thrust them into Galen's upper arm, slicing through the heavy fire coat as if it was paper.

Pain ripped through every nerve...

"Galen! Galen, snap out of it!"

Kerri's voice shook him free of the nightmare. He looked around to find himself still standing in the midst of his body on the bed. Uncomfortable with the surreal position, he retreated to the center of the room. And saw that the amber stone had shattered into several pieces. "What the hell happened? What *was* that?" he demanded.

"What you saw, Galen—what we all saw—was what *really* happened to you in that building," explained Libby. She walked briskly around the bed, and pushed the sleeve back from his body's limp right arm. Examining the skin, she murmured a few Latin-sounding words. "Here it is. Come over and see for yourself."

Galen didn't know what to think. On the back of his tricep were four long crescent-shaped scars in a row. *Like I tangled with a damn mountain lion.* "I've never seen those. The doctors didn't see them either. How could that be?"

"A small and simple spell," said Libby. "Just like the one we used to get into the hospital. It doesn't make things invisible, it simply deflects attention."

"Then I was right about that guy! I knew something was off about him, but I never imagined those claws…and those teeth. What the hell *is* he?"

To Galen's surprise, Libby shook her head. "I'm not ready to hazard a guess," she said. "But I have some ideas to explore."

"It bothers me that he clawed you," said Kerri. "He obviously enjoyed causing you pain, but he talked about needing an ingredient for his recipe, his *spell*. Skin, blood, muscle, whatever sample he could get. He didn't seem picky as long as he got some of your cells."

"He wanted my goddamn DNA? What the hell for?" He was already furious that some bizarre creature had walked right up to him and stolen his life. For some odd reason, amid the onrush of memories now bombarding his brain, it was the possible theft of his genetic code that infuriated him the most. *It just seems so much more personal…or does it?*

There was a question somewhere in there that he couldn't quite articulate, and he filed the thought away for later.

Meanwhile, Libby was shaking her head. "A sorcerer couldn't care less about your DNA, Galen. He simply needed something that was intimately connected with you in order to complete his evil work."

"Which is what, exactly?"

"We don't know that part yet," said Kerri. "Some nasty spells can be made with something that you've touched, some can be made with an item that you own. But the darkest magic would require—"

"A piece of me," finished Galen. "I get it. But hey, maybe it's not magic at all. Maybe he's growing goddamn clones of me in a giant petri dish somewhere."

He moved to the window then, staring out at the cityscape with his back to the women while he got his temper under control. *Quit thinking about yourself, McAllister. That frickin'* thing *is still running around loose out there.*

What if he's doing this to other people too?

* * * * *

The police officer looked uneasy and rubbed the back of her neck, as if some latent instinct was trying to warn her about the shadow that clung to the dark side of a nearby building. Nah'mindhe, the Unspoken One, watched the uniformed woman shake off the sensation and focus on her task once more—directing traffic around a three-vehicle accident. From his vantage point, several stories off the ground, Nah'mindhe could see other professionals on the scene as well, including a contingent of firemen. He was particularly curious about *those*.

Out of the countless humans available to him, he'd always selected the young and the strong. Now, however, Mr. McAllister had given him almost as much food for thought as *shi* to consume. What if there was more to consider than simple physical condition? After all, hadn't the fireman lasted far longer than any of the others?

Perhaps firefighters are different in some way, thought Nah'mindhe. *Time to search for a suitable subject, and find out.* What a worthy experiment that would be! It was a shame he wouldn't be able to compare his new subject to Mr. McAllister, however. The ancient spell was effective but limiting, and could only run its course. The man's end was inevitable, but at least it would be glorious. *For me.* Mr. McAllister would simply be dead, a spiritless husk devoid of—

Something pushed at him, and the shadow on the wall whipped around with enough fury to send a group of rats scurrying from the trash bins far below. *What is this?* Energy buffeted him, shoved at him insistently and then abruptly merged with him. In an instant, Nah'mindhe understood. It was a small remnant of his own dark energy. Someone had rebuffed it, causing it to wing its way back to him!

How could this be? It had been centuries since any mortal had done such a thing. *Since any mortal* dared. He didn't know where it came from, but it wasn't difficult to guess. However well-versed they might be in magic, no human possessed the power to send energy over any great distance.

He glanced back at the firemen wistfully and sighed. His experiment would simply have to wait. *Fortunately, an immortal has plenty of time!* With a rasping chuckle that would have chilled the blood of any creature that heard it, the Unspoken One pulled away from his dark perch and headed west.

Nah'mindhe didn't hurry. He never hurried. Haste was for lesser beings. And he certainly didn't fear whatever mortal had gained his attention in such a brazen way. But his thoughts were uncharacteristically excited as he traveled. After such a lengthy existence, something truly interesting was difficult to come by—and Mr. McAllister was proving to be very, *very* interesting.

At Sacred Heart Hospital, he lingered in the deep shadows across from the building he sought, prepared to assume an unremarkable humanoid form. It was a perfect time of night to come here—no one coming and going, no movement, no sound at all except for the occasional ambulance with its flashing lights and annoying sirens—

Two women suddenly emerged from the double sliding doors. And between them walked McAllister. Incredibly, the three of them were talking together as if they were all on the same plane of existence. Stunned, Nah'mindhe reached out with preternatural senses honed over millennia. It was indeed the fireman and yet *not*. The man was as insubstantial as the Unspoken One himself, but not what the mortals called a ghost. He exuded far too much energy, and even possessed an aura. *What mystery is this?* Of all the humans Nah'mindhe had fed from over the centuries, most remained trapped within the shell of their body, hopelessly lost in dreams and unable to find a way to wake up. Few escaped their physical confines. And none had ever been strong enough to connect with the living.

The younger woman caught his attention then, and he studied her appraisingly. Her *shi* shone brightly, as strong as the fireman's had been. *Perhaps more so.* Nah'mindhe stared intently until her aura was revealed to his gaze as well. It matched McAllister's: vivid blue shot through with brilliant streaks of gold. *Rare colors indeed, and rarer still to find a pair.* The aura of the older woman was no less powerful, but it was vibrant green; perhaps she was a healer.

The Unspoken One changed his mind about visiting the still body in the room upstairs. As the group got into a vehicle and left the parking lot, the blackest of shadows detached itself from its surroundings and followed them.

NINE

A vast labyrinth of bookshelves stretched before Kerri as far as the eye could see. They towered over her, reaching up to impossible heights as if they belonged to Jack's giant. If there was a ceiling, she couldn't spare the time to look for it. Instead, Kerri dashed through the rows, turning this way and that, yanking out one huge dusty volume after another. Again and again, she opened a book but the yellow pages within were utterly blank. No matter how promising the title, not a word remained in any of them. Had the print faded away with age? Or had the brittle paper always been bereft of words?

I won't stop looking. Somewhere in one of these tomes was the key to freeing Galen...

Without warning, a clock appeared on a shelf in front of her face. As she moved along the stacks, more clocks appeared. From tiny travel alarm clocks to ponderous mantel clocks, they were wedged between the musty books, stacked on top of them, squeezed under them. Wall clocks and pocket watches now hung from the edges of the shelves, and some dangled from wires that disappeared into the zenith. Kerri stopped still as she realized their significance: *Time is running out. Whose time? What—*

BANG!

Something between thunder and an earthquake jolted the strange library, shivered up through the floor beneath her feet, and shook the gargantuan shelves around her.

BANG!

Like the tolling of a monstrous doomsday bell, the powerful vibrations caused hairline cracks to appear in the marble floor. Heavy books began falling throughout the library. *No! Not now!* Kerri tried to press on until an entire shelf of books crashed near her in an explosion of leather-bound pages and dust. Quickly, she cleared off a bottom shelf and tried to squeeze herself inside for protection. But it was too small, and she couldn't make herself fit.

BANG!

Her surroundings shook again. As the sound died away this time, a continuing tremor lingered on. She could feel its vibration travel up her spine until it throbbed in her teeth and pounded inside her head. The mountainous shelves creaked and groaned horribly, then slowly, inexorably, tilted inward…

With the sudden force of a rockslide, all the books and clocks tumbled down at once. Her arms were flimsy and useless to protect her as the hard-edged books beat against her, as their weight combined to crush her. She couldn't escape, couldn't move. With her last breath, she screamed as she was buried alive in the darkness—

"*Kerri!*"

Someone was pulling at her, trying to tug her free of the rubble. Didn't they know it was hopeless?

"Kerri, look at me!"

She knew that deep voice, knew the resonance and tone of it. It had touched something primal in her from the moment she first heard it. It touched her now. Her eyes flew open— yet the darkness remained. She gasped, then dragged in a great greedy lungful of air. And another until a coughing fit took over. It seemed like every speck of dust from the collapsed library had settled into her lungs... *Wait a minute, that's not possible!*

"Just take it easy and breathe. I've got you."

And he did. She couldn't see a damn thing, but she could feel Galen's strong arms around her, holding tight. Sheltering her. Her eyes were already watering as she struggled to get her wind back, but a few real tears of pure relief mingled in.

"Here, let's shed some light on the subject." The little bedside lamp winked on, and Kerri blinked at the familiar surroundings: she was in her own house, in her own room. And her own rescuer was scrutinizing her with deep concern in his golden-brown eyes.

"Better?" he asked. "Now take a nice slow breath for me, will you?"

She complied and offered him a shaky smile. Relief replaced the worry on his brow, and he leaned in to kiss her—

Suddenly his striking features were replaced by a worried pair of buggy eyes set above a flat wrinkled muzzle that promptly sneezed in her face.

"Way to ruin a moment, Waldo!" Kerri scrubbed her lips vigorously with a pajama sleeve. "Get off me, will you?" The pug had climbed in her lap, and stood with his feet poking into her chest so he could study her at close range. She tried shooing the determined little dog away without success, and managed to set off another coughing fit.

"Over here, buddy." Galen somehow coaxed Waldo into sitting on the floor beside them. The anxious pug settled for gluing himself to her side like a hairy limpet and earnestly licked her elbow as she caught her breath.

"Thanks." She rubbed Waldo's round furry head, and got her hand washed as well.

"He just wants to know if you're okay," said Galen. "Me too." He brushed her forehead with his lips, a soft cool tingle against her skin. "You had one helluva bad dream."

"That's an understatement." She couldn't remember *ever* having such a whopper. "It was so damn real…but I'm okay now, I think. Just let me sit up." Her head cleared as soon as she was upright, enough to realize that there was no soft mattress under her. "What on earth am I doing down *here*?"

"Beats me. When I came in, you were tangled in your blankets and trying to crawl under the bed. Good thing you've got too many boxes stored under there to let you get far."

Images from the dream flashed through her mind, and she shivered, only to have her anxious pug try wiggling into her lap again. The coughing began once more as she blocked his determined path.

"Here, I think you need this."

A cool glass of water was placed in her hands and she drank all of it. Kerri could feel the spasms ease until she felt almost normal. She took a deep breath. "Omigosh, that's better. I guess my throat was dry."

"Or you inhaled a lot of dust bunnies."

"There's no dust under my bed!" *Was there?*

Galen took the empty glass from her and pulled her close. "Come on, let's get you off the floor before you get cold." He drew her smoothly to her feet. They lingered like that for a long moment, and Kerri ran her hands over the strong arms that surrounded her so securely. They looked solid and yet were not. *How is he doing this?* Like a football linebacker, Galen's muscles were clearly visible even through the fabric of the hooded sweatshirt he wore, but her fingers couldn't seem to trace their contours. *Energy,* she realized suddenly. *He's holding me up with pure energy.* She tested her theory by reaching her arms around his broad back—and felt nothing at all! She looked up and tried cupping his face with her palm, but her fingers passed right on through.

He grinned but there was sadness in his eyes just the same. "You don't know how much I'd like to feel that."

"You will. We'll find a way, I prom—"

BANG!

Only Galen's tight hold on her kept Kerri from screaming as the entire house shook and the little lamp went out. Waldo started barking furiously, but the pug's voice was greatly muffled. She couldn't see him—she couldn't see *anything*— but it was easy to guess that the little pug had burrowed under the heap of blankets on the floor. She wished she could join him. The darkness in the room suddenly seemed downright oppressive, as if the air had thickened and was pressing down on her...

BANG!

She gritted her teeth so they wouldn't chatter, and stared into the darkness, willing her eyes to adjust, telling herself over and over that she was awake. That nightmares didn't come to life.

"I was going to mention that," Galen whispered in her ear. "There's some asshole ghost outside who wants in."

"A *ghost* is doing this? You're kidding me."

"Nope, not kidding," he said. "Everett and I were in the middle of checking it out until we heard you."

"And we both came running," declared a familiar voice from the direction of the hallway. "You all right, Kerri-girl?"

"I was a lot more *all right* before I heard *this*," she said. The idea that a spirit would be so rude really annoyed her. She pulled away from Galen and took a couple of steps forward to look out the window. No one, incorporeal or otherwise, was in sight. She noticed then that although the streetlights were still on, their yellow glow didn't seem to be penetrating the glass. It was every bit as dark in her bedroom as if the power grid had gone down all over the city. *How is that possible?*

"Look, I want to know that you're safe in here," said Galen. "You said your house had some kind of protection."

She nodded. "Aunt Libby created the wards herself. And she never does anything by halves." *I hope whoever it is gets a headache from beating on my poor house. Heaven knows, I'm getting one.*

BANG!

This noise had come from a different area of the house. Probably the sunporch, she thought. The last time, it seemed to be the roof, and before that, maybe the front of the house. Even Galen, when she'd "locked him out," hadn't made such a terrible ruckus as he searched for a way in. *But Galen wasn't angry.* Whoever was out there now was extremely pissed, she was sure of it. "Who could it be? None of my clients would be this obnoxious." *And none of them could manifest this powerfully in the physical world.*

"It ain't no ghost," snorted Everett. "Figured that's what it was at first, that maybe somebody didn't like the rules and was making a fuss about it. I was gonna go give 'em a piece of my mind while Galen was checking on you. Didn't feel right, though."

"What do you mean?"

"Well, I can't exactly explain it. One of my old friends woulda called it *bad juju,* so I thought it best to do a little recon first, you know? When I peeked out, there's this guy, all in black, pacing back and forth on the front lawn. Had his hat down low so I couldn't see his face—then suddenly he looks up like he could see *me* plain as day. Didn't say a word, just snarled like some kind of animal. Damned if he didn't have teeth like one too! And those eyes...nothing has eyes like that. Nothing *should* have eyes like that."

Kerri could feel the blood drain from her face, and was grateful for Galen's steadying hand on her shoulder. "Omigod, it's him, isn't it?" she breathed.

"Who?" asked Everett. "You *know* that monster out there?"

"You could say that. He's the bastard who stole my life." Galen's voice was tight and grim. "Kerri, you're absolutely certain that your house is defended?"

"Yes. Just let me—"

"Good. Then you'll be safe with Everett while I go have a word with—"

"NO!" She almost screamed it, and although she could barely see him in the darkness, she could feel him turn towards her. "No way. He's too powerful. You can't go out there."

"Like hell I can't. What do you want me to do, hide in here while he gets away?"

"Galen, please think it through," she said. "That thing *stole your body* the first time you met him. Who knows what he could do now? Please trust me that you're going to need magic, a boatload of it, on your side before you confront him."

Galen sounded impatient. "What if you and your aunt can't find a goddamn spell that works? Then I've lost my chance to—"

BANG!

"Son," Everett broke in, "I don't like to interfere, but I saw that thing's *face*. Trust me, you won't have to go looking for him. Whatever he is, he wants something real bad, and he's bound to keep coming back until he gets it. You want to fight him? I'm with you all the way. But if you go out there unprepared, it'd be no better than giving up."

Kerri held her breath and hoped. She didn't want to have to try to stop Galen.

"Fine," Galen growled at last. "But for God's sake, if we're going to be under siege, can't we at least pour boiling oil off the roof or something?"

"I like the way you think," she said. Actually, she liked the idea a lot. She was getting damn tired of the constant noise, and the intrusion on the sanctuary of her house. "Because of the work I do with spirits, my aunt gave me a few spells in case of emergency."

"To do what?"

"I'm not completely sure. I've never had to use one before. But if we're lucky, maybe we can give Mr. Tall-Dark-and-Nasty a black eye."

Everett sounded concerned. "Might be like poking a grizzly with a stick."

"Maybe. But he'll know we're not helpless, and that's something."

"Go for it," said Galen.

She sat on the bed, closed her eyes, and put her fingers to her forehead in an effort to concentrate. Her aunt had made her memorize the spells, but only one would come to mind. *I sure hope that's because it's the right one to use in this situation.* Kerri took a deep breath, focused her intent, and recited:

"Walls of wood and glass and stone,

Shelter all within this home.

Stand as fortress, fight our fight.

Banish evil from our sight.

Cast off dark and set light free

By the power of three times three."

She opened her eyes and was disappointed to discover it was still dark. Just as she wondered if she should try the spell again, the entire house suddenly shook itself like a dog. Books and pictures crashed to the floor around her...and blinding blue light split the night like a silent thunderbolt. The lingering flash was so intense that purple afterimages danced on the inside of Kerri's eyelids. Somewhere outside, an inhuman moan quickly grew into a scream of pure rage. She covered her ears with her hands as the wail intensified to a frequency that had every dog in the neighborhood barking at once...

Then, just as abruptly, all was still.

The power came back on and held steady. Only the clock radio flashed on and off: twelve-zero-zero. *Damn, I meant to put a backup battery in that thing.*

"Holy shit, that was something!" Galen was already peering out the window, and stuck his head partly through the glass to get a better view. "Damned if Everett isn't already outside with his baseball bat—you oughta lecture *him* about playing it safe!"

"Believe me, I will."

He pulled back into the room. "I just got the *thumbs up* from him. I guess that means we're all clear. You did it."

Kerri managed a smile as he sat on the bed and put an arm around her. "Don't get too excited," she said. "We only won the first round."

"Yeah, I know. Everett was right when he said it's bound to come back." Galen sighed. "And now I've put you on that monster's radar too. I'd go someplace else but—"

"But it's too late for that," she finished. "And I wouldn't let you go anyway. We're stronger together, and we're both safe here." *I hope.* "Come on, let's go downstairs. I need to get out of this room for a while."

"Midnight snack?"

Truthfully, she felt that a glass of wine—or something a whole lot stronger—would be more appropriate under the circumstances. In the end, she decided it was better to stay sharp, so she settled for making cocoa in a saucepan as Galen and Everett sat at the kitchen table and discussed the night's events. Waldo was curled up snoring at their feet. They looked like more than friends. *Like family.* So perfectly normal. *I can use a whole lot of* normal *after a night like this!*

The aroma of chocolate soothed her, and the act of cooking it up from scratch was grounding. Tomorrow they would figure things out with Aunt Libby but for what was left of the night, Kerri would take comfort in simple pleasures, in Everett's loyal friendship and in her growing feelings for Galen McAllister.

* * * * *

Rage tore at the Unspoken One, flooded his mind and took him over. *How dare they!* It was humiliating enough to need anything from these mortals, to be utterly dependent on the life force they harbored within their weak bodies. But to be repelled in such a manner…

A *magical* manner.

Magic.

Slowly the violence ebbed from his corporeal form as the wrathful haze cleared from his mind. Few humans in this time commanded true magic. But the skill hadn't always been so rare. Millennia ago, when Nah'mindhe first entered this plane of existence, most mortals were familiar enough with sorcery to practice some form of it in their daily lives. The existence of unseen worlds was a given. Medicine and magic worked together to solve the maladies of their own physical world, and to recognize and repulse those ills created by otherworldly beings such as he. If Nah'mindhe was careless, if he consumed too much from a single victim and weakened them, their families or friends were quick to notice. Rituals and incantations were immediately applied. Most spells were simply annoying to him. But some had real power...

Like the one that had just sent him reeling to the other side of town. It could only have come from one of the women that McAllister had left the hospital with—but the older one, the healer, had departed the tall old house soon after arriving. *So it is the younger one who worked the spell, the one with the bright aura.*

Consumed with his thoughts, Nah'mindhe gazed without seeing at what remained of the three humans at his feet. He'd vented some of his fury by draining them of every ounce of *shi*, then by tearing them to pieces with claws and teeth. Blood now painted the narrow street with broad dark strokes. Usually he would have taken the time to cleanse the area with a spell and to hide the bodies. Instead, he allowed himself to fade to his natural state. The blood that had coated his claws, his arms, his clothing, hung in the air as a red mist for a long moment before raining to the ground. As for himself, he glided along the walls of the lightless buildings, a darker shadow among many.

The influx of so much *shi* gradually buoyed his mood until he was more amused than angry. Humans with magic might be rare, but novelty was an even scarcer commodity for the Unspoken One. The firefighter had been unique, truly something to savor, as an uncommon vintage of wine was valued among mortals. But that bottle was on its last dregs.

The gifted young woman, however...

Nah'mindhe began to laugh, the harsh sound startling a flock of pigeons into fleeing their evening roost. His initial impulse had been to systematically assault the warded house where McAllister was, to slay those who dared to oppose the Unspoken One. But spellcasting on such a scale would require a great deal of energy—and he realized now that he didn't need to spend any in order to achieve his goals. *McAllister's physical body is not going anywhere*, he thought. *And sooner or later, the little sorceress will surely return to Room 440.*

He would enjoy her even more than he'd enjoyed the fireman.

TEN

There was very little smiling and chitchat when Aunt Libby arrived during breakfast. The mischievous spark in her pale blue eyes had been replaced with indignation and a focused intensity that would give a charging lion pause. *Like a mother bear after someone dared to mess with her cub,* thought Galen. *But she's gonna have to get in line.*

It didn't sit well with him that the dark creature had discovered where Kerri lived. *I led it straight to her.* After all this time, the damned thing must have been watching him and simply followed him here from the hospital. *And then I encouraged her to blast it. Way to go, McAllister—now it's pissed at her too.* He'd argued with Kerri twice more since daybreak, certain that the best thing he could do was leave. He hadn't won a single round, though. Her logic had been unassailable, but that didn't mean he felt good about it.

"Have a little faith," she'd said at last. "The universe brought you here for a reason." Which sounded fine as long as the universe was on his side and not the monster's.

It wasn't surprising that the four of them—Kerri, her aunt, Everett, and himself—ended up sitting around the kitchen table rather than the living room. His mother had always said that kitchens were the true nerve center of a home, more like an HQ than simply a place to feed people. And didn't *that* fit in with their mission? They weren't having a discussion, or even a pre-game huddle. This was a council of war.

Galen levitated a coffee cup just in time as Libby spread a thick sheaf of papers over the table. "I've been buried in books ever since I left here," she said. "And based on what Galen described plus Everett's eyewitness account this morning, I'm pretty sure I've found what we're looking for." She placed a series of photos of ancient stone walls carved with intricate reliefs. "We're dealing with something that's been around for a long, long time."

Kerri picked up a picture and studied it. "It's not Egyptian."

"No," said her aunt. "It's much older. This artwork was created by the Sumerians, who lived in Mesopotamia almost six thousand years ago. In fact, Sumer has often been credited as humanity's very first civilization, although that's being debated now that we've found new sites to study. Regardless, these people built amazing cities, developed a written language, and a complex culture. Their religion acknowledged hundreds of gods and lesser gods."

Galen studied the photos until one caught his attention. "This weird star here, the one with the eight arms like a starfish? It's just like the one drawn on the floor of that burned-out apartment."

"Good," said Libby. "That helps confirm my suspicions. I told you that the Sumerians worshipped many gods, but they also recognized their opposites." She placed a new picture on top of the pile. It wasn't a photo but an illustration: a man-like creature with a wide mouth filled with long sharp teeth. His—*its*—eyes were completely black with no whites at all.

"Ugly bugger," said Everett. "That's pretty damn close to the thing that growled at me last night."

Galen could only nod. If he was capable of a physical reaction, he'd be having the worst case of skin-crawling *heebie jeebies* this side of a Stephen King novel. As it was, the image was damn tough to look at. Flashbacks assaulted his mind, and he was grateful when Kerri turned the picture face down.

"Last night I went from creeped out to angry," she said to her aunt. "If I stare at that picture any longer, I'll be right back to *creeped out*. But I want to hear every detail you know about this thing."

"Especially the part where we kick its ass," muttered Everett.

Libby nodded and waved a hand at the face-down picture. "The name for this creature is *Rabisu*, and it was believed to be a demon that wandered between worlds."

Worlds? Plural? Galen was certain that his eyebrows had just merged with his hairline. "Please tell me we're not talking about aliens."

"Not the way you mean," said Kerri. "Not the outer space, interplanetary types. It's more likely that the Rabisu is an interdimensional traveler."

As Galen silently mouthed the word *interdimensional*, Everett leaned towards him. "Remember what I said about the rhododendron, son?" he whispered.

Right. A bush that's really a part-time portal... But then, here he was separated from his physical body, so who was he to say what was weird and what wasn't? As if sensing his distress, Kerri slid her hand close to his on the table, and he focused on sending energy to his fingertips where she would feel it. The smile that lit her face made him feel a little better, even lighter, despite the gravity of the situation.

"All I could find was an artist's representation," continued Libby. "While there aren't any known images made by the Sumerians themselves, we still know what the creature looks like from their descriptions of it. The people spent a lot of time writing spells on cuneiform tablets, and making amulets and talismans, to protect themselves from the Rabisu."

"Okay, so they had a name for this monster," said Galen. "And they had spells and whatnot to protect themselves from it. But what about undoing the damage it caused? Did they know how to do that?"

"Believe me, I'll get to that, I promise, but first we all need to understand what we're up against."

Emotionally, he'd rather cut to the chase, but she was right of course. Galen had studied fire science, even had a degree in it—and still, out of all that knowledge, the most basic principle remained the most important: you had to know what you were dealing with before you tried to fight a blaze. Putting water on a chemical fire, for instance, would only make things worse. He stuffed his impatience into a locker in his mind, hoped like hell it would hold, and nodded at Libby.

"The word *rabisu* means to seize or to grab," she continued. "According to the Sumerians, the Rabisu fed on the life force of human beings. It hunted by hiding in the dark and waiting for a chance to grab its prey. Some accounts tell of it attacking people as they slept, siphoning off their energy. One thing all the records agree on is that the more energy the Rabisu ingests, the more power it has to affect things in the physical world."

"And it's been feeding off Galen!" Kerri looked horrified. He found the notion pretty repulsive too.

Libby nodded. "Just as psychic vampires do."

Vampires now? *What the hell?* Immediately, he hoped he hadn't said that out loud, but everyone was looking at him. Of course, it could just be the dumb look he was certain he was wearing...

"We're not talking *Dracula* here," whispered Kerri. "No blood is involved."

"Good," Galen said and meant it. "Because I was definitely 'Team Jacob' when *Twilight* came out." Nobody laughed at his lame joke, but Kerri's eye roll made it worth it.

"Blood or no blood, it's a parasitic relationship just the same," said Libby. "We've all been in a crowd, perhaps a store, an elevator, or a bus, and suddenly felt drained for no reason. Most of us brush it off as a bug, a sudden onset of the flu or a cold, maybe lack of sleep or even something we ate. We might feel tired for an hour or exhausted for days. In truth, it's often because someone has stolen some of our energy. Or, as the Sumerians called it, our *shi*, the breath of life."

"And this creature, this Rabisu, must be doing the same thing," added Kerri.

"Is that why he didn't kill me outright?" asked Galen. "So he could drop by and have lunch whenever the hell he felt like it?" He got up and paced the kitchen, as his mind put together some of the puzzle pieces. "You know, it's been bugging me for a while that it wasn't personal. The creep in the burned-out apartment addressed me by name but he really didn't know me. In fact, I don't think he gave a shit who I was. I was just some kind of—what did he say?" He fought to remember the exact words. "A *subject.* That's it. He set the fire because he was hoping for *subjects to keep him going.* And he said I'd serve the purpose. Now I know what he meant."

That's when a new realization dawned. "Actually, he said I'd do nicely *for a while.* So, I was right, he's doing this to other people too." *Way to go, McAllister. All wrapped up in your own problems while that thing racks up five thousand goddamn years of stealing lives...* Dear God, just how many deaths were on its hands?

"We have no way of knowing what the Rabisu's needs are," said Libby. "It's impossible to guess how many other people might be in your situation at present. But I'd be very surprised if you're the only one he's feeding from."

"We've got to find him and stop him," Galen declared. "Whether you can undo what's happened to me or not, we have to stop him from doing this to anyone else. Isn't there a spell to kill this thing?"

"That's not the kind of magic we practice," Libby said firmly. "And even if we did, it's far beyond our abilities to accomplish."

"Are you kidding me? You—you created a frickin' *force field* around the entire house! And Kerri's spell forced the Rabisu to leave in one helluva hurry. I don't understand how it works, but you and Kerri have real power."

"Galen, trying to reunite you with your body will take everything we have, and it still might not be enough," Libby said. "It's true that I've studied magic my entire life, and Kerri is very accomplished for her age. But we're talking about a being that even the Sumerians themselves couldn't get rid of with their most powerful sorceries."

"But you just said they had all kinds of spells!"

She shook her head. "All they could hope for was to repel it for a time. And by the way, this is a creature that's had *thousands* of years in which to practice its own magic.

"Quite frankly, we're no match for it."

* * * * *

As her aunt revealed more and more details from her research, Kerri proposed that they move to her office. The plot points for her novel-in-progress were pinned to an enormous cork board that covered one wall, and it didn't seem to take long before her existing outline was almost completely covered with notes on ancient Sumerian energy vamps. *Maybe I should write a book about* that *instead,* she thought. Publishers were always asking for something different...but they probably would find an energy-sucking demon far too fantastical a concept.

Kerri only wished it was.

Aunt Libby had indeed come up with a spell to reunite Galen with his physical body. She'd even managed to round up some of the more exotic ingredients for it. As with any incantation, however, it would come down to *intent*. A great deal of focus would be required of all of them. Plus, like it or not, they simply had to have one more person in order to pull this off.

Everett had volunteered, bless him, but his abilities were limited. The spell had to be performed where Galen's body *was*—and although Kerri had often tried to take her dear old friend on outings, it seldom worked out well. He didn't seem to mind visiting Libby's house on occasion. Anything else, however, was just too far out of Everett's comfort zone. As she pinned yet another note to the board, she resolved to approach Fred, the nurse at Sacred Family. *He has a family connection to magic and a respect for it. And he cares about Galen.*

"Tomorrow night will be our first night," said Libby, bringing Kerri back to the present.

"Our first night for what?" asked Galen.

"The magic that imprisons you is extremely powerful. One ritual might not be sufficient to unmake it. I suggest a casting of three times three."

He looked puzzled and Kerri quickly translated: "We're going to perform the spell every night for the next nine days. Nine's a very powerful number."

"Sounds good to me," he said. "I figure the more mojo, the better."

She looked over at her aunt. "Are you sure we can be ready by tomorrow night? Maybe we need a little more time to prepare." The sudden distraught expression on Libby's face caught Kerri by surprise.

"The truth is, hon, I don't think we have that luxury."

It was on the tip of Kerri's tongue to ask *why not*. Instead, she barely managed to stifle a gasp as the significance of all the clocks in her terrible nightmare suddenly became clear. Stunned, she put down the papers and thumbtacks before she dropped them, and carefully returned to her chair.

Libby's attention was all on Galen now. "Some spells are time sensitive," she said gently.

He frowned. "What's that mean? Is it going to expire or something?"

"I wish it was, but I'm afraid it's like an expiry date in reverse. Some spells are strengthened the longer they remain in place. And evil always gets stronger the longer it's unchallenged."

"And?" pressed Galen.

It was Everett who was brave enough to fill in the rest: "She means that if the spell isn't unmade by a certain time, it'll become permanent, son."

Kerri moved closer to Galen, but it was all she could do. The news had obviously hit him like a two by four, yet she couldn't touch him.

"How long?" he managed.

Libby looked him squarely in the eye. "Usually only a year. The basic principles are the same no matter what type of magic you're dealing with. And so, the anniversary date is most likely the key that locks in the spell."

"Christmas Day. This happened to me on Christmas. That's only—"

"Ten days away," finished Kerri's aunt. "Including today, we have ten days to unmake this spell."

He swallowed, hard, before regaining his composure. "And you're going to do it nine times. We've got exactly the right number of days," he said. "I guess we'll just keep swinging until the very end."

"Damn right we will," said Everett. "I'll loan you my bat."

"I just might need it." Galen laughed a little, then reached over and took first Kerri's hand, then Libby's. Kerri felt the warm tingle as energy enclosed her fingers. "It's a good plan," he said. "Thanks. Whichever way it goes, thanks."

* * * * *

By the time Aunt Libby left to teach her evening class, Kerri had a pounding headache. Lack of sleep, the frightening events of the night before, and the new discovery that they only had a very small window in which to free Galen, all combined to make her put her head on her desk. Her lids practically *fell* shut and she left them that way. At least she wouldn't have to look at the accusingly blank screen of her laptop. She was pages behind on her latest novel, but she had to have some peace, had to breathe, had to concentrate, had to think, dammit!

Because she couldn't accept that there might be a future in which there was no Galen.

At least he seems to be taking it well. She'd watched his eyes when her aunt told him about the time limit. The appalling news had taken him by surprise, but the knee-jerk fear had been quickly replaced with solid determination. This was a man who would go down fighting to regain the life that had been stolen from him, and it warmed her with respect and something more...

As if on cue, tiny pulses of energy soft as a whisper, planted themselves along the exposed skin of her neck. Every delicate hair on her body instantly stood on end as if straining to capture each nuance, each vibration. She stifled a moan but a hint of it squeaked out just the same.

A deep voice murmured, "It's been a long day." It tickled her ear with the same cool sweet energy that his kisses held.

"I thought you were playing cards with Everett," said Kerri, opening one eye and enjoying the sight of him. His dark gray hoodie lent intriguing shadows to his strong-featured face. *I can't believe I'm attracted by a sweatshirt, but he makes it look downright sexy.* And if she was truthful, those phantom kisses on her neck had aroused her more than a little.

"Well, we worked at it for a while, but I can tell it frustrates him that he can't hold a single card yet. He said his favorite show was coming on and I took it as a cue that he'd had enough practice for the moment."

"You're probably right."

"Know what else I'm right about?"

"What?"

"That you're exhausted. You didn't sleep for the rest of the night after the Rabisu showed up. And you've beaten a path to the coffee maker ever since."

She sighed. "I admit to feeling like a little kid afraid of the dark. I didn't want to go back to sleep in case that horrible creature came back."

"There's nothing wrong with that. Some things are worth being afraid of, like fire. Fear keeps you on your toes, keeps you alert. If you're not afraid, you get careless."

"Well, I'm not in any danger of being careless then."

"I can tell. When I kissed your neck, I noticed that you have a big knot of tension right at the base of it." He leaned closer. "I can fix that for you."

The automatic refusal died on her lips when an invisible hand began to circle the muscles between her shoulder blades. "Oh, no fair…" As protests went, it sounded pretty feeble even to her.

"Move just a little. Keep your head down but rest it on your hands. That's the way." He eased behind her and his fingertips moved in sublime *figure eights* all along her spine from the top of her neck to the bottom of her hips, and back. "Now just relax."

"I can see…that resistance…is futile," she managed. It was true. She felt utterly helpless against the delicious pressure that miraculously made each muscle untie itself. Galen found every bit of tension and released it as if by magic, leaving soothing warmth in its place. *Omigod, this is better than sex*, she thought, and immediately wished that particular subject hadn't crossed her mind. Perhaps it crossed Galen's too, because without any warning the massage blossomed into a burst of liquid heat that rocketed through her entire body.

Her last coherent thought was how glad she was that she was sitting down…

ELEVEN

Kerri woke with a loud rumbling sound in her ears. Automatically she reached out a foot and nudged the snoring pug on her bed. As always, it was like trying to budge a furry cannonball, but at last Waldo shifted and his buzz saw racket gave way to light wheezing. She rolled over and stared at her alarm clock on the nightstand.

Five a.m. *Five* a.m. *What the hell?* Trying to do the math made her brain plead for coffee, but the rest of her felt incredibly refreshed and relaxed. She had to have slept between ten and twelve hours, undoubtedly due to Galen's bone-melting massage—not to mention that little surprise finish! Just thinking about it brought on a delicious whole-body shiver. There was probably some etiquette book somewhere that said the man had stepped over the line a tad, but she certainly wasn't going to complain.

Of slightly more concern was the fact that she couldn't seem to remember anything after that orgasmic back rub. How on earth had she gotten herself upstairs to bed? Galen had solemnly promised he wouldn't carry her again without permission—and she was pretty sure she hadn't given it. *I must have been on auto-pilot and went to bed on my own. I've made coffee lots of times and not remembered that I did it.* And a hundred other little things too, *familiar tasks oft repeated*, or however that old saying went.

There had been nothing automatic about her dreams, however. No weird libraries and falling books this time, just a long string of normal, pleasant, everyday activities—

painting the house, shopping at the market, wading in the waves at the beach, even washing the dishes (and who in their right mind dreamed about washing dishes?) But in every scenario, Galen was at her side, warm and tangible and *real*. Her palm still pulsed with the memory of his hand surrounding hers. She'd been held close in strong, loving arms that felt like, well, *arms* instead of simply energy.

And she wanted that dream with everything that was in her. *I'm in love*, she thought, and her wonder was mixed with a touch of dismay. She'd been attracted to Galen from the moment she met him, and accepted that her feelings were growing. But surely she'd held back a little? Knowing the enormous risk, knowing the odds were heavily stacked against having a normal relationship with him, Kerri was certain she'd been keeping some part of her heart safe. *The joke's on me*, she thought. *You can't parcel out bits of your heart like you're rationing water in a desert.* The stakes with Galen were a little higher than most—okay, they were damn daunting—but didn't everyone who dared to love risk devastation? She loved him, and she would love him with a whole heart for whatever time they were granted...

Which reminded her of tonight's mission, when they would begin the spell that might free him. "Please let it work," she whispered fervently as she sat on the edge of the bed and felt around for her slippers with her toes. *Please let it work.*

Kerri shuffled to the dresser mirror and noticed two things in the reflection at once. One was behind her. Waldo had somehow found his way to a forbidden pillow when she wasn't looking, and was snoring as if he'd been there all night. *How does he do that?* She sighed and decided not to shoo him off. After ten years, her pug was no longer an early riser, and deserved to sleep until midmorning. Even if it meant she'd have to wash dog hair off her pillows.

The scarier thing in the mirror was her own hair. Sleep had flattened the wild auburn curls on one side of her head and frizzed them into a lion's mane on the other. *Okay, so skipping a shower is not an option today.* While her hair would never be truly tamed, washing and conditioning would restore some sort of symmetrical shape. As she stepped into the tub, she mentally crossed her fingers that the aged and ailing hot water heater would cooperate.

Things went well at first. Then, just as she was ready to rinse the soap from her hair, the water sputtered to liquid ice. She flailed blindly to turn off the freezing spray even as she was trying to dance away from it. She hadn't yet found the knob when the water suddenly warmed again. The stream became full, and the temperature was exactly right. Kerri took a deep breath and began rinsing her hair as quickly as she could. There was no telling how long the hot water would last. She imagined the cantankerous water heater laughing evilly, trying to lull her into a false security so it could freeze her again. But the water remained steady. She even dared to enjoy massaging the conditioner into her long spiraling curls. Rinse again. Still good.

It wasn't until she pushed the clean, wet curls from her face that she spotted the handheld showerhead floating above its cradle. "Galen!" she yelled and snatched a towel that was draped over the glass doors. In answer, the long hose coiled briefly into the shape of a heart. "Very funny, now what are you doing in my bathroom?"

She sensed him right behind her then, and his deep voice rumbled oh-so-pleasantly in her ear. "I was hoping to pick up where I left off last night," he said, and carefully swept her hair aside to expose the back of her neck. "Let me make you feel good."

The cool energy of his unique kisses traveled skillfully over her sensitive nape, and her nipples tightened beneath the now soggy towel she clutched to herself. As expected, the sensible side of her brain protested loudly and trotted out the usual arguments—that it wasn't a good idea, that it was too soon to be feeling all the emotions she felt, that a relationship was out of the question until the man was back in his body…but as the phantom kisses traveled over her shoulders and worked their way down, she ordered her annoying inner voice to be *silent*. She was sure of just how deeply she felt about Galen, and she was sure of what she wanted. Which was whatever he was offering. *Anything. Everything.*

Out of the corner of her eye, her new bath puff appeared to be lathering itself with her best rosemary soap. A delicious little thrill ran down her spine. "Don't I get to see you?" she asked.

"Nope. Not yet. This is all about *feeling*. Just concentrate on that."

"Mmm…I think I can do that."

The kisses were replaced by the lightly circling puff, which left a trail of soft lather and tingling sensations behind as it worked its way down her back. She expected the shower head to follow, but it remained in its cradle. Instead, a wide ribbon of water emerged from it, looped up and around her, and rinsed away the soap. Her plain-Jane shower didn't boast a massage feature, but somehow Galen was making the water do amazing things to her skin—and that simple nylon puff was now in a class by itself. Kerri extended an arm to give both more access. The puff spun gently around her wrist and traveled up and down her arm. Deliciously warm water stroked close behind. She closed her eyes and lifted her other arm, allowing the towel to fall to her feet.

Both puff and water paused. "God, you're beautiful," whispered Galen.

She smiled as he resumed his sensual ministrations. *And you are sooo good at this.* He was finding so many sensitive spots she'd never even thought about. Who expected an elbow to be erotic? As ribbons of water and scented soap swirled around her breasts, spiraled over her hips and drizzled wonderfully down her legs, she found herself wishing she knew how to purr.

But it was only the beginning....

Unseen hands nudged her to a wider stance and she braced her own hands on the tiled walls. The puff slipped between her legs and she moaned as it stroked her ever so lightly, its soft lather foaming and tickling. Gently arousing, softly pleasing, coaxing her to greater excitement.

The water wasn't so subtle. The spinning rope of it licked hotly between her folds and slicked over her clit, causing her to gasp aloud. Even more intense pleasure awaited, when the water splayed into clever fingers and pressed into her. *Omigod, omigod, omigod...* She peaked, hips rocking helplessly as sensation shuddered through her.

Kerri opened her eyes to find Galen standing in front of her. Naked. If she looked hard enough, the tiles of the shower wall were still visible through his powerful body yet that didn't stop the spike of fresh arousal in her blood. She was still pulsing from the orgasm, yet she ached for him to touch her again.

He smiled then, slowly, lazily. Before her astonished eyes, the water from the shower appeared to pour into him, quickly filling every inch of him as if he were a tall glass. From head to toe, from fingertip to the tip of a very rampant cock, he appeared almost substantial. And when he stroked a hand down the side of her face, it was wet, it was warm, it was *amazing.*

She tried to grab his hand to look at it, but that didn't work. Her fingers clutched right through the watery shape. Instead, he obligingly held out a hand for her inspection. "This is incredible," Kerri murmured, running her fingertips lightly over his palm, discovering just the right amount of pressure that would allow her to skim the surface without breaking through. The water within him seemed to be moving, circulating rapidly yet was contained within the shape—*for now.* "Hey, this isn't going to turn out like the milk thing, is it? Because I don't swim all that well."

"Ten bucks says it'll hold. Trust me, I've been practicing."

"I just got my ten bucks *back* from you," she laughed. "Exactly how much practicing have you done?"

"I spent most of last night in the downstairs shower figuring out a technique and finessing it." His voice dropped to a whisper that made her toes curl. "So I could do *this.*" His hands circled her breasts, warming and sensitizing the skin. He bent his head to them and she felt the impression of masculine lips—and not the cool impressions of energy she'd experienced until now. These kisses were hot, wet and needy on her nipples, and Kerri moaned aloud.

All coherent thought disappeared like soap bubbles as Galen used both energy and water to wrap a powerful supporting arm around her waist—and the other hand slid slyly between her legs. Warm liquid caressed her pearl like a skillful mouth, thrumming like a subtle vibrator, and she opened readily, wanting, asking for more.

Nothing prepared her, however, for the powerful energy that suddenly suspended her, pinning her securely in place against the shower wall. But she was more than ready for Galen as he thrust into her. *Yes, yes, oh yes...* His water-cock filled her again and again, and she chanted his name as she shattered not once but twice more.

When awareness returned, she was sitting on the floor of the shower trying to catch her breath. Every bone in her body seemed made of limp spaghetti. The water was off, Galen had disappeared, and a persistent thumping noise came from the room beyond. No, wait, that was a knock, *someone is knocking.* She staggered to her feet, threw a bathrobe around herself and stumbled out to see Waldo with his flat nose pressed to the bottom of the door, his curled tail waggling with pure pugly anticipation of greeting whoever was on the other side.

It was Everett. "Sorry to bother you, Kerri-girl. But your first client's here. Should I tell them to come back?"

"No, no, that's fine. Thanks." She could feel her cheeks flame, but if Everett noticed anything, he gave no sign. "I just need a minute to get dressed and I'll be right down."

She waited until Waldo followed the old ghost down the hallway before she closed the door, then sagged against it for support. It was going to take a supreme effort to overcome her post-sex languor if she wanted to make her appointment. Had she *ever* felt this relaxed in her entire life? Kerri staggered to the dresser and pulled out some jeans and a t-shirt. *I probably don't have to worry about walking down the stairs. I can just pour myself over them like a waterfall!*

Dressed, she combed her hair with her fingers and left the room. *Where the hell is Galen?* It puzzled her that he wasn't in the hallway, or waiting at the bottom of the stairs for her. He wasn't in the kitchen—and she had to admit to more than a little disappointment that there was no fresh coffee for her either. Although it was hard to complain after he'd rocked her world (and then some), it still seemed a little callous, even rude, for him to disappear without a word.

So much for the afterglow...

* * * * *

Galen stared out the living room window at the snowy morning. Every big Victorian house in the cul-de-sac—even the purple one—looked Christmas-card perfect. Kerri looked damn perfect too as she hurried to her office for her first appointment of the day, a young man wearing a skater's cap backwards and baggy pants low enough to reveal colorful boxers.

She hadn't seen Galen at all.

He sighed and glanced down at Waldo, who was busy adoring him with big puggy eyes, although he probably couldn't do more than sense Galen's presence. "Sorry I can't help you out with a belly rub, buddy. I haven't got enough energy left to blow out a candle." It had never occurred to him that he might have limits. He'd never considered that the energy he commanded could be finite, or that perhaps his powers ought to be budgeted. And now, he had no idea when or *if* his energy would return. *Pretty hard to be sorry about what I spent it on, though.*

Everett wandered by with yet another client, a short thin woman wearing an apron and a hairnet. The nervous little ghost reminded Galen of one of the lunch ladies from his high school days, and he hoped Kerri could help her. His pugly companion trotted off after the pair, no doubt to provide moral support. *A therapy dog for the supernatural,* he thought. *Who'd have thunk it?*

Of course, there was a helluva lot he'd never thought of before. Ghosts. Magic. Demons. Spells. Never in his wildest dreams could Galen have imagined that this stuff was real. But then, he hadn't imagined it possible to be locked out of his body either. Now? If someone announced that Santa Claus existed, he'd be willing to entertain the notion. *I'd probably believe anything if it meant a chance to get my life back.* He'd wanted that from the beginning of course. But there was no denying that his reasons had changed.

I want to share a life with Kerri.

The woman used magic, sure, but in a very real way she *was* magic—and he was bespelled by her in the very best sense of the word. He loved the sound of her voice and how her laugh lit up a room. Loved her inherent kindness. Loved the way she was both fun to be with and deeply grounded. Plus, that little interlude in the shower had been nothing short of incredible. *Kerri* was incredible. He'd thoroughly enjoyed pleasuring her, coaxing her to feel more, take more. Her every response had fascinated and delighted him…

Too bad I couldn't feel a damn thing myself. It was beyond frustrating to be so divorced from his body, devoid of touch, of sensation, of pleasure. Especially when he couldn't stop thinking about it, when it was driving him crazy wondering what it would feel like to have Kerri's luscious curvy body pressed close against his skin. What would she smell like, taste like? He had to know. He had to get back into his body, and *know* what it was to have this woman in his arms. And find a way to keep her there.

"Galen!"

He turned to see Kerri, alarm written on her features. "What's wrong?"

"I can hardly see you at all, that's what's wrong! What hap—" Her voice trailed off as she made the connection. "You used up your energy. In the shower this morning, you nearly spent it all, didn't you? And dear God, I let you." She put her hand to her head. "I'm *so* sorry."

"Hey, it was my idea and I enjoyed every minute. Don't you dare be sorry. Unless of course you didn't like it." He grinned as color blushed along her neckline and into her face. The smile he was so fond of failed to appear, however.

"This is why you took off on me, isn't it?"

He didn't really want to tell her but there wasn't any way around the truth. "I never left," he admitted. "I was right beside you when suddenly I had some kind of weird power outage. You couldn't see me or even hear me when I spoke to you. But believe me, *I was still there*. I came downstairs when you did."

Kerri stared at him for a long moment, then sank onto the couch. "Galen, I have a pretty powerful gift. Do you know how far gone you'd have to be to completely vanish from my radar?"

He sat beside her. "That bad, huh? But look, I'm already recharging."

"Oh really? Maybe you're not totally invisible, but you might as well be made of glass. I could read a fine-print book through you without even squinting. And your voice sounds like it's coming from another room altogether." She shook her head. "We can't risk this again. It's already bothering me that I don't know how to make *you* feel good when you don't have a body yet. I have *orgasm guilt* for crying out loud! And now this."

No damn way did he want her to regret what they'd done. "I feel plenty in my mind and in my heart, things I hadn't even imagined, all because of you," he said. "And as far as the sex goes, believe me, I enjoyed the hell out of it." Galen leaned closer, still determined to tease a smile from her. "In fact, I've already been working on ideas for next time!"

"No! I just told you, there's no *next time*." Kerri put her hands up as if to ward him off. "Nobody has an unlimited amount of energy, no matter what dimension you exist in. We don't know how dangerous it could be for you to expend so much. Galen, what if it affects our spell tonight?"

He sobered at once. "Christ, I didn't think of that."

"Neither did I, but I should have. Like I told you, I've never met anyone who can do the things that you can. Oh sure, there are a few ghosts who can throw things around, slam doors and such. But you? You can finesse things—"

"Like I finessed you?"

She tried to ignore that comment, but it was hard. "I'm saying that you have unbelievable control. And that has to require tons more energy than the average poltergeist."

"Well, I pride myself on being above average, you know."

Kerri rolled her eyes. "Dammit, are you taking this seriously at all?"

More than you know. But I don't want to talk about it. Not now. "What I'm hearing is *no more nookie in the shower* until I've got my body back." He leaned close to her and stage-whispered. "And then we'll spend a week in there!"

He won a small smile from her at last. "We'd be prunes!" she said.

"Very satisfied prunes. I'm willing to take the risk, how about you?"

"Let's focus on getting your body back, water boy, and then we'll talk."

TWELVE

By the time Kerri's aunt arrived to pick them up, Galen had recovered quite a bit of his strength. Not enough, however, to prevent Libby from *also* noticing something was off.

"Galen McAllister!" She folded her arms and fixed him with a look she might have borrowed from his third-grade teacher. "What on earth have you been doing? I don't see you as well as Kerri does to begin with, but now I can barely see you at all!" The ensuing lecture on the importance of conserving his energy could have peeled paint from the walls, and he couldn't disagree with a single word of it. The only good part was that she didn't allow him a word in edgewise—because he sure as hell didn't want to explain *how* he'd spent his energy. As it was, he could see Kerri in the background looking guilty as hell.

It was Libby's last words however, delivered before she stormed to the kitchen in search of coffee, that had the most impact on Galen: "If I didn't have other gifts to tell me you were there, I might walk right by without even noticing you."

Without noticing me. That little notion would do more to keep him in line than anything else, he thought. What if he became invisible permanently, forever unable to connect with Kerri in any way? It would be unendurable. He'd have to leave, would have to go wherever real ghosts went…just as he'd planned to do after the monster showed up at her house. But he'd allowed Kerri to talk him out of it, instead of doing what was best for her. And as for the Great Shower Incident? *I should have left before things went so far between us.*

Too late, too damn late, for any of that. Whether it was a good idea or not, their feelings for each other were undeniable—and he would *not* break her heart by trying to leave now. But could he avoid breaking her heart in the future? What chance did they have if his condition was irreparable? He and Kerri existed on different planes. Surely, they'd be torn apart in the end. And that was assuming that some remnant of him even survived the malicious spell...

What if I cease to exist altogether?

It was eleven p.m. when Fred met Kerri and Libby in Room 440. With his hands on his hips and his brow heavily furrowed, the big man reminded Galen of his deputy chief. "I don't know how you gals get into the building or how you make it all the way up here without somebody noticing, and I don't ever *want* to know," he said sternly. "If anyone ever asks, I never saw you before in my life."

His expression melted when Kerri hugged him. "No problem, Fred. I can't thank you enough for agreeing to help us. To help Galen."

"We know you're taking a big risk," added Libby, putting down the bags she was carrying.

Fred shrugged. "I figure it falls somewhere under my oath, the part about *devoting myself to the welfare of those committed to my care.* Somebody's gotta help Mr. McAllister, and it's plain that mainstream medicine can't do it."

"We're not sure we can either, to be honest," said the older woman. "But we're sure gonna give it our best shot."

"Can't ask for more than that." Fred directed her to an extra bed-table parked to one side of the door, and helped her unpack her things.

Galen leaned towards Kerri. "Tell him I'm sorry I was late getting here this afternoon. I only heard the last part of the story, but it sounded great."

"What story?" she asked.

Ah, what the hell. He was supposed to be conserving his energy, but he didn't want to play the message game. If Fred was brave enough and committed enough to try to help him, then he deserved to know that his patient was present and accounted for. Galen motioned towards the locker on the opposite wall and a newspaper sprang from it like a newly freed bird. It flapped through the air towards a wide-eyed Fred, opened itself and folded back to reveal—

"*NASA Plans to Put Humans on Mars,*" Kerri read aloud.

"I…I thought it was interesting," said Fred, glancing around in case Galen might suddenly appear. He cleared his throat. "When I was a kid, I read a lot of Ray Bradbury books, *The Chronicles of Mars* and stuff like that. Always wanted to see the *red planet.*"

"Tell him it was a good choice," said Galen. "And thanks for reading it to me. Thanks for everything in fact."

Kerri started to relay the words, but Fred put his hand up. "Son, I don't know where you're hiding, but you can thank me best by getting your lily-white butt outta that bed and buying me a beer!"

Galen clapped Fred on the shoulder. To his credit, the man didn't jump—although his eyebrows nearly met his hairline.

"Did I really hear that?" he asked Kerri. "Did he just say *you're on?*"

"He certainly did," she laughed.

The nurse mopped his brow with a paper towel. "I always believed he was still with us, but this is gonna take some gettin' used to," he said. "You're gonna owe me *two* beers now, McAllister. And a darn big plate of buffalo wings to go with 'em."

Kerri used a ceremonial broom of bundled ash twigs—a "besom" she'd called it—to sweep negative energy from the room. As she worked, Libby and Fred pulled the bed containing Galen's still, pale body, plus all the monitoring equipment attached to it, as close to the center of the room as the electrical cords would permit. Together, they carefully laid out the items required for tonight's casting.

And his own contribution? *Nada.* Galen stood watching from a corner where Aunt Libby had banished him with strict instructions not to expend "one more iota" of energy unless she told him to. He watched as his friends rolled the reading table over to the bed and positioned it across his feet. *His feet. His body.* He almost felt like he didn't know it anymore, that he had no connection to the figure connected to by wires and tubes to noisy machines. Uncomfortable, Galen chose to focus on Libby as she stood at the foot of the bed and spread a small woven white cloth on the table. Next, she placed a series of tiny clay bowls on it, then some small, corked bottles, containing water, salt and herbs.

Fred added a metal incense burner to her collection. He pulled a lighter from his pocket and as the first tendrils of scented smoke began to waft upwards, he frowned and shook his head. "This is bound to set off the sprinkler system, you know."

"Trust me, it won't," Libby said simply. "Would you please set out the candles too?"

The big man did as she asked, setting nine tall white pillar candles around the room. Each candle was notched, divided into nine sections, one for each night they would perform the spell. Fred still looked a little dubious, but he lit them all.

No alarms sounded.

Meanwhile, Kerri finished her task and hung the bundled twigs on the wall above a chair where a bare picture hook protruded. To his surprise, she added a few sprigs of plastic holly and a big red velvet bow.

"Um. Looks festive?" Galen attempted.

"That's the idea. Everyone will think it's a Christmas decoration, and—"

The light went on. "And it'll be hidden in plain sight for us to use every night," he finished. "If this spell works, I promise we'll give your broom a permanent place of honor over the fireplace."

"It's a *besom*," she corrected, but beamed at him until her aunt motioned them over.

"We need all the help that we can get," said Libby. "And thus we'll begin by petitioning the assistance of the four directions before we cast our circle."

Galen tried to follow along as everyone faced north, then east, south and west. He'd seen something like it once before when a Native American friend in college had performed a sweetgrass ceremony. At the time Galen had thought it was merely a respectful tribute to history. Now he wasn't so sure. How many times in his life, he wondered, had magic crossed his path and he hadn't realized it?

Libby handed Kerri a small fan of white feathers. "Be careful not to trip on the cords, hon. We can't draw a physical circle on the floor, but we'll create one just the same by invoking the elements."

Kerri nodded. She held the feathers in front of her, flicking her wrist to fan the air as she walked slowly clockwise around the room—taking care to step carefully over the cables and tubes which anchored both bed and machinery to the wall.

"Element of air, as I circle all about,

Bring us courage, lift our hearts, and cast away all doubt."

Fred was next. He grinned a little sheepishly as he took a bowl of salt from Libby. "My grandfather must be laughing at me from the other side. I kept telling him I wasn't interested in magic, that I wanted to work in medicine. He kept telling me that magic *was* medicine." The big man followed the path that Kerri had traveled, and his baritone voice was strong and sure.

"Element of earth, as I circle once again,

Cast out fear and bring in hope, and consecrate this plane."

Libby took the next circuit with a small pitcher of water.

"Element of water, as I pace this circle round,

Banish darkness, banish harm, and consecrate this ground."

Kerri gave Galen an encouraging smile. Carefully he lifted the incense burner by its bail, allowing it to swing slowly before him as he walked. It was like trying to carry a damn bowling ball with his little finger. Not because the delicate bronze filigree of the burner was heavy, but because he was still low on energy. If anything, it underscored what he was fighting for, what they were all fighting for with him.

"Element of fire, lend this circle strength and light.

Protect all those who stand within and guard our task this night."

As Kerri gave him a thumbs-up, Galen suddenly detected a subtle thrumming, like a quiet vibration from an unseen source. Was the room brighter? Just as he was about to ask questions, Libby took up her cane—and unsheathed a slender silver sword from it! *Holy shit, she really* is *Indiana Jones!* The device might appear in every cheesy adventure movie ever made, but the older woman held the sword with quiet dignity. Slowly, silently, she walked the circle again, drawing the gleaming metal tip lightly along the floor, lifting it only to clear the cords. To Galen's amazement, a line of blue-white light began to glow where the sword had touched. And when she finished, every candle abruptly flared up until their narrow flames nearly reached the ceiling.

Libby resumed her place at the foot of the bed. The candles returned to normal. The circle of light faded. Yet he knew the power was still there. He could feel it all around him.

"Galen," she said. "Please stand in the center just like you did before."

So not *my favorite thing.* It had weirded him out the first time he'd stood in the middle of his body, but he was determined to do anything that was asked of him. Anything that might help him to regain his life again—especially if it meant a chance to share that life. But for a moment he looked down at that face, *his* face, pale and motionless and intubated to the max. If it wasn't for the respirator causing his chest to rise and fall, somebody could mistake him for dead. *Not your best look, buddy...*

"Galen," whispered Kerri, shaking him out of his study. She stood on his right side, and Fred and Libby were on his left. Together they joined hands with each other, encompassing Galen where he stood. A circle within a circle.

"We gather here upon this night, the three of us a wrong to right.

By the power of three times three, no longer shall this binding be.

Free to live and free to soar, let him walk as man once more..."

They spoke in unison, calmly and quietly, yet Galen felt every word as if a great bell had been rung. There could be no question that real power had been brought to bear in this room. Still, his faith was centered not in the spell that was being cast but in these people who had selflessly rallied to his aid. He focused on joining any energy he could muster to theirs.

* * * * *

A utilities truck with flashing yellow lights was parked a few blocks away, its four-man crew laboring to locate the cause of the outage. Nah'mindhe was unconcerned. Mortals were *powerless* in more ways than one, and could do nothing to return light to the little city of Colfax until he permitted it. Likewise, they could neither prevent nor disturb the Unspoken One's purpose this night...

The overcast sky created a deeper, more complete darkness. Save for the occasional glare of headlights in the distance, it was reminiscent of the shadowy world he'd left behind millennia ago. He gloried in the cool sweet shadows and glided openly along the sidewalks until he reached a small green and white house that had fallen into disrepair. There, it was the work of a moment to slip between the door and the jamb, to float along the walls and slide soundlessly beneath the bedroom door.

The woman was in her bed of course. The Unspoken One had steadily supped upon her energy ever since he'd followed her home last year. Now, he waited in utter stillness for what he knew would surely come this night: the last breath, the departure of the soul, and with them, the *Ezebu Shi*—the final burst of energy as the woman died. It was like the passing of a minor star.

The natural patience of a predator was absent this night however. Nah'mindhe found himself anxious for the injection of power. More, he was frustrated that it would have to last until he could attend the final moments of another mortal. There was nothing wrong with the system he'd created. In fact, it worked flawlessly. The unseen conduits of energy that flowed to him from his collection of stricken prey sustained him very well for a time. In recent months, however, he found himself constantly hungering for more and more…until now, only regular infusions of *Ezebu Shi* could fully assuage his appetite. Where once it had been an occasional indulgence, a delicacy, it now seemed essential to his strength and power.

Again, the Unspoken One considered his numberless years as the source of his increasing needs. And again, he rejected the idea. He was timeless, ageless, immortal. He would not succumb to non-existence. He would transcend all, no matter what it required.

Including the consumption of *Ezebu Shi* several times a day.

Nah'mindhe smiled at the thought. To achieve such a thing, he would need many, *many* more victims. Of necessity he had been cautious in the past. He'd always been careful to spread out his kills lest a concentration of prey in one place drew unwanted attention. But now, with his strength renewed and growing, who did he have to fear? His powers were such that he was once more a god among helpless cattle.

And he would begin his grand plan with the humans who were trying to aid Galen McAllister. As soon as Nah'mindhe consumed the firefighter's dying energy, he would turn his attention to the women, particularly the young one. He was still tempted to drain her dry, feasting on her shining vigor like a great lion on a slender antelope—but he was having second thoughts. She would make a fine beginning to his enhanced collection, and he would still get to experience her

Ezebu Shi in time. Likewise, the woman who traveled with her, the healer, plus the older man who had joined them…

Nah'mindhe was perfectly aware of the trio's efforts at Sacred Family Hospital. Despite the distance, he could feel the faint but frantic tug on his energies the way a spider could sense a fly struggling in its web. And, like the fly, their little exertions were futile. Ancient magic such as his could not be overturned, and in a scant few days, his work would be unassailable. *Let them do what they will. I will take Mr. McAllister's shi—and then I will take* theirs *as well.*

All of it.

In the meantime, however, it might prove entertaining to watch them…

THIRTEEN

The morning sun coaxed glints of gold from the snowy fields as Kerri directed her little red car onto the highway exit that would take them northeast. Galen was in the passenger seat. If she squinted, she could still see right through him to the scenery passing by, yet it seemed the most natural thing in the world to have him by her side. In fact, the only weird thing in the whole scenario was his lack of a seatbelt…which of course he had no need of.

"Are we there yet?" he asked for the third time.

"Not trying to make me sorry I brought you, are you?" She took a quick swig of coffee from her travel mug. *Yuck. I should have let Galen make it.* "We're barely past the city limits."

"Hey, somebody has to ask the question or it's not officially a family event. You said Yule was a family thing."

"I *said* our family celebrates it. Didn't you notice all the phone calls?"

"I couldn't miss them. You talked to your mom and dad for nearly two hours."

"It wasn't long enough, believe me. They're in Guangzhou for a couple of months right now, visiting my brother, Ryan, and his new wife, Daiyu. I can hardly wait for them to move back to Seattle next summer, so we can all get together *here* again."

"I often thought it must be fun to have a big family at Christmastime. There was usually just me and my mom. Although we had a lot of fun, I often wished I had some siblings to play with."

"I don't know about sisters, but I found brothers to be highly overrated when I was growing up. They used to tease me all the time, and do unspeakable things to my dolls."

Galen grinned. "I probably would have helped them."

She laughed as she pictured him conspiring with Ryan and Ben and Baxter, the perfect partners in crime. They'd adopt him readily, no doubt of that. *But is the world ready? If they ever get together, they'll be like a force of nature!* Kerri hoped Galen got the chance to experience having brothers— and her mirth abruptly faded. They were doing all they could do, but the future was still uncertain. Smoothly (she hoped), she changed the subject. "Where's Everett?"

"Probably still practicing. While you were chatting, I gave him another lesson in *prestidigitation*."

Deliberately, Kerri took another long sip of coffee. "It's way too early in the morning for words that big," she grumbled, but inside she was relieved that he hadn't overheard her conversation with her folks. How would he feel if he knew that she'd been asking for their help on his behalf? *But we need all the help we can get!* Once mobilized, the Tollbrook clan's assistance would be considerable too. Every relative she had would send positive energy as a matter of course, but now they would also dedicate the unique magic of the season to Galen's cause.

It was December 21st, and the date was known by many names. Solstice. Yule. Midwinter's Eve. Tonight would be the longest night of the year and, by tiny degrees, the daylight hours would increase from this point on. It was a time to welcome the return of the sun to the wintry earth, and to celebrate the triumph of light over dark. Kerri hoped the ageless symbolism of Yule would lend them strength in their battle against the darkness that held the man she loved captive.

Tonight, they would perform the spell for the sixth time. Five nights in a row, an hour before midnight, the four of them—Aunt Libby, Fred, Galen, and herself—had gathered in the dim hospital room, cast a circle, and invoked the elements. Sought the aid of spirit and light, appealed to higher powers to help them. The magic they were striving to create must be the polar opposite of the demon's sorcery. *The Rabisu doesn't ask, it just takes. It forces energies to obey it—and it's very, very strong.*

Galen knew it too. It had been difficult to convince him that they would be safe in Kerri's car, that her aunt had warded it with the same powerful spells that protected Libby's old boat of a Lincoln. He had faith in Kerri's own magical ability, though, citing the night the monster attacked the house. She wasn't half as confident in her talents as he was—but she wasn't going to live in fear of the Rabisu either, afraid to leave her house.

"Okay, that's it. Pull over," said Galen.

"What? What's wrong?"

"You heard me." The natural humor in his voice had been replaced by pure steel. "This is the fourth time you've wandered too close to the center line. I told you this trip was a bad idea when you're so tired."

"No fair to pull the I-told-you-so card." *Even if you did tell me so. Repeatedly.* He'd argued in favor of purchasing a tree from a lot that was only a few blocks from her house. And on the surface, it was a perfectly sound idea—if all they wanted was a simple Christmas tree. She'd tried hard to explain the finer points of a Yule tree, and that they didn't come pre-cut! She sighed. "Galen, I'm not going home. This is too important. We need every bit of positive energy we can get from celebrating the Solstice. I know it'll help our magic."

"I didn't say we were going home, but you sure as hell haven't got the energy to drive."

She didn't have the energy to argue anymore either, especially when deep down she knew he was right. In addition to the late hours, she hadn't been sleeping well. As her feelings for Galen had grown, so had her anxiety about losing him. During the day, she could resist the stress and worry. But at night, she was just too tired to keep it at bay. Kerri checked her mirrors and slowly pulled off onto the shoulder of the road. She put the car into park and sighed. "I'll just take a catnap, then I'll be good to go again."

He gave her a look. "We don't have time for that. I'll take the wheel."

"Wait a minute—you're not supposed to use up your energy, remember? Aunt Libby will strangle us both if you show up tonight on half-wattage."

"Trust me, a machine doesn't require a lot of energy to operate. Or finesse." He leaned close and his deep voice dropped to a whisper. "It's not like making love, you know."

Kerri tried to look stern, but a delicate shiver ran through her, and beneath all the layers she was wearing, her nipples tightened. "Fine. I'm trusting you to drive. *Sanely and within the speed limit*, thank you. I don't want to get pulled over."

Galen laughed. "Deal. Just stay where you are, and put your hands in your lap."

"But—"

"Other drivers can't see below your shoulder. They'll just assume you hold the wheel low."

I guess that makes sense. Kerri dropped her hands and expected Galen to drive from his side of the vehicle, just as he had in the parking lot of the shopping mall the night she met him. But he surprised her by somehow slipping into the driver's seat with her. *Omigod.* She could see his hands on the wheel in front of her, but the rest of him was somehow around her, in her, through her, and yet separate. It was intimate beyond anything she'd ever imagined—and they'd been pretty damn *intimate* in the shower! This was different though, a gentle melding of auras, perhaps even of souls...

"Are you comfortable with this?" he asked softly, and she was hard-pressed to define where his voice originated. Beside her head—or in it?

"Kind of gives a whole new meaning to *invading my space*." She made quotations marks in the air.

"Not quite what I was going for," he laughed. "I just figured it makes more sense for me to drive from *here* like I'm used to. As long as it's not weirding you out. Okay?"

Still marveling at the profound sensation of oneness, she just nodded. A moment later, her car pulled smoothly back onto the highway. It was unexpectedly easy. Except for giving a few directions, she didn't have to do a single thing—and gradually, any remaining reservations disappeared. "You know, this is really kind of nice."

"Sitting with me or driving with me?"

"Both," she laughed. "I feel like I'm in a Galen cocoon, all warm and comfy and safe. And I have no complaints about your driving. Maybe I should just hire you to be my chauffeur."

"I could get into that. Dark shades, a *men-in-black* suit like the Secret Service. You've got to get a more dignified vehicle, though. This is a toy."

"It is not! I love this car!"

He attempted to make a case for a big black SUV with four-wheel drive, and Kerri wasn't all that certain he was kidding. They were still arguing when they arrived at the end of a long country lane that hadn't seen a lot of traffic, judging by the amount of snow down the center of it.

Galen surveyed the surroundings. "You know, I was expecting a tree farm, not a forest. We're not re-enacting the *Griswold family Christmas*, are we?"

"Come on, where's your sense of adventure?"

"I get plenty on the job, believe me. Please tell me you've been here before because I sure as hell didn't bring any breadcrumbs. I'm already wishing we had that SUV."

She rolled her eyes. "One of my friends owns this land, and she lets me choose a tree from it every year. I come here quite a bit in the summer too. So yes, I know the place." Kerri loved it too. "In fact, I've dreamed for years about building a house here, maybe having a little hobby farm." That sparked a new thought. *What are Galen's dreams?* He must have had goals, dreams, or maybe even a bucket list of sorts before his body was stolen. She made a mental note to ask him, but right now, the quest for the perfect tree needed all her attention.

Her backpack swung from one shoulder as they trudged through the snow. In reality, *she* did all the trudging. Galen was unimpeded by the drifted trails, and had insisted on carrying the saw "for safety's sake." He pointed out the merits of potential trees along the way, but none of them felt right to her.

Thirty minutes later he asked: "Are you sure you're not just being picky? Because that last fir was a beauty. A perfect pyramid, and not a single bare spot anywhere."

"I know, but it's not appearance that counts."

"Yeah, well, *time* counts. I don't want you out here too long. You need to rest."

"Hey, *Mr. Bossypants*, some things can't be rushed!"

"See? Now you're cranky."

It was on the tip of her tongue to deny it, when she realized how childish that would sound—and how right he was. *Good grief.* Instead, she took a deep breath and explained: "I'm looking for something special, a tree that calls out to me because it knows that we need it."

Galen stopped in his tracks (or rather *her* tracks, since he didn't make any). "You talk about them like they're aware."

"They are." She waved a hand at the forest around them. "All the trees are. In fact, most things are to some degree."

"Sooo…you're not looking for a perfect tree, you're looking for a *volunteer*?"

"You could put it that way. We're not walking up to just any old tree and taking it. The tree is offering up its life freely, so we can observe the Solstice." She expected Galen to ask more questions but although his eyebrows lifted slightly, he simply motioned for her to carry on. *Does that mean he's beginning to understand? That he feels more comfortable with magic and able to trust it?* With her luck, he'd probably concluded that she was crazy, and he should just humor her.

Kerri pushed all of that out of her mind and focused. Around her, the air was clear and cold, refreshing rather than uncomfortable. The snow alternately sparkled in the sun and cast blue shadows. Here and there were the footprints of many birds, a rabbit, and three or four deer. It was peaceful, and she allowed that peace to seep into her…

It was only a few minutes later that she felt a faint vibration, one that barely skimmed the edges of her awareness. Following it, she worked her way around a prickly thicket of wild rose bushes and came upon its source.

"You gotta be kidding me," said Galen.

"Shh." Kerri pulled off a glove and gently touched the evergreen branches. The soundless thrum of life was in the boughs, slowed by the winter cold. But was there something more? "We need your help," she whispered to the tree. In her mind's eye, she saw the silvery wisp of energy even as she felt it flow softly over her fingers.

"Thank you," she breathed.

It was big—and the damnedest ugliest tree Galen had ever seen. Outside of being some kind of short-needled evergreen, it couldn't look *less* like a holiday decoration. There were ragged cones still dangling from the boughs and at least three old bird nests inside it. No shortage of bare spots, more than a few dead twigs and branches, plus near its base a big swatch of bark had been charred from some long-ago fire. The oddest thing was its trunk, however. It divided into a nearly perfect *U* halfway up, resulting in a pair of crowns instead of one.

Great, a two-headed tree, Galen thought. Where the hell do you put the star? The guys at the station would have razzed him for the rest of his natural life if he'd brought in something like this. Even Charlie Brown wouldn't pick this tree. Hell, Frankenstein wouldn't choose it.

But Kerri loved it, and that was all that mattered. He didn't understand everything she'd explained about Yule and the Solstice, but if she said it was important, then he trusted that it was. Because of her, he'd been introduced to a wider world, one that he had never known existed outside of old fairy tales and fantasy novels. He watched from a respectful distance as she cast a large circle around the tree, not with salt or sword, but with birdseed, alfalfa cubes, and dried apple slices as a gift to the wildlife that lived here. Finally, she addressed the tree itself:

"Forest tree touched by water and fire,

Please shed your light on darkness dire.

Forest tree touched by earth and air,

We ask you for your life to share.

Still evergreen despite your scars,

Please merge your energy with ours.

This time when day wins over night

Loan us your strength to win our fight."

She nodded to Galen and he entered the circle, placing the saw at the base of the tree. He felt something then—a strange expectancy as if the tree was, indeed, patiently waiting for the cut. outside the circle, he could see that Kerri was occupied with getting something else out of her pack, so Galen took a moment to whisper to the tree. "Sorry to do this, bud, and I sure hope it doesn't hurt much," he said. "But we really need the help, and she says you're the one. So, thank you. and I promise I'll do my damnedest to make you the best-looking tree on the block."

When the deed was done, Galen carefully levitated the tree out of the circle. Kerri was holding a small spade and a handful of weird beige sticks the size of carrots. "What on earth are those?" he asked.

"Fertilizer stakes. I'm burying them within the circle. The roots of this tree are strong, and they'll send up shoots in the spring," she said. "In the balance of things, new life always wins out over death. just like today, when the year rolls around from darkness to light."

He turned those words over in his mind as he watched her go about her task. thought about them the whole time they walked back to the car, and during the process of carefully bundling the tree with a roll of burlap. It was even bigger and more awkward than it looked, and it was a job and a half to make it as narrow as possible for the trip home. Finally, they tied—and then retied—the tree securely onto the car roof rack. Their prize dwarfed the little red vehicle of course, but it was balanced enough to be safe.

Balance. in the balance of things, new life always wins out over death…

When Kerri reached for the door of the car, Galen put his hand over hers. the winter sun was bright, but he wrapped an aura of warmth around her like a blanket just the same. "Kerri, we really need to talk. if anything happens to me—"

"Don't," she said. "We can't think that way."

"Hey, I'm all for being positive, but we can't shy away from the truth either. When I first came to the station, one of the older guys on the crew, Art Peters, told me two things— that you need to live each day like it was your last, and *especially* that you have to tell the people you care about what you want them to know. It was something I'd already learned from my mom. She was upfront about dying, and it freed us both to say the things we needed to, so that when she was gone, there were no loose ends, and no regrets for either of us.

"So now I need to say some things, and I need you to hear them."

Kerri studied the ground for a long moment, then nodded. "All right, Galen. I'm listening."

When she lifted her head again, her hazel eyes seemed to borrow both the rich blue of the sky overhead and the green of the spruce forest around them. He'd never imagined such a vibrant color—or the strength of the emotions that shone so clearly through it. God, he felt like he needed to clear his throat, even though technically he didn't have a physical throat to clear. He didn't have a physical knot in the middle of his chest making it hard to breathe either, but that didn't stop the emotional sensation…

Still, he pressed on. "If this doesn't go the way we want it to, I want you to know that it was worth it," he said. "More than worth it. It was the best day of my whole damn life when I met you. And I need you to know that I'm going to fight as hard as I can to stay with you because I love you."

"I love you too. And I'm fighting for you with everything I have."

It would be so easy to just kiss her now, and to hell with the rest of the speech. The words that had sounded so simple and sensible in the middle of the night now seemed totally inadequate, but he forced them out anyway. "You've been on my side from the moment we met. But we need to face the fact that we might not win, and I don't know what happens after that, what losing really means. I have a gut feeling that I won't be here, not even like *this*, like some kind of ghost. In fact, I don't think I'll be here at all."

"Galen," she began, but he "touched" his finger to her lips and shook his head.

"Here's the thing. My mom made me promise to live my life to the fullest for both of us. There's been a lot of times when that's helped me push forward, especially when I didn't want to or didn't feel like it. *And I want that same promise from you.* I don't know what the future holds, but if we aren't together, then I need to know that you won't let it stop you from having a life. A real life, Kerri, with everything—and every*one*—that might entail."

Moisture welled in her eyes, though she held it back. "I don't want to think of a life without you in it."

Oh baby, I can't stand the thought of being without you either. Quickly, he pressed an energy-laden kiss to her forehead, then continued along her brow and down her temple. He was just tracing her delicate cheekbone with his lips when he encountered a runaway tear that nearly undid him. "You don't have to think about it now. I'm saying it *just in case*, remember? It's like—well, it's like packing a survival bag for emergencies. If everything goes south, and we don't get our chance together, you'll have that promise in your bag. I even made up a bucket list to go with it. And one day, when the time is right and you're ready, you'll pull out the promise and the list, and use them to move on. For both of us."

"Okay. Okay, I get it." She scrubbed at her face with her hands. "And I'll make the damn promise, too. I will. I'll even check off whatever goofy things you've got on your damn list—and it better not entail any strip clubs in Vegas, mister." A deep and shaky breath followed. "But I've had enough of this 'just in case' and 'moving forward' stuff. We've had the talk now. We know what we're facing and what we're up against, so let's not bring it up again. Deal?"

"Deal," he said, and pulled her to him for a long, lingering kiss that was as much to comfort him as her. He wasn't afraid of dying. It was the idea of leaving Kerri that threatened to tear his heart out by the roots.

FOURTEEN

With Everett supervising, Galen and Kerri unwrapped the tree in the living room and set it in a bright red stand—not an easy task as Waldo insisted on inspecting its bark as closely as his flat little nose would allow. She snatched up the chubby canine and held him, so they could stand back and survey their handiwork.

"Yup, it's a real dandy, Kerri-girl," said Everett. "Biggest one you ever brought home."

That was true enough. The double-crowned spruce was even taller than she thought it would be, but the high ceiling of the old house still accommodated it easily. "Maybe that's a good thing. Maybe a big tree will equal big magic for us."

The old ghost nodded. "Makes sense. You know, I never much bothered with trees and such when I lived here, but I never seen one quite that—er—*shape* before."

"This is the tree that offered itself to us," she said. "So that makes it very special."

"Yeah, two heads are better than one," Galen whispered in her ear, and Kerri smacked him—or she would have if her hand hadn't gone right through him.

"Just for that, smart guy, I'm making *you* bring the decorations down from the attic."

"Works for me. Ten bucks says I'm better at decorating than you are anyway."

"You're on. Everett can tell you where the boxes are, and then you can go crazy."

"Wait a minute, aren't you doing it with me?"

"Hey, I have edits on my novel to finish, and then I have to set up the Yule altar before Aunt Libby arrives." Kerri paused and took a deep breath, letting the fresh pungent scent of evergreen fill her senses. "That is *so* good."

"Now I'm jealous," said Galen. "I miss that smell."

"After you get your body back, we'll go to the woods and you can smell every one of the trees," she said. "Just like Waldo."

"You can pee on them too if you want," added Everett, and guffawed as Galen rolled his eyes.

"Yeah, I'll be sure to put that right at the top of my list," he said, then began making small circular motions in the air with his hands. Kerri watched, fascinated, as all the burlap and rope, plus several hundred spruce needles that had been rubbed off in transit, speedily rolled themselves into a tidy bundle. A large white garbage bag floated in from the kitchen like an airborne jellyfish and engulfed the debris.

"Nice work. And I thought your coffee was good," laughed Kerri. "Do you do windows too?"

"Maybe." Galen lowered his voice and leaned into her. "Especially if I'm properly motivated."

"I think I'll be heading upstairs for a while," Everett announced suddenly. "I got an episode of NCIS that's calling my name."

As the old man vanished from sight, Kerri asked, "Did I hear that right?"

Galen shrugged. "Hey, he likes cop shows, and he's already seen everything there is to see on that vintage network. So last night I talked him into watching NCIS. You can find a rerun at any time of the day or night, so it's perfect for him. It'll be even better once he learns to operate the remote."

"How's that going?"

"So far he keeps hitting several buttons on the pad at once. And he doesn't quite understand it either, so that makes it harder."

She frowned. "That stupid remote is designed for rocket scientists, never mind somebody who's never used one in his entire life. Maybe I could pick up a simpler one, with extra-large buttons. What do you think?"

"I think," he said, wrapping his arms around her. "That you've got the biggest heart of anyone I've ever met. And if we didn't have to conserve our energy for yule-tiding and spellcasting tonight, I'd be making some serious advances right now." He sighed and pressed a tingling kiss to her forehead. "Which reminds me, you promised you would rest."

"As if you'd let me forget," she said, and picked up a heavy knitted throw from the couch and a computer tablet from the coffee table. "See? I'll just relax right here while I finish these edits."

"That's not resting, that's work."

"Hey, I'll be curled up in a cozy chair." She put on her most sincere expression. "Editing is just like reading, honest."

He brushed tingly kisses over her eyelids. "I don't believe that for one minute, but make sure these gorgeous peepers close for a little while, okay? I'm going to hang out with Everett before I bring the decorations down. Our mutant tree needs a couple hours to warm up anyway. Sometime after four o'clock work for you?"

She nodded, and he disappeared, Kerri studied the tree and murmured a few words to make certain it remained upright in its stand. Galen had been right about the tree. It needed time to relax, time for its branches to soften and unfurl, so she nestled into her favorite chair. She could use a little unfurling herself.

Normally Waldo would do a puggy cannonball into her lap and try to get under the blanket with her. Instead, he remained perched on the back of the couch, leaning precariously to get as close to the tree as possible. All he could reach was the very tip of one branch, but it had his complete and undivided attention. When Kerri finished with a chapter and looked up, he was *still* sniffing the tree branch intently. To a dog, she supposed it might be like reading a newspaper. Or maybe a travel brochure. *Or maybe he's just high on evergreen fumes.*

She turned her attention back to her tablet, but soon found herself rereading the same paragraph over and over. Her eyes closed…

Until a burst of staccato yaps and yowls roused her. Kerri sat up quickly, confused to find herself in the dark, as Waldo barked furiously at the living room window.

"What? What's wrong?" A glance at the glowing clock on the mantel showed *four thirty-three*. The scant daylight hours had already given way to early evening. Kerri ran her fingers through her hair several times as if it might stimulate her brain to wake up fully—but it was hard to think with all that barking. "Waldo, knock it off!" If the neighborhood kids were playing street hockey again, or someone was walking a strange dog past the house, her pug might bark once or twice, but only in "I want to play too" excitement. Now, however, his hackles were up, the fur around his wrinkled neck and along his spine stood on end, and he growled and snarled as if an army of polar bears were advancing on the house. "Dammit, settle down, Waldo! You're making me deaf!"

Her words had no effect at all on the pug. He bounced along the top of the couch and clawed at the glass, while his barking grew more frenzied. Kerri rose and looked out the window. *No polar bears. No wolves. No serial killers.* In fact, the cul-de-sac looked like a Christmas card, with snow falling softly on lovely old houses decorated with countless strings of colored lights. The street lamps lent a golden glow to the scene, and silhouetted the big trees that lined the road. The kids weren't out playing hockey yet but there were several people strolling along the sidewalks, enjoying the holiday ambience. Ghosts were out and about too, and Kerri recognized several of them, but they couldn't be the source of Waldo's distress. Too many of them were his friends.

She studied the tranquil scene, trying to bring all her senses to bear. The walls between realms known and unknown were paper-thin at this time, permitting more than mere spirits to roam the earth freely. Temporary portals formed invisibly in the most unlikely places—including the freezer section of the corner MiniMart. There was even a doorway where the rhodie bush grew in her very own backyard. The phenomenon was cause for wonder (plus a little common-sense caution), but not usually cause for alarm.

Suddenly she spotted a shadow between the big houses across the street. In the presence of so many festive lights, it was far darker than any shadow had a right to be, so dark that light seemed to disappear when it touched it.

Kerri reached into the neck of her blouse and withdrew a clear quartz pendent.

"Clarity I ask for, to see what seeks to hide,

Reveal to me the truth, and draw the curtains wide."

A thread of ice shot through her veins as the darkness resolved itself into a shape—a tall figure in a long coat. *The Rabisu!* His hat was pulled low over his face, yet she knew without doubt that he was staring right at her.

"You cocky bastard, you know what we're trying to do, don't you?" *And here I thought there were no serial killers outside...* For a moment she considered working a spell to repel him, but it would be a waste of magic. After the creature's attack on Kerri's home, Aunt Libby had added additional protections. Not only was the house fortified, but so was every square inch of the yard and driveway, plus the fenced perimeter, and every tree and shrub that grew within it. The Rabisu could not set foot on the property again. As for her aunt, her big old tan-colored Lincoln had always had formidable defenses. She wouldn't have any trouble getting to and from Kerri's house no matter how many demons stood in the way.

A flash of glowing red appeared under the broad brim of the hat. Eyes? Kerri shivered but stuck her chin out and refused to look away. *I think you like attention, and I'll bet you feed on fear too. And I'm not going to grace you with either one.* Instead, she scooped up Waldo—still barking wildly and showing every crooked tooth he had—and tucked him under her arm. With her free hand, she lowered the blinds and made herself walk slowly, casually, upstairs to see what the guys were up to.

The pug quieted at last and hung heavily on her hip like a rolled-up sleeping bag. "I need a sling for your bowling ball butt," she muttered. Waldo simply grinned widely, tongue lolling, enjoying the ride. No one would ever guess he'd just been threatening a monster with bodily harm.

At the landing, she realized she couldn't hear a television. Everett's viewing habits usually provided the backdrop for most of her daily routine. She *could* hear the old ghost cussing with apparent frustration, however, and quickened her pace. As she reached his open door, a flurry of cards abruptly flew past her face like an explosion of quail from a thicket and she nearly dropped Waldo on his head. Only quick reflexes allowed her to regain enough of a hold on his stocky body to set him down awkwardly but gently. The pug ran straight into the room of course.

She was a little more cautious. "Should I wear a helmet?" she asked as she peeked around the door jamb.

"Naw, I'm sorry, Kerri-girl," said Everett. He looked sheepish, and sank even deeper into his armchair until only his knees and upper torso were visible. "Didn't know you were there. I just got fed up, is all."

Galen sat across from him, busily rubbing the dog's velvety ears. "This guy's being way too hard on himself. Did you know he can hold three cards now?"

"That's amazing!"

Everett was less enthused about his accomplishment. "What the hell good are three cards? We're playing two-handed pinochle!" He shrugged. "It's probably time for my show anyway."

Across the room, the television powered on by itself. "Did you do that, Everett?" she asked.

He brightened somewhat. "Yeah, that young man of yours helped me figure that much out. Badgered me into watching some new show too, and now he's got me hooked on it."

Kerri laughed. "Well, it's time to trim the tree, so you might want to show Galen where the decorations are stored before you get too involved in your program. Aunt Libby will be here about seven." *No sense in worrying the guys about the Rabisu,* she decided. While it creeped her out knowing the creature was out there watching them, no one was in any danger within the house. And at the hospital, they were completely safe within the circle they cast. But did the demon know that? Was that why he hadn't tried again to attack them? No doubt he was simply waiting for them to make a mistake.

But somehow it didn't feel like that. In fact, if she had to put a word on what she sensed from him, she'd say he was *gloating.* It made no sense to her.

Unless he thinks he's already won.

* * * * *

Galen came downstairs with a caravan of boxes floating along behind him, but stopped at the door to the living room and gave a low whistle. The tree had expanded in the indoor warmth all right—to near-epic proportions! Its shape seemed even stranger, and the vee in the trunk was more prominent. The double tops were no longer symmetrical at all. In fact, one looked more like a freakish twin growing out of the side of the spruce. *Great. Just great. It'd be easier to decorate Godzilla. At least he's only got one head.*

Waldo and Everett caught up to him. "Holy Moley," said the old man. "What're you going to do with *that*?"

Hide it, was his first thought. This was like some weird reality show test of his abilities. Trimming the tree had always been one of his favorite activities, but Galen would have felt far more comfortable wading into a burning building than trying to dress up the ugly evergreen.

Still...

I guess the poor thing can't help what it looks like. Besides, it volunteered to help me. "What we're going to do, bud, is make this tree a sight to behold," he said aloud.

As Everett muttered something about it already being a sight, Galen squared his shoulders and started opening boxes. Not only did he have a bet with Kerri to win, he'd made a solemn promise to this particular tree.

Hope the guys at the station never hear about that.

* * * * *

"Okay, I admit it. You've won your ten bucks, hands down." Kerri stared up at the glittering tree, the charred block of firewood in her garden-gloved hands temporarily forgotten. She'd brought the Yule log inside, the small remnant of last year's Solstice blaze, and was on her way to the fireplace when the sight of the fully-decorated tree had stopped her in her tracks.

The transformation was nothing short of astonishing. There wasn't a square inch that didn't feature a sparkling ball or a loop of garland, and hundreds of lights twinkled from deep within the spruce as well as from the tips of every branch. And *both* of the tree's crowns boasted a glowing star, artistically offset to create a pleasing, if unusual, picture. She was certain that the evergreen itself was standing a little straighter as if proud of its finery. "You know, I didn't think we owned that many ornaments and light strings."

"Everett found some in the basement that were left over from a previous owner, so we incorporated them. And, you're just in time for the finishing touch."

"More? It's already gorgeous."

"You'll like this, trust me." Galen stood back with Kerri and she could feel the warm tingle of energy as he put an arm around her shoulders. The wood in her hands was suddenly weightless and she knew he was hefting it for her. He nodded at Everett. "Go for it, bro."

The old ghost looked nervous, but reached for a palm-sized ornament on the coffee table. It was a unique piece, half silver moon and half golden sun, the perfect symbol of the Solstice. Its braided ribbon rose by slow degrees, following the direction of Everett's gnarled fingers, until the decoration itself bobbed in the air.

Kerri held her breath…but she needn't have worried. The ribbon looped neatly over a branch, and the ornament hung securely. "Omigod, Everett, you did it!"

"Guess I did, didn't I?" he said, and hooked his thumbs in his belt loops. His expression was a mixture of satisfaction and pure relief.

"I'm so proud of you!" She tried to pat him on the shoulder, but of course that didn't work. They both laughed.

"Well, I wouldn't have tried it at all if you hadn't replaced all the decorations with plastic 'cause of Waldo." He shrugged. "It's not so scary when you know you can't break anything."

"Um, *right*. Good thing I did that." Then and there she decided she wasn't going to tell her friend that the Solstice ornament was handmade—and the *one* thing made of glass that she had kept. Instead, she smiled at Galen. "My pug used to think that all the things on the tree were toys for him."

"Yeah, well he still does. We would have been done an hour ago if it hadn't been for chasing Waldo. He even dragged one of the stars under the couch when we weren't looking."

The pug waggled his curly-tailed butt at the mention of his name, completely unrepentant.

"Speaking of things dragged, I almost forgot I brought this in," she said, indicating the wood she still held in her hands. "It's been in the yard under the porch since last year." Kerri knelt by the fireplace, laying the small log carefully on top of a stack of kindling that a boy scout could be proud of. It wasn't strictly necessary to have a big blaze at Yule. These days many people simply decorated logs with candles and pinecones. But for Galen's sake, she wanted every ounce of Solstice magic she could possibly attract. The words came straight from her heart:

"The wheel of the year has turned again,

The earth will slowly warm.

Darkness must give up its hold

And shadows lose their form.

Welcome all that brings new life.

Welcome sun and daylight bright.

The wheel will turn, and fire burn,

And warm us all with inner light."

The kindling was just beginning to catch fire when the front door flew open with a crash. Aunt Libby was in the living room before Everett even got a chance to announce her.

"Did you see that *thing* out there?" she demanded, depositing an armload of bags and packages into Galen's arms. The pile bobbled for a split-second until he tapped into the energy needed to hold them up.

"What thing?" he asked, quickly rebalancing the top package.

"The Rabisu," said Libby. "It's standing right across the street, smug as a Cheshire Cat. The foul creature even tipped its hat at me as I drove by."

Kerri sighed. "Waldo spotted it earlier. It's been there since it got dark."

"*What?*" Galen stared at her. "Why the hell didn't you say something?"

"Why spoil everyone's fun?" demanded Kerri. "The Rabisu would get a real kick out of disrupting our celebration on this night of all nights."

"What, you think he's just trying to psych us out because it's a goddamn holiday?"

"Maybe. I mean, he's probably always looking for an opportunity to get at us somehow. But tonight is different, and I'm sure he knows exactly what we're doing."

"Of course he does," said Libby. "The ancient Sumerians observed *Nardoqan*, the winter Solstice, as a time when the old sun weakens and is destroyed by evil powers, and a new, stronger sun is created by the gods. There would be countless wardings created, and incantations made to hold back the powers of darkness at that time."

Galen frowned. "You're saying that whatever we're doing is no big surprise to our friendly neighborhood monster." The older woman nodded.

"I'll bet the Rabisu can even *feel* our magic," said Kerri.

"I say we make damn certain that he can," declared Libby. "I see the fire is lit and—oh, that's *quite* the tree!" She studied at it approvingly before asking: "Where's the altar, hon?"

"In the dining room." Kerri led the way. As in most homes, the dining room didn't see a lot of use. Unless her brothers or her parents were visiting, she ate most of her meals in the kitchen. But the round oak table with its enormous lion-paw feet was an ideal spot for an altar, and she'd put a great deal of effort into planning this one for the Yule.

The broad wooden surface was draped in white linen embroidered with red and gold thread, and layered with live cedar boughs. Apples, oranges, pomegranates and all kinds of nuts and pinecones were artfully arranged with braided stalks of wheat, and sprigs of living holly, ivy, and even mistletoe. In the center was a large spiral made of smooth round stones, carefully placed from largest to smallest, and interspersed with glittering crystals of every color. Around the perimeter, perfectly spaced, sat eight tall glistening jars. Each contained a beeswax candle, waiting to be lit.

Galen leaned over to study the intricate pattern in the center of the arrangement. "It's really pretty. Reminds me of a galaxy or something," he said. "What does it do?"

"The spiral represents the cycle of seasons, and of life. The circle of candles represents the Wheel of the Year, one for each of the *sabbats* or celebrations," said Kerri. "Yule is just one of them, but it's the longest night of the whole year. We light every candle and let them burn until the sun comes up. Aunt Libby, will you do the honors?"

The older woman nodded. Kerri brought her a long twig that had been set alight from the Yule log, and Libby recited the traditional words as she touched the twig to each wick. The beeswax smelled sweet as it warmed. Kerri could feel the magic growing in the room—strong and steady, life-infusing, enlightening. The last candle in the circle was lit—

And Galen disappeared.

FIFTEEN

Without warning everything and everyone around him vanished, and Galen was plunged into total darkness. He struggled blindly, but the blackness resisted him and pressed against him, almost as if he was submerged in deep water. As he fought, he gradually became aware of a bright white glow above him that pierced the dark yet revealed nothing. A cacophony of strange noises competed for his attention: whooshing, thumping, pounding, swishing. And above it all, a loud mechanical gasping.

That's when he heard Waldo, barking like a pug possessed, his deep grumbling *woof* penetrating the thick fog that seemed to hold Galen in thrall. Focusing on the dog's voice, he blinked and—

Suddenly the dining room swam back into focus, the eight glowing candles a reassuring sight after the alien darkness. He knelt and hugged the still-barking pug, rumpling his ears and rubbing him all over. "Thanks, buddy."

He was just wondering where everyone was when Everett appeared and clasped Galen's hand with a burst of energy. "It's about damn time you showed up, son. We've been looking all over creation for you."

Libby rushed in as well, looking every bit as rattled as Everett. It wasn't until Kerri entered the room, however, that Galen's world finally righted.

"Where the hell did you go?" she demanded, and he couldn't do anything for a long moment but grin like an idiot just because she was *there*. Finally, he slid an arm around her and deposited a kiss on the very top of her reddish curls.

"I didn't go anywhere," he said.

"You weren't here. I couldn't *feel* you," said Kerri. "And Aunt Libby couldn't even locate you with a spell!"

"But I didn't leave," he insisted. "Why would I?"

Everett pulled a handkerchief from his back pocket and mopped his brow, although Galen was pretty sure that ghosts didn't sweat. "I dunno, son, but I was damned afraid you'd crossed over or some such thing. Maybe even wandered into that damned rhododendron bush for all we knew. You've been gone for over two hours."

Two hours? "Wait, that's not possible. I—I was right here." Wasn't he? Galen suddenly wasn't so sure. The strange experience hadn't been like the aftermath of the Great Shower Incident. He'd faded out then too, but he didn't lose any time. More importantly, *he had been able to see and hear Kerri.* All he'd heard this time was...

"The respirator!" he burst out. "I heard the respirator in the hospital room. At least I think so. Holy shit, I might have been in my body for a second!" If he'd been in a body now, he'd definitely be sitting down. Implications crowded into his brain. "What does it mean?"

"Maybe it means we're winning?" offered Kerri. She smiled for the first time then, and it felt damn good to see it. "*You're* winning!"

Libby nodded. "You just might be starting to wake up, Galen McAllister. The repetition of our spell each night, plus the Yule magic we've invited into the house, could be strengthening you."

Without warning, Kerri's oh-so-welcome smile faded into consternation, and she quickly left the room.

"Hey, wait just a minute—I thought that was *good* news!" Galen followed her into the living room and watched as she raised the blind on the front window. "Is Mr. Ugly still out there?"

She shook her head. "I don't see it anywhere." Together they scanned the pleasant streetscape, but there was no sign of the creature, no shadows any darker than they should be. All was peaceful and bright.

"Maybe the thing got bored and left," he ventured.

"Maybe." Kerri ran her hands through her hair as if composing herself. "I didn't mean to charge off like that. I just had to check, you know? I've been so worried that the Rabisu had found a way to get at us after all, that *it* was behind your disappearance."

I should have thought of that. "Sorry to scare you."

"It wasn't your fault. And hey, isn't it a good thing that you finally got visitation rights to your body?"

He whispered into her ear. "I'll be happier when I have visiting rights to *yours.*"

"Galen!" She couldn't maintain her mock indignation however, and relaxed into his energy-filled embrace. He could sense the tension leaving her as they watched the snowflakes fall outside. As for himself, however, he'd feel better knowing where the damn Rabisu was. *And what the hell it's doing.*

They heard the sirens at the same time.

* * * * *

The gentle ambience of Christmas lights and quiet snow was eclipsed by the roar and rush of bright flames against a dark sky. Fire erupted from the upper story of the big rose-colored house at the top of the street, and burst from the attic window of the green house on the opposite corner.

From her front yard, Kerri watched the twin blazes with a mix of horror and sorrow—but she couldn't look away. Instead, she held Waldo tightly and laid her face against his thick fur. The pug's familiar snorting and wheezing in her ear was comforting, as was Libby's elbow interlocked with hers in family solidarity. The residents of the entire street were likewise gathered in small tight groups, huddling close as the disaster unfolded, as teams of firefighters did battle, and policemen put up barricades...

And as Galen and Everett did one last invisible sweep of the buildings for survivors. As spirits, the two were impervious to smoke and flame, but Kerri still breathed a sigh of relief when they finally reappeared beside her.

"Everybody's out," declared the old ghost.

Galen's arms surrounded her and her aunt, and of course, the wiggling Waldo, with energizing warmth. Together, they watched as more trucks arrived on the grim scene.

"What about the houses? Can they save them?" whispered Kerri. Galen shook his head and her heart sank. *The street's going to look so bare, so wrong, without them...*

Libby sighed deeply. "McCraneys have lived in the rose house for generations," she said. "Their family built it right after the railroad first came here. John's father just restored the house a few years ago, and even found some of the original furnishings. It's a terrible loss." Her voice was hushed, subdued. Everett stood close beside her with his head bowed.

It feels like a funeral, thought Kerri. Fortunately, there would be no actual funerals. Jim and Judy McCraney and their three cats had already been safely outside, being cared for by other neighbors, before Galen had arrived to search their house. "What about the Websters? Are they okay? They only moved in a few months ago."

"All safe, even Sully," said Galen.

She frowned. "I don't remember a Sully. Isn't their little boy's name *Mason?*"

"That's what the sign says on the bedroom door, but inside I found a big bearded lizard basking under a heat lamp like a sunbather on a beach. The scaly guy had no idea just how hot it was about to get for him. I levitated his entire tank to the back porch where the firefighters would find it in a hurry." He managed a hint of a smile. "Actually, I scared the hell out of them. One minute the porch was empty, and the next, a big-ass aquarium was on the top step in front of them."

"I'd love to have seen their faces." The only thing Kerri had been able to see from her distant vantage point was that the little boy appeared to be cuddling something under the blanket he was wrapped in. She'd assumed it was a plush animal or some other beloved toy, but Galen assured her it was indeed Mason's lizard pal, Sully. A few moments later, she saw the Websters—reptile tank and all—ushered into Margaret Callahan's house.

All present, all accounted for, all safe. "But why two fires? And why tonight of all nights?" She feared she already knew the answer but shoved the thought away. *Not that. Please, anything but that...*

"Because they aren't natural fires," said Galen, dashing her hopes. "Too hot, too fast, and no single point of origin. Look there, and *there*, and over there." He pointed to several places on the blazing buildings. "When I was inside, I could see that the flames didn't commence from a single location in either house. It wasn't a pot that was left on the stove too long, or faulty wiring, or a sooty chimney that caused this. Not with fresh fires springing up everywhere in both homes."

"Maybe they're just burning fast because they're so old."

"Not necessarily. The latest studies confirm what most firefighters already know—new homes often burn faster than older ones because of the synthetic materials used to build them. Besides," he persisted, "even if the physical evidence added up, what are the odds that two residences with a whole paved street between them would ignite at exactly the same time?"

"Maybe a spark? A spark could have flown from one to the other." She was grasping for straws and she knew it.

"Wind's wrong," Everett piped up. "Some damned idiot set those fires on purpose!"

"Or some damned *demon*," said Libby, finally putting Kerri's worst fears into words. "Let's not forget that Galen was trapped during a fire that was started by the Rabisu."

The old man nodded. "Just like the bad guys on NCIS. Setting fires is probably that toothy bastard's MO. In fact, Kerri and me would probably be sitting on the curb right now if it weren't for Libby's protection spells. And I'm too stuck in my ways to find a new place to haunt."

Despite Galen's arms around her and the warmth he generated, Kerri shivered. She shifted Waldo to her hip although the stocky pug was getting heavier by the minute, but she couldn't make herself put him down. She needed something solid to hang on to. "The Rabisu did this to get back at us. He couldn't harm our house, so he…" Her voice caught, and she couldn't continue.

"Acted like a typical bully," finished Everett. "And attacked our neighbors out of pure spite."

Libby was doubtful. "I don't know if spite had much to do with it. The creature is very old, and he's had a lot of time to observe humans. He may have guessed that harming those families would hurt us as much or more than if he'd burned *this* house down." Suddenly she looked older than her years. "I wish I could have warded the entire street, but—"

"But you can't," said Kerri. Her arms were full of dog, so she settled for leaning over to press her forehead to her aunt's. "You told me that when I was six, that magic doesn't work that way," she murmured. "Remember? I had it in my head that all the cars on the street should be pink, and you explained about *spheres of influence.*"

"What's that?" asked Galen.

"It just means that Libby isn't Superwoman," said Everett, and patted the older woman's arm. "No matter how much she'd like to protect us all."

Galen looked at Kerri. "I get that. When I was a kid, I always thought of *magic* as being able to do anything you wanted to."

She smiled weakly. "I did too, at first. But I soon learned that magic has rules and boundaries." *Just like everything else in life. Unless you're a damn Rabisu...* What the hell were the rules for ancient demons?

Libby and Everett left the yard together and went inside. Kerri started to follow them, but Galen paused on the front porch to look back at the firefighters.

"I should have asked you before," she said. "Is that your crew?"

"No, but I know quite a few of them. It's Mel Rutherford's company." He pointed. "The guy directing the others, see? He was in the same class as Brody and me..." Galen's voice trailed off and he simply shrugged.

Kerri tried to imagine what it was like for him. Even if he'd had real family left, the firefighters would still be like his brothers. "You miss Brody. You miss them all."

He nodded. "I do. And I miss the job as well, every day."

"You'll get back to it soon," she said. "In fact, it's time for us to go to the hospital now. Come on, we've got a spell to cast." She reached out a hand—

"Son of a bitch!" he yelled, and ran out to the road. Waldo was at his heels, barking excitedly.

There was nothing to do but run after them. "What? What is it?" demanded Kerri.

"You live on a dead-end street!" he shouted.

"It's called a *cul-de-sac*, not—" And then it struck her. The only way out had been very effectively blocked by a veritable wall of emergency vehicles, hoses, and equipment.

* * * * *

The Unspoken One glided up the tall narrow walls of the hospital stairwell. His insubstantial form was a tarry black smear against the stark white paint, a shadow that the bright fluorescent light was powerless to penetrate. At the heavy fire door that led to the fourth floor, he assumed a humanoid shape. For a long time, he'd been forced to reserve his physical form for feeding, since it required so much energy to sustain it. *But not now.* Strength and power radiated from him, boosted by the life he'd so recently devoured—and besides, it amused him to mimic mortals. It had been a long time since Nah'mindhe had afforded himself so much entertainment.

Too long.

He struck a casual pose with his clawed hands tucked into the pockets of his coat before heading to his destination. It wasn't necessary to glance at the numbers to find the room. The gossamer riverlet of cool, sweet energy that linked him with his victim was a thread he could follow from anywhere. The Rabisu rounded a corner—

And leapt back again, his jagged teeth scissoring against each other in his frustration. Despite the lateness of the hour, a flurry of activity was taking place in and around the room he sought. Doctors conferred in excited whispers, nurses wheeled equipment in and out.

So, the impossible is indeed true. Galen McAllister was attempting to shake free of a Rabisu spell. This was what the Unspoken One had sensed, as he stood watching Kerri Tollbrook's well-warded house. But he had not believed it.

McAllister's resistance was both fascinating and unsettling. How many centuries had passed since any man had dared to fight back? Not that such paltry efforts would do any good. Even the Sumerians had never been able to keep him at bay forever. *He is aided by simple Nardoqan spells that cannot last the month,* Nah'mindhe told himself. The Solstice season would pass, and so too would the potency of its magic. *This human may be stronger than most, but he will not succeed in escaping me. And neither will those who have aided him.*

Of course, Nah'mindhe had already punished their actions. They would be late in arriving tonight, late in casting their sixth spell. *Perhaps even* too *late...*

That possibility pleased him immensely. He dissolved into shadow and slid beneath an empty stainless-steel cart in the hallway to wait. Every word spoken in Room 440, no matter how softly uttered, was effortlessly picked up by his preternatural hearing. And he was aware when the focus of all those conversations slipped back into a dreamless torpor.

See? McAllister has not the strength to resist me for long. The man was a fascinating experiment at best, an interesting diversion at worst. *And nothing more.*

With their patient once again unresponsive, his attendants lost interest and dispersed, leaving the lights dimmed for the night. At last, the Unspoken One floated through the open door. Naturally, he didn't attempt to approach the body in the bed—the glowing blue-white circle, invisible to physical eyes, had been drawn on the floor with potent magic. Nah'mindhe could not cross it at present, but it was only a temporary nuisance. Time was firmly on his side. The spell with which he had bound his victim would be sealed in four days' time, and no amount of magic would prevent Nah'mindhe from consuming that final glorious rush of *shi* as it fled the dying body.

"I can be patient, Mr. McAllister, because you cannot elude me," he hissed aloud. "And because your final moments promise to be worth the wait. I expect great things from you."

Even more pleasurable, however, was the anticipation of enlarging his collection of victims with McAllister's unique circle of friends. *Strong in magic means strong in shi.* He'd already decided to begin with the powerful young woman who had dared to meet his eyes from her window…

Nah'mindhe wouldn't need her right away of course. He could afford to take his time, attending the *Ezebu Shi* of another victim in a neighboring state before returning here for McAllister's last breath. Should he take the woman then? Dark and silent, the Unspoken One lingered in the room for a long time, contemplating one delicious possibility after another.

Until his black gaze fell upon an innocuous little detail. A fresh scenario unfolded in his mind, simple yet highly entertaining, and his face split into a predator's toothy grin.

* * * * *

When they finally arrived at the hospital, Fred was pacing the hall. To Kerri's surprise, he ran up and hugged both her and Libby. "Why didn't you answer your phone?" demanded the big man. "You missed all the excitement. I've been just about busting with all kinds of good news."

"We've had a little excitement of our own," muttered Galen, too low for Fred to hear.

There's an understatement, thought Kerri. Unable to leave her street by car, they'd been forced to resort to climbing fences through a maze of backyards. *If I ever move to another house, I'm picking one with a back-alley exit.*

Galen had helped her aunt while Kerri charmed an unending number of surprised dogs, and even a human who had been taking empty beer bottles to a garden shed. Finally, they'd arrived at a quiet road far from the din of the emergency vehicles, and were relieved to find the cab they'd called ready and waiting as if by magic.

In truth, it was just plain luck.

The vehicle wasn't magically warded, either. Not like the old Lincoln or Kerri's little car. Aunt Libby performed a basic protection ceremony on the fly with Galen's awkward help, while Kerri leaned forward and distracted the driver with questions about his family.

Now, Galen followed behind as Fred shepherded her and Libby to an alcove that had been made into a waiting area. "Cindy—that's the night nurse at the other end of the floor— she's on a well-deserved break, so I can talk freely for a few minutes," said Fred. "And as for *you*—" His big finger wavered for a moment, then pointed unerringly at Galen.

"There you are. I can feel you now. I'm surprised you're out here, son. I thought *for sure* you were inside your body."

"I think I was, for a little while," said Galen. Kerri could sense him focusing his energy as he spoke.

The effect was immediate: Fred lit up as the words became clear to him. "Well, I'm betting that was about seven-thirty, right?" Everyone nodded, and he continued. "I was just making Mrs. Garnecki comfortable when your alarm sounded. We have it set in case the machines detect changes in heart rhythm, respiration, oxygen levels, all that stuff. Me and Cindy sprinted for your room like it was on fire."

"Was he okay? He wasn't in trouble, was he?" asked Kerri. Dammit, she'd turned her cell phone off during the Solstice ritual.

"Heck, *no*. He was moving his fingers! Toes! Fluttering his eyelids! Not having a seizure either—'cause sometimes that can happen—but deliberate-like. Dr. Suri, your neurologist, was on call, and came on the run. He was just as excited as we were."

Excitement was too mild a word for the emotions that bubbled up like a fountain within Kerri. She had questions, dozens of them, but the words stuck in her throat as she tried to take in the good news. A reassuring tingle of energy encircled her shoulders as Galen slid his arm around her.

"He really *is* waking up then!" Libby spoke for all of them. "We hoped that was the case. The man disappeared for close to two hours."

"I didn't know what was going on, though," said Galen. "Didn't realize where I was until later."

"Didn't you hear us?" Fred asked him. "We sure called your name enough."

"No. No voices. Just some noise and, like I said, the machine."

"Too bad. I told you one of my best jokes, too. Well, Dr. Suri checked all of your reflexes, and you've been upgraded, son!"

"What's that mean?" Kerri managed to ask, but it was Galen who answered her question.

"There's a scale of one to fifteen that measures your level of consciousness. The doctors tested me a lot for the first couple of months. Not so often now."

"It's eye, verbal and motor testing," added Fred. "They're assessing degrees of responsiveness. You, me, and Libby would be rated at fifteen—that's a fully conscious person. Our boy's been in a deep coma-like state, hovering around two. And let me tell you, no one really expects a person to recover from that.

"But tonight his responses were measuring between three and four. Three and four! Best darn score since he got here. I thought Dr. Suri was gonna start dancing." Fred grinned and chuckled as if picturing it. "It was late, but he called in a couple other doctors anyway just to witness Galen's responses, and they had a pretty good confab about it.

"'Course, all the movements seemed to fizzle out after a while, almost like Galen was falling deeper asleep. But they've scheduled an EEG and a couple other labs and tests for tomorrow morning. Everyone agreed they were *very encouraged*." He made quotation marks in the air with his big fingers.

Kerri was far more than encouraged. She was giddy, exhilarated, flying high on the amazing news. *It's exactly what we'd hoped for, and after only five castings of the spell!* How much better would Galen be once they'd completed all nine? Strangely, though, he didn't seem very excited.

"What's the other shoe, Fred?" he asked suddenly. "I've been kicking around this hospital long enough to know your face."

"That so? Remind me never to play poker with you then," said the nurse.

Kerri looked from one to the other. "Is something wrong?" *Say no, please say no…*

"After all the excitement died down and the doctors left, Cindy was heading to the supply room and caught sight of a strange character in a long black coat at the end of the hallway," said Fred. "Scared her bad, but she's a real pro— she kept herself together. Called security, and then me. I ran to the stairs where she said the thing went, but when I opened the door, every light was out—even the emergency and the exit lights—all the way down."

"You didn't go in there, did you?" asked Libby, with real alarm in her voice.

Fred shook his head. "I know better than to chase things that go bump in the night. Heck, I didn't even go in there when the lights came on by themselves. Security did a thorough search of the entire building, and they left extra guys downstairs for the night."

"But what about Galen's body? Is it, is *he*, okay?" The thought of the demon in Galen's room made Kerri ill. *You wretched thing, now I know why you left the neighborhood,* she thought. It hadn't simply sensed the magic they were making for the Solstice, it must have realized that its victim was shaking loose of the spell! "Did the creature do anything to him?"

"Not that I can see. I checked him over really well, took all his vitals. And then I checked the security camera—we can watch Galen from the nurse's station. All I saw was a tall black shadow in one corner, no details. It didn't even move, didn't try to cross our circle or anything."

Kerri exchanged glances with her aunt. "Did the creature say anything?" she asked. What if it had somehow reinforced its binding spell? Or worse, nullified the magic they'd begun? *There isn't enough time for us to start over from scratch.*

"I ran the tape—well, I guess it's all digital now, but you know what I mean—and I didn't hear a sound. The creepy thing just seemed to be hovering there. Almost reminded me of a movie villain."

"Great," said Galen. "Nothing like having Emperor Palpatine watching me in my sleep." He looked at Kerri and winked. She didn't believe for one minute that he wasn't as worried as she was, but she loved him for trying to lighten the mood.

"Now ask me what I *felt*," said Fred. "You can tell that evil's been visiting that room. I swear it's actually darker in there than it was before. Like a haze in the air that you can almost touch."

Libby checked her watch. "At least that's something we can deal with. The room will simply have to be cleansed again—and quickly, so we can finish today's spell casting at its appointed time. The Solstice affords us some leeway, but we still have to hurry."

"I'm on it," said Kerri. Nothing was going to stand in the way of Galen's progress if she could help it. *Nothing.*

SIXTEEN

From the far side of Room 440, Galen watched the now-familiar preparations for the spell. He hadn't felt one bit different after the first night. In fact, he hadn't felt any different after the fifth night. Sure, there was that weird episode earlier in the day where he'd lost two hours like some kind of alien abductee. And Fred had witnessed the body in the bed actually moving, and exhibiting signs of rising consciousness.

But Galen hadn't sensed a damn thing at the time. He certainly hadn't commanded his body to move. Even when he thought he *might* be inside it, he'd had to guess his location from the sounds around him. And what if he'd guessed wrong? After all, he'd been every bit as disconnected from his body then as he had been when he first found himself standing outside of it twelve months earlier.

Just as he glanced at the clock and wondered if there was anything to that *longest night of the year* stuff, something suddenly changed.

As she always did, Kerri leaned close to the still body in the bed, the body he felt so distant from, and whispered to it. He couldn't perceive the words with his physical ears of course but relied on overhearing them. Kind things, little reassurances. Sweet nothings that were everything. They warmed his heart and added to the wonder and love he felt for this compassionate woman—

And without warning, his incorporeal hand rose involuntarily to his head because *something was tickling his ear!* The physical hand on the bed remained slack and motionless, naturally, but the more Kerri talked to his body, the more he had the urge to rub his ear. *What the hell?* Before he could say a word, he saw her smooth the hair from his body's pale forehead and kiss it.

And dear God, he felt something. For the first time in nearly a year, he felt something. It was faint, as if there was a thick blanket between his skin and her lips, but it was still flat-out terrific.

Another sensation followed, powerful and terrifying at the same time. Like a tsunami, it overwhelmed every thought, every vestige of his strange existence, every trace of self.

Hope.

The next day was a busy one for his unconscious body. Fred kept them apprised of what the doctors were doing, but Galen went straight to the source. *Sometimes it's handy to be invisible.* He observed each test, then easily located his reports and read every last word of them himself. Nothing but good news. He'd been upgraded yet again on the neurological scale. The lab results were better than expected. The doc had even ordered an MRI and the results for that were also positive.

Best of all, they repeated some of the low-tech testing like pinching his nailbeds, and squirting cold water in his ear. His body flinched and jolted! He could feel it! Sensations were still faint, but they were real. *Who'd have thought it could be so exciting to have people jab your toes with pins?*

After the seventh and eighth nights Galen could feel even more. And by focusing his energy he found that he could finally move a toe, the tip of a finger. He still wasn't inside his body, still not commanding it from within, but the small bit of progress brought him immense hope. And not a little fear. There was only one spell left to perform. Just *one* before the final day, the day he would awaken or the day the Rabisu would win. It seemed like a helluva long way between moving a digit and waking up.

Was just one more spell going to be enough?

It has to be, he thought as he sat in the darkened living room alone. *It has to be.* He hadn't known Kerri Tollbrook an entire two weeks yet, and out of everything he would miss about his life, he would miss her the most. She already owned his heart. Hell, she'd become part of it. And within a few rhyming words, a scattering of herbs, an arrangement of candles, and three people clasping hands, lay his only chance of a future with her.

The wild card, of course, was the Rabisu. The creature appeared to have given up staking out the house after the night of the Solstice—and the fires. No one had sensed its negative presence in the hospital room again either. Libby had suggested the demon was too busy with its other victims, a thought that made Galen shudder.

If he became fully human once more, what then? The damn monster would still be roaming free, preying on the lives of others. But what could he do to stop it? What power did he have against something that didn't conform to physical rules?

Since the day she'd met him, Aunt Libby had spent an immense amount of time researching how to reunite Galen with his physical body. Since the night of the fires, however, the priority had shifted. Kerri and her aunt had been working almost around the clock, poring over old books, scanning the internet, online-conferencing with experts in history and magic, and conferring with gifted friends and family members. Even now, at three a.m., the pair were still in the office, searching for answers, clues, even tiny hints as to how to fight the Rabisu.

Everett had taken a different approach, canvassing the ghostly grapevine for information, even old rumors and urban legends. Sadly, the old man's questions turned up nothing of use. While he'd definitely found people who had passed on during comas, no one reported any encounters with a monster.

As for himself, Galen had tried to help out in every way he could, but it was tough to feel useful when you didn't know what you were looking for—and likely wouldn't recognize it if you did. For him, the realm of magic was not just a strange country with an unknown language, but an entirely new *planet*. He was determined to learn, and confident in his ability to study. After all, hadn't he been an honor student throughout his school years? But after laboring through every archaic word of a 300-year-old handwritten volume of transformation spells, he gratefully accepted the assignment of *chief cook and bottle washer*. Hell, it felt like a promotion.

In the end, they were left with the original plan, to *put one foot in front of the other*, as Libby phrased it. To refuse to be intimidated and simply move forward with the final spell. To break the curse, and restore Galen to his body, and his life. It made as much sense as anything was going to. So why was his apprehension growing with every passing second? *I've got to be missing something...*

Everett had aptly described the demon as a predator. A mountain lion would wait until the odds were in its favor before it pounced, right? In this case, that would be Christmas Day, the time when the binding spell finally became permanent. *So why did it come to the house? Why was it watching us? Why the hell did it come back to the hospital?*

Maybe Fred was right, and the creepy thing just liked to gloat. Maybe it had nothing better to do. If it was virtually immortal, maybe it got bored. But what if that wasn't the reason? *If the Rabisu is as old as Libby says, then it's got to be smart. It's probably got bigger plans*, Galen thought. *Bigger than me—*

The sudden realization was a bare-knuckle punch to the heart and the gut at the same time. *That damn thing's going to take Kerri too. It's going to take all of them.* He knew it as surely as he knew he had to find a way to stop that from happening. His mind scattered in a dozen frantic directions at once, desperate for an idea. At last he realized he was spinning his own wheels. *Quit this shit, McAllister! You're supposed to be a professional, and here you are acting like a goddamn rookie,* he reprimanded himself, wishing it was possible to smack himself in the head. *You'd never approach a fire call like this.*

Immediately his thoughts shifted gears, became clear and focused. A fire call was a perfect analogy. Galen analyzed what he knew, and compared it to his training. Firefighter

101 said that if you deprived a fire of fuel or oxygen, it would starve and go out. *What would happen,* he wondered, *if the Rabisu ever got cut off from any source of energy?* Would it also starve?

Before he could wonder how the hell such a thing could be achieved, a baleful whine echoed from somewhere upstairs. "Waldo? Are you okay, bud? Where are you, Waldo?" Instantly he groaned at his own question. *Remind me to buy you a red-striped shirt...*

The pug had been contentedly passed out on Everett's favorite chair—with Everett on top of him—when Kerri, Galen, and Libby came home from the latest spellcasting. Kerri decided to leave the small snoring beast where he was, rather than move him to her bed. *Waldo's probably just not used to waking up without her.*

The whine sounded again, followed by a long *woo-wooing* howl, and Galen rushed to the source: the little dog had planted his pudgy butt in front of Kerri's door.

"She's not in there, buddy, she's downstairs. Shall we go find her?"

Dragging the gutted remains of a large plush toy— possibly a purple cow once—the pug huffed his way over to sit at Galen's feet and look up at him imploringly. Automatically, he reached to rub Waldo's ears, but paused. *Something doesn't look right here.* "Hey, you don't have that toy, that toy's got you!"

He knelt to investigate. Sure enough, a long thread had become caught in Waldo's teeth, making it impossible for him to release his prize.

"Hold still for me." The pug must have been desperate, because he *did* sit still as Galen struggled to help. "How the hell did you get it wedged in there so tight?" The thread was tougher than it looked. It was wrapped around an upper canine, and a pug's mouth was a very cramped place to work in even if your fingers *could* pass right through it. Finally, Galen resorted to his ghost-like bag of tricks, lowering himself through the floor and looking up into Waldo's drooling mouth like a mechanic looking up at a car on a hoist. The new vantage point helped immensely, and soon the little dog was free of his plush "albatross."

Waldo yipped and raced up and down the hallway several times, before coming to rest in front of Galen with an expectant look on his wrinkled face.

"I think I'd better keep this, bud," said Galen, still holding the shredded purple cow. There were a lot more threads sticking out of it. "You'll just get yourself in trouble again."

The pug barked as if he understood, and ran for Everett's room. He emerged momentarily with a big red rubber pacifier in his mouth, then disappeared again.

"I've got to talk to your owner about getting you some more dignified toys." Galen regarded the plush cow and drew out the long thick thread that had so effectively captured the pug. *A thread...* He thought again of what he'd once said to Everett about energy. *It's like pulling on a thread until the whole sweater is in your hand.*

"Energy," he said aloud. "The key is energy. It has to be." There was some kind of an answer here, if only he could figure out what it was...

A flash of intuition illuminated his mind, as sudden and brilliant as lightning revealing a dark room. He *knew*. He understood. And with that understanding, he also knew what he had to do.

* * * * *

Galen was edgy enough to wonder if his body over on the bed was developing sweaty palms. Eight days, eight nights, eight castings—all had hurtled by surprisingly fast. But today? The tension at the house had been thick. No matter how normally he and Kerri had tried to behave, the specter of tonight's final spell hung between them like a heavy curtain. At least she'd been able to keep busy by counseling a roster of disembodied clients. This close to Christmas, there seemed to be a greater demand for her services than ever.

As for Galen, he'd already baked three batches of his mom's cookies. He couldn't taste them, of course, couldn't even smell them. But it had been their ritual when she was alive, and so far, he'd kept the custom going every year. *I wonder where she is?* He'd asked Kerri that question, but she felt certain that his mother had most likely moved on. It made sense—she'd left no unfinished business behind. As for him? *If things go bad tonight, I don't know where I'll end up.*

He cleaned the house, top to bottom. That was a pre-Christmas tradition too. No silverware in the house to polish, though. He'd hated that job as a kid, but today he would have welcomed it, just to help fill the time.

Between clients, Kerri usually stayed in her office, but not today. The waiting was wearing on her too. All they could do was reach for each other at every opportunity as the day dragged on and on. There was nothing left to say. Galen simply held her close, comforting them both.

Libby had been subdued when she arrived, and there had been near-silence in the car on the way over to Sacred Family. Even Fred had been solemn as a funeral. *Wish I hadn't thought of it quite that way*, thought Galen. If they failed, it would be his own funeral for certain, but he'd come to terms with that. It was the danger to the others, especially Kerri, that was uppermost in his mind. He still didn't want her to risk herself, yet he couldn't help but respect her resolve. And love her all the more for it.

Would she be as understanding about his own resolve, and the decision he'd come to in the early morning hours? *Hell, no.* But his mind was made up as he watched Kerri, her aunt, and their new friend, Fred, carefully cast the circle for the ninth and final time.

This one's for all the marbles.

Galen no longer needed a nod from Libby to tell him when to take his place. And it was no longer so foreign and distasteful to stand in the center of his physical body. The face behind all the tubes wasn't as pallid now, and every now and then an eyelid fluttered or a hand twitched. *You look a whole lot less dead, buddy.* Once Galen was in position, the three moved to either side of the bed and joined hands around him. It was almost like a dance, or perhaps a well-rehearsed play.

Although the candles had already flared and died down, the room seemed brighter than ever. He could sense the magic now, pulsing through him, around him, under, above. Kerri had explained that the circle they created wasn't one-dimensional, not a ring at all but more like an immense bubble that encased them completely. He pictured it as a force field, shielding them, protecting them, holding in the enormous energy. *It's going to be enough.* He knew it, he felt it.

And he was ready—

Without warning, the door opened and a middle-aged woman in purple scrubs stood there with a clipboard in her hands. "Fred? What's going on here?"

Galen could see everyone's hands tighten as they smiled in unison at the unknowing intruder—and Fred, bless him, didn't miss a beat. "Hi there, Cindy. How are you tonight?" he said smoothly. "I'm just helping with a special religious observance for Mr. McAllister for Christmas Eve. Kind of like a *midnight mass.*"

"Oh," she said, suddenly flustered. "I'm so sorry, I didn't mean to interrupt anyone. I just came in to see if there was any spare tubing in the cabinet—the supply room's out of the size I need. I'll call downstairs for some. And I'll make sure no one bothers you."

"A Merry Christmas to you, Cindy," Fred called after her as she closed the door. Kerri and Libby let out the breath they'd been holding.

"I thought for sure she was going to say something about all the candles and the incense," whispered Kerri.

Fred shrugged. "Naw. Mrs. Bertolli just down the hall had her priest in today, and I swear there was a cathedral's worth of candles in there. Sure, they're against the rules but sometimes we look the other way. People need comfort, especially at this time of year. So no, Cindy wouldn't have been too concerned about that. I just think she's still a little on edge after running into that *tall, dark stranger* a couple nights ago."

Kerri nodded. "I think we all are."

"At least we didn't let go of each other's hands," said Libby. "That's the kind of concentration we need. Hopefully we're done with interruptions for the night."

Human ones at least, thought Galen.

"Okay, let's all take a deep breath and a moment of stillness to center ourselves, to regain our focus," she continued. "Then we'll begin. And remember, we must continue to recite the spell until Galen is safely inside his body. Three times or thirty, or a hundred and thirty, whatever it takes."

"Whatever it takes," Kerri repeated, and her gaze met Galen's. Devotion and determination radiated from her in equal parts, as resolute and unyielding as a vow.

"Whatever it takes," he agreed, and meant it, knowing that she needed to hear that from him, needed to believe that he was fully on board with their efforts tonight. *Whatever it takes.*

But he had a very different idea of what might be required...

Libby rang a small crystal bell, and began reciting the ninth and final spell. Fred and Kerri joined in the incantation, not only speaking the words of power in perfect unison, but with perfect intent. Every syllable was infused with their energies, their wills, their hearts, their minds. For him, all for *him*, and it wrung the strands of Galen's heart. No matter that his time with them had been short, he felt unbelievably lucky to have known them, and especially to be so cared for, so *loved*...

The power around him was building, throbbing like a giant's heartbeat, just as it had on other nights. Then, without warning, it swelled to unimaginable proportions. Surely everyone in the building could feel it! He glanced around the room, expecting...

Yet no demon had appeared. *You* have *to come, you bastard. I know you can feel this.* If the damn thing lived on energy, surely they'd just rung the dinner bell. *Come on!*

Nothing. Was it possible it wouldn't show up?

Libby nodded at Galen. She'd instructed him to try to reclaim his physical shell, to attempt to get back inside it when she signaled. It wasn't part of his private plan, not now, but he just couldn't resist giving his body a half-hearted push with his mind—and was surprised to discover that he could move far more than just a finger or toe. Galen found himself lifting his hand, clenching and unclenching the fingers at will. For a single glowing instant, he was both within and without his body, still standing on the outside yet with a new awareness dawning, a new sense of *himself*. Giddy with the unexpected accomplishment, he reached for Kerri with his physical hand and grasped her wrist. *Warmth. Softness.* Her quickened pulse beat beneath his fingertips. *Life.* Elation flooded through him, through her, and there were joyful tears on her cheeks. He felt something on his own then—and turned to look in amazement as a single glistening droplet followed the contours of the still face on the pillow.

"Kerri," he began. "Kerri, I—"

He sensed it before he saw it: an oil-black shadow flowing under the door. In the split second it took for Galen to recognize it, the living darkness had already twined upwards and resolved into an all too familiar figure in a long, black coat.

Kerri's eyes widened as she, too, spotted the evil creature—but she didn't flinch. She didn't stop reciting the spell either. Instead, her chin came up and she deliberately closed her eyes. So did Libby and Fred. The trio continued to hold fast to each other's hands, and their voices became louder, more determined, more urgent, as they recited the life-giving words of the spell.

Only Galen watched the Rabisu. It didn't attempt to enter farther into the room, didn't approach the circle or the people in it. Didn't seem to move at all. Yet one by one, the candle flames extinguished until the only light in the room came from the blue-white glimmer of the magic circle, the tiny lights and screens on the medical equipment, and the eerie red glow of the creature's eyes beneath the brim of its hat. The inhuman face split apart in a nightmare grin then, exposing double rows of long needle teeth, as the demon made a nearly imperceptible gesture with its clawed hand...

All the candles leapt into the air at once. They bounced soundlessly off the invisible shield of the circle, only to spin away and hurl themselves at it repeatedly until they shattered into tiny fragments of wax that rattled to the floor like hail. Incredibly, no one wavered in their efforts, though Fred seemed quite a bit paler. The three pressed on with their plan. As for himself, Galen had a plan too—the minute he figured out how to implement it.

I thought I had this figured out, dammit!

Thinking was even more difficult as the creature escalated its assault. Coats, clothing, cards, and flowers whipped around the room as if caught in a vortex. Cabinet doors flew open and medical supplies became projectiles, ricocheting wildly. Pictures flung themselves from the walls, dashing their frames apart, and splintering the glass into knife-edged shards. Fabric blinds pulled themselves away from the windows, and tall privacy curtains tore free of their overhead rings. They beat like giant moths against the sphere of magic surrounding the bed. Even the heavy armchair, where Fred had sat countless times to read the newspaper to Galen, now floated ponderously to the high ceiling, then swooped down at the circle, again and again. It made a sickening thud, like an angry bull ramming a fence, every time it bounced off the protective bubble.

Everyone's eyes remained squeezed tightly shut but couldn't they *hear* the bombardment? How the hell were Kerri, Libby and Fred coping with this? They had to be scared, yet they carried on with their task—and suddenly Galen realized he'd allowed himself to be distracted from his own.

Focus, dammit! he growled at himself. *Don't think about them, don't think about Kerri. She's safe in the circle. She's safe in the circle...* And she'd continue to be safe, as long as he did what he'd set out to do. He turned, forcing himself to ignore the maelstrom that was tearing apart the hospital room, only to have his gaze fall on something more subtle and sinister.

The electrical cords that powered the equipment that monitored and sustained his body, the tube that brought the oxygen to the respirator…these were the only things that crossed the circle. And one by one, they were slowly pulling themselves free of the outlets! He couldn't help but glance at the bank of machines, expecting battery backups to kick in. Instead, the screens went blank and the lights winked out like fireflies dying.

He was out of time. And his plan, which had seemed so solid in the early hours of the morning, now seemed to be missing a crucial detail. How the hell was he going to—

"—your body, Galen!"

It was Kerri. Fred and Libby continued incanting the spell, but Kerri's eyes were wide open now. "Grab hold of it now! Take control! You can do this!"

Grab hold... The clue he sought was in her words, the same words he'd said to Everett: *Like grabbing hold of a string...* Without hesitation, Galen shook off his newfound connection to his physical body. Instead of drawing breath, he swiftly drew in every ounce of power and energy from within the circle—

And lunged straight at the Rabisu.

SEVENTEEN

Kerri wrested her hand from Libby, and instinctively reached out as Galen shot past, though her brain hadn't enough time to realize his intent, or even to remember that she couldn't physically stop him. A scream rose in her throat but there was no time for that either, as a sudden brilliant burst of green light blinded her, and a soundless explosion slammed her into a wall. Dazed, she slid to the floor, but her scream was shaken loose when the floor itself heaved beneath her, and the entire building groaned like a behemoth. Darkness swallowed the room as if the world was ending.

The circle! The circle is broken!

That thought brought her senses back to her like a slap. As she took a shaky breath, the hospital's auxiliary power kicked on, illuminating the room with a strange half-light and revealing Libby lying on the floor by the foot of the bed. Immediately Kerri scrambled to her aunt's side, broken glass be damned. "We gotta move."

"Gimme a minute," murmured Libby, waving her away.

A quick glance upwards confirmed Kerri's fears and shot adrenaline through her veins. "We don't have a minute! Come on, come on. *Hurry!*" She half-dragged the groggy woman beneath the overhang of the bed and covered her body with her own as much as possible. It was a tight fit, and if the bed hadn't been fully raised, they'd have never managed it. As it was, they'd barely tucked their feet in when the big armchair crashed to the floor just inches away.

Objects large and small began to rain from the ceiling. There was no longer any sphere of magic to repel them.

And no energy in the room to hold them in place, she thought. *Galen, what did you—*

The building heaved again. And again. She clutched Libby tightly as the falling debris was joined by pebbles of shattered glass from the windows. Several beads bounced up and struck the back of Kerri's sweater. Another stung the back of her head and she could feel a droplet—*blood*—trickle down the back of her neck. "Where's Fred?" she shouted into Libby's ear over the din.

"I don't know! I can feel that he's still here, but I can't see a damn—"

The room tipped crazily then. The broken armchair slid over to the wall, and an I.V. pole fell over, taking one of the monitors with it. They followed the chair. The brakes on the bed's wheels kept it from sliding after them, but for a breathless moment, Kerri thought the heavy bed might topple over. A low vibration, a powerful resonance from an unknown source, made her very bones tremble—though she was certain she was already shaking. *Omigod, is the building coming down?* "Hang on," she managed through chattering teeth. "Just hang on!"

The emergency lights flickered, and suddenly reality righted itself. The last of the suspended objects succumbed to gravity and clattered to the floor. It took a lot longer before the floor itself seemed solid again. At long last, all shaking ceased, and the building lapsed into a sudden eerie quiet. Seconds later, the vacuum of silence was filled by screams and shouts, and running footsteps in the hallway.

Kerri crawled out from the cramped space, and nearly forgot to give her aunt a hand up when she saw the bed. Galen's body was entirely hidden beneath an enormous tangled cocoon of window blinds and privacy curtains—and something big was struggling within! Together, the woman pulled and tugged the heavy material away, revealing a gasping Fred performing CPR on Galen's body. "I need one of you to take over *now!*" he ordered, already climbing down.

"I can." Kerri moved fast to take the big man's place, but not as fast as he did. He'd already slapped the red emergency button on the wall, and was fighting to reattach cords and reboot the respirator, as she straddled the pale figure on the bed.

Adrenaline pumped through her as she interlocked her hands and began compressing the sternum directly above the heart. *Press! Press! Press! Press!* She took a refresher course yearly, but had always been afraid that she'd forget the training if she ever had to use it. Instead, her head cleared as she found the rhythm.

Libby stood close with a hand on the pale forehead, murmuring a familiar healing spell. "Don't we need to do mouth-to-mouth too?" she whispered between verses.

"That's the old way," Kerri managed to answer. It was hard to talk—she had to put all her strength into her task. "S'all compression now." She thanked her stars for that because she had no idea how she'd do otherwise with the plastic breathing tube in the way. Suddenly the respirator kicked in. A nurse and a doctor arrived with a crash cart, and Kerri slid from the bed. She joined her aunt in a corner of the room, where they clung together like storm survivors as the medical staff worked with Fred to stabilize the man on the bed.

When they finished, Kerri felt like she needed reviving herself. Her knees felt rubbery and in her anxiety, she'd been holding her breath far too much. The newcomers left quickly to help other patients, but Fred lingered just long enough to put his big arms around both women and give them a squeeze. "He'll probably be just fine," he said. "I threw myself over him the minute things started dropping from the sky. Everything's back online now. His heartbeat is strong and regular, and he's getting plenty of oxygen." The big man was himself bleeding in several places. Libby reached out a hand, but he shook his head. "I gotta go—there's a lot of frightened people here, maybe some injuries—but I'll keep a good eye on our man here, and the nurse's desk has him on live video as well. Are *you* all right?"

Even as she nodded, Kerri felt she would never be *all right* again. She waited for Fred to leave before she slowly approached the figure on the bed. She stroked the familiar masculine face, squeezed the once-strong fingers, but there was no response. She hadn't expected one. Her worst fears had already been confirmed the moment she'd put her hands on his broad chest, placed them over his heart. And confirmed again when Fred had failed to use his patient's name. *He knows it too.*

"Galen's not here." She forced herself to say the words out loud, even as a huge chasm of emptiness gaped within her. *Omigod, omigod, this can't be right. His body is alive, but it's just as vacant as it was when we started.* "I can't feel him. Not in his body, not in this room. He's not here at all."

Libby nodded slowly.

"But where is he? What happened to him? And where is that goddamn Rabisu?" Kerri intuited the answers already, but her brain refused to process them. Her voice had been reasonably steady to this point, but now the rising lump in her throat made it hard to ask the question: *"What did we do wrong?"*

"Nothing was wrong, hon." Her aunt gently grasped her hand with both of hers. "We did all we knew how to do. We kept the integrity of the circle, we maintained integrity of purpose. I'm so proud of you and Fred. Every single one of the spells was *perfectly* done. There was a great deal of gathered power in this last circle, the culmination of three times three castings."

"But—"

"Galen could have taken back his body, he'd already made the connection. But he made a different choice."

This can't be happening. "He used all the power against the Rabisu, didn't he?"

Libby nodded. "That's why the circle shattered. It was the sudden release of all that magical energy. And when it collided with a creature of purest darkness, the backlash probably caused the quake."

"But—but Galen doesn't know *anything* about magic. How could he know what to do?"

"I don't believe he did, not completely. His instinct was to protect us, to protect *you*, and there isn't a more powerful magic than to sacrifice oneself on behalf of another. I doubt that even a monster like the Rabisu could withstand such pure intent. And with the punch of all that power behind it? I believe Galen succeeded in destroying it."

Sacrifice... Kerri pressed her hands to her eyes, unwilling to let the tears fall. If she started crying now, she might never stop. "What about the other victims?" she managed. "We knew there had to have been more."

"Anyone still living would have been released from the creature's power when it died. Galen's freed them."

"I really thought it would free *him*," she blurted.

"He's free, hon, just not the way we planned. Your young man was at the very heart of that collision." It was Libby who fumbled for a Kleenex first. "And I am so, so sorry that I couldn't do more to save him."

Her aunt's sudden tears galvanized Kerri into putting her own grief aside. Later she would cry, but right now, she had to think of Libby: the older woman looked exhausted. How many nights had she gone without sleep? How much energy had she expended in spellcasting? "Galen would be the first one to tell you not to think like that. If it wasn't for you, we'd never have had a chance at all." Kerri put an arm around her. "Come on. We need to go home, at least for now," she said.

It took more than a few minutes to pick their belongings out of the room's debris. And most of the rooms they passed on the way out of the hospital were just as bad. For Kerri, the scattered and broken items on every floor mirrored their own dashed hopes. There was no time left in which to work the spell again, no second chance. They had done everything possible and failed. *No—worse than failed, whether it was our fault or not.* Not only was Galen not reunited his body, everything that made Galen who he was, his spirit, his essence—all was totally, utterly gone. And she didn't even know *where*.

Outside, the night was unexpectedly clear and bright as a full moon silvered the snow. It was long past midnight and Christmas was officially upon them.

Unofficially, it was the worst damn day of her life.

* * * * *

Like the greedy maw of a tornado, the greenish light swallowed Nah'mindhe whole and bore him away. He felt no fear, but howled with frustration and rage that his plans had been disrupted. The strange phenomenon was akin to his arrival in the human world. Yet no bridge between dimensions existed on the fourth floor of the Sacred Family Hospital. *I would have known, would have sensed. This cannot be happening.*

All movement abruptly ceased then, but not because Nah'mindhe had willed it. The sickly light vanished, leaving him—*where?* There was neither day nor darkness here, no features of sky or earth or water. In every direction, there was only a strange mist the deep color of Sumerian apricots as they dried in the desert sun.

It was then that the Unspoken One, the living shadow that struck terror into mortal hearts, felt the first tremors of unease. *If this world has no form, then I cannot take one!*

Suddenly a familiar voice interrupted his thoughts. "Great. Just great. Of all the roommates in all the world, I gotta get stuck with *you*."

Nah'mindhe whirled to face Galen McAllister. Or tried to. Instead, he could only turn very slowly, his movements

labored and weak. He was without substance, incorporeal—
and desperate for energy from any source. Where had all his
strength gone? He'd feasted well in the human world, drained
the *Ezebu Shi* from not one or two but several mortals in
recent days. He should be at the very peak of his might, a
god.

"You're not looking so good." McAllister stood calmly
amid the sunset-colored fog. Strangely, though still a spirit,
he appeared more solid than ever, radiant with—

"*You!*" Nah'mindhe hissed out, and his voice was barely
more than a strangled whisper. "You robbed me of my
power! You took it from me!"

"You bet I did, you soul-sucking bastard. And, *newsflash*,
all that energy was never yours to start with," said
McAllister. "How many lives did you steal over the years?
How many people weakened and died, all because of you?"

"Think you to lecture me?" he rasped, and threw out a
shadowy hand as if to seize the insolent human. Instead, grey
wisps unraveled from his fingers and flew towards
McAllister, disappearing like storm clouds dispersing in the
sun. His unease turned to something entirely new to him—
raw fear. *Not only was he unable to feed in his shadow form,
he could not draw energy from non-physical beings.*
Nah'mindhe could not retrieve his power from this insolent
human. Still, he snarled in defiance. "I walk between the
worlds as you cannot. I am ancient beyond your imagining.
For millennia, I have feasted upon your kind, as mortals feast
upon cattle."

"Yeah, I figured as much. And I also figure you've had
your turn."

"What can you do against such as I?"

"This." McAllister stretched out his hand.

Without warning, Nah'mindhe's already shadowy form began to fragment under the tug of an invisible force. "What—*what are you doing!*"

"Just pulling a string."

"The power is of no use to you. You will never escape this place!"

"Fine with me, as long as you don't."

The last vestiges of his failing strength, his essence, his very being, were dissolving! "Nooooo!" he screamed soundlessly. "I am the Unspoken One! I am immortal! And I am—"

No more!

EIGHTEEN

Kerri's legs felt leaden as she walked up the steps and into her house without Galen. It felt wrong to be without him, wrong that he wasn't at her side teasing her, or giving her a tender energy-laden version of a hug, and a whispered proposition. Wrong to see the shining tree still green and glowing with life, wrong to have carefully-wrapped presents waiting beneath it. And wrong that the old man standing beside needed to be given such terrible news.

"I'm so sorry, Everett," she began, but he held up his hand.

"No, Kerri-girl, *I'm* sorry. I saw you get out of the car by yourself, with the weight of the world on your shoulders." He sniffed loudly, and snatched his handkerchief out of his back pocket. The big red cloth failed to hide the grief that crumpled his face. "Wasn't hard to guess things didn't go our way."

"No. No, they didn't." Her body sank bonelessly into the wingchair. "We lost Galen. We tried our best, and we lost him." She related the events of the evening, surprised she could do so. Maybe she was in shock, or just plain numb. Even Waldo was subdued, laying across her feet and not even begging to get into her lap.

Finally, Everett nodded, and put his handkerchief away. "You didn't lose Galen, you know. He gave his all. There's a difference."

"Did you know? Did he tell you what he was going to do?"

"Nope. But I guessed he might make that choice, considering the kind of man he was."

Was. Aunt Libby had told her repeatedly to blame the Rabisu, not herself. Kerri had no trouble summoning up all kinds of anger towards the murderous creature. She was glad Galen had somehow killed the evil thing, glad that it would never again steal innocent lives. Proud of the man she loved for the hero he was, for the stand he had selflessly taken. But surely, she ought to have done something, said something, thought of something...*more.*

Kerri managed to stay dry-eyed until she dragged herself to her room and shut the door behind her. The subtle *clunch* sound of the old latch had a terrible finality to it. Part of her life had just ended, a room in her heart had just been closed. There was no keeping the memories inside it, however. She'd barely taken three steps forward when she caught sight of the shower—and was undone. Tears broke loose like a dam giving way. Sinking to the floor, Kerri clutched her arms and rocked back and forth as great shuddering sobs shook her very bones until there was nothing left inside. Agony hollowed her from head to toe, pain carved out her soul like a Halloween pumpkin.

Finally, exhaustion dropped her into darkness, and she slept for a day and half on the floor in front of the bathroom.

After that initial catharsis, everyday life settled into what Kerri called *numb with periods of bleak* during the daylight hours. With Everett's encouragement, she reduced her counseling hours. After all, it was tough to be effective when she was as empty, barren, and stripped of substance as her otherworldly clients. Writing was impossible, and she was glad to be in the copyediting stages of her latest manuscript. Punctuation and formatting? That she could do like an emotionless robot.

All bets were off after night fell, however. Despite her best efforts, her defenses fell too, and grief could ravage her at will. Nightmares plagued her until she began staying awake until dawn, watching TV with Everett until she could be assured of a short but blessedly dreamless sleep. *Thank all the stars for Waldo.* She was exhausted, but she'd never have been able to face her bed at all without her loyal little pug. He seemed to understand her grief and all but glued himself to her side, twenty-four seven. His familiar wheezing and snoring was reassuring whenever she woke up, and his stocky little body felt solid and warm and comforting in her arms while he licked the tears from her cheeks. *Better than any teddy bear.*

But not better than what she was sorely missing…

How could she have forged such a powerful bond with a man she'd known for less than a month? The connection wasn't as simple as two halves of a whole. Instead, the sum of them together equaled something enormous and exceptional, far beyond anything she'd ever dared hope for.

She searched for that connection every time she went to the hospital, but couldn't find it. Galen's body still breathed, thanks to the respirator. Fred had hugged her and assured her that the strong body was still in excellent shape, but they both left the obvious unspoken—that it couldn't last. And she didn't need to ask to know that Galen's level of consciousness had been downgraded on the neurological scale.

During each visit, Kerri squeezed Galen's fingers, stroked his hands and face. Kissed his cheeks, his brow, the tip of his nose. *If only the spell could be broken with a kiss, like in the old fairy tales...* Sadly, it reminded her more and more of a trip to a wax museum with her cousins as a teenager. On a dare, she'd kissed one of the more realistic celebrity figures. *Elvis* had been neither cold nor warm, as empty of life as a big plastic doll. Galen's body wasn't much different. It was a representation, an image, a replica, of the man she loved.

And nothing more.

At home, Everett worked hard to be as helpful as possible. Thanks to the skills Galen had taught him, he picked up a lot of the slack in the cleaning department so her home didn't fall into complete ruin. Libby visited at least a couple times a week, bringing meals to share with Kerri, but the rest of the time, Everett managed to concoct variations on toast and eggs and canned soup. Best of all, he made coffee. It wasn't quite the magical brew that Galen had achieved, but it was pretty good. The old ghost brought refills to her office throughout the day as she worked on the latest copyedits she'd received for her manuscript.

Normally he left quickly after his "caffeine deliveries" so she could work, but today Everett lingered after she thanked him. "Kerri, you and I are friends, right? Good friends?"

She looked up in surprise. "Of course we are. In fact, we're family!"

"Well then, good friends or family would be saying what I'm saying now. It's been three months, and you've barely left the house. You hardly even leave your office except to watch TV with me. And you're still not sleeping much. You've got shadows under your eyes that Waldo could hide in. Not to mention that it's *March,* for Pete's sake, and there's a damn Christmas tree still standing in the living room. Now lemme finish—" He put up a hand as she tried to protest. "I know full well it's a little soon for anything to feel normal. In fact, after knowing and losing a man like Galen, I figure nothing's ever going to be quite the same again. And it shouldn't be. But you can't hide away from life forever."

"I'm *not* hiding, I'm working."

"I mean a *real* life."

"My work is important. My clients need me."

He nodded. "Can't deny that. You and that big, wise heart of yours are damn good at what you do. But you have to remember that *you need you* too."

"I don't get it."

"Look, you know some terrific dead people—present company included, of course—but if you're not careful, you just might bury yourself with us. Think about it. If you had a regular job, you'd have to take time for yourself, now wouldn't you? Vacations, weekends, hobbies, friends, that kind of thing."

It sounded overwhelming and her face must have shown it, because the old ghost raised a calming hand.

"Now, I'm not saying you should run off to Vegas or Tijuana. That's not your style. I'm just saying that you need to ease yourself back into life outside this house. Might take a year, might take ten, but Kerri-girl, *you gotta make a start.*

I figured it was time to bring you this." He held out an envelope with her name on it in bold masculine print, and her hands were suddenly nerveless. Understanding, Everett placed it carefully on the desk in front of her.

"He gave it to me before you left for the hospital that last night, just in case he didn't make it. Said I'd know when to give it to you. Like I said, seems like the right time."

He disappeared before she could do more than nod. Swallowing hard, Kerri fumbled for a letter opener.

* * * * *

Galen wasn't sure which he hated more, the infernal roiling mist or the weird rusty-orange color of it. *It's like being on Mars.* Except Mars would at least have something to see, places to go. He could count craters, or throw rocks, or even draw pictures in the sand to startle earth-bound astronomers. Instead, he was getting damned tired of all this nothingness. No up, no down, and no sense of time either. He had no idea if he'd been here a day, a month, or a whole frickin' year.

At least he didn't have to put up with Mr. Pointy Teeth. Galen had to admit that it had been satisfying to drain that soul-sucking monster dry, to wring every last particle of energy from the Rabisu until it dissipated like *a fart in a windstorm* (to borrow a favored phrase from his friend, Brody). And he was also honest enough to wish that the creature had suffered just a little more—hell, a *lot* more—for all the pain and sorrow and death it had brought to the human race.

Still, the important thing was that no one else would die because of it. No more lives destroyed, no more families mourning. *Except Kerri.* She was safe, he'd seen to that, and if he had to live in this wretched orange nothingness forever, it was well worth it. *But is she okay?* Dear god, he missed her... He might not be in a physical body, but it didn't keep him from hurting constantly like something vital had been amputated without anesthesia.

And what *had* happened to his body? *Am I dead now?* If so, this wasn't like any description of the afterlife he'd ever read. Surely his mom wouldn't have gone to a weird place like this. Besides, there was no one here but him. The monster had spoken of *walking between the worlds.* How many worlds were there? Had he broken through into some other dimension altogether, like a character in a science fiction story? Answerless, Galen wandered through the deep orange mists, hoping against hope he could find some physical feature, anything, even a frickin' ant hill, that might help him orient himself. But there didn't seem to be any solid ground. No sky either. *Even the Twilight Zone had stars...*

He smiled then, thinking of the letter he'd left with Everett.

* * * * *

"Number 12: Star-gazing at Natural Bridges National Monument in Utah," read Kerri. The envelope had contained "Galen McAllister's All-Purpose Bucket List", and she was genuinely intrigued by some of the entries. *Designated an International Dark Sky Park, the skies are free of light pollution. The Milky Way is readily visible most nights.* She'd often watched the moon from the back porch, enjoyed what stars she could see on clear winter nights. She'd gone camping a few times as a kid and marveled at the night sky— but had she *ever* seen the Milky Way?

It wasn't what she expected from a bucket list. There were no grandiose wishes at all—no trip to Europe, no crossing the Atlantic in a rowboat, no base jumping off a New York skyscraper. Most were simple pleasures, like looking for glass fishing floats on an Oregon beach, and spending a weekend on a Wisconsin dairy farm and sleeping in a hay loft. Some were little kindnesses like paying for a stranger's groceries, or taking coffee to a homeless person. And a few were downright ridiculous. *Number twenty-two: Fill a mayonnaise jar with vanilla pudding, and eat it with a spoon in public—*

For the first time in months, she laughed. Out loud. And the grief inside her eased just a little bit, allowing her to breathe without pain for a moment. With it came clarity in the form of a memory. Galen had extracted a promise from her the day they went looking for the Yule tree. *I'm supposed to be living for both of us…* Kerri looked down at her flannel pajamas, and ran a hand through her unruly hair, yelping as her fingers caught in a tangle. The clock said it was four in the afternoon, and she wasn't sure when she'd last showered. *Good grief. So far, I'm really falling down on the job.*

No wonder poor Everett had staged an intervention. The old ghost was right, she had to make a start. And the *how* was right here in her hands. "Okay, okay, I get it." Slowly, Kerri stood up. "It's not going to be easy, you know," she said, as if Galen was in the room with her. "I'm not going to feel like it sometimes. I'm still going to have bad days when I just can't stand that you're gone. But Galen McAllister, I'm going to do every last thing on your damn bucket list. Except maybe the mayo thing."

Oh, what the hell, maybe I'll do that too!

NINETEEN

"Well, it's not much of a change, but I'll take it." In truth, Galen was downright relieved to see the heavy orange mist gradually lighten and thin out in spots. Not that it was revealing anything to look at yet… He didn't know how long he'd been wandering, but he was starved for variety. Who'd have thought the afterlife would be so damn boring? Not to mention silent as a—well, as a *grave*. "Might as well look at the bright side, at least I'm getting sensory deprivation therapy for free. Some people have to pay for—"

He froze. Had he heard something? Galen strained to listen, hoping the sound would repeat itself. After a long moment, he sighed. "Great. Now my imagination is messing with me."

Suddenly he heard it again, faint but unmistakable: a dog was barking. *What the hell is a dog doing here of all places?* But he was already moving fast towards the sound. As he got closer, the orange fog dissipated until it was translucent in places. Light poured through it here and there, like dozens of opaque windows. He could hear the dog clearly now, its voice a low-pitched rumbling woof.

Dear God, it's Waldo!

It made no sense, but Galen didn't care. He shouted the pug's name, and was rewarded with a flurry of rapid-fire barks and excited yips that were easy to home in on. Sort of. Instead of finding the canine, Galen found a place where the retreating mist had revealed a large and fiery oval suspended vertically in mid-air like a mirror hung on a wall. Of course, there *was* no wall. He circled it warily, unable to determine what was holding it up. He couldn't see through the strange phenomenon either, but he could certainly hear the dog going berserk somewhere on the other side—or rather, within it—*and then he heard a human voice.*

"What in blue blazes has gotten into you, Waldo? You're supposed to be taking a leak, not raising the dead. Now shush, before the neighbors start complaining."

"*Everett!*" Galen shouted with everything he had. "Everett, over here!"

"Holy Moley. Galen-boy, is that you?"

"Yeah, it's me. I'm right here!" He could hear the old man trying to hush the near-hysterical pug.

Finally, Everett simply hollered over the incessant barking, "*Where* here? How come I can't see you?"

Shit. Galen didn't know the answer to either question. Before he could think of something, his friend spoke again—and his voice sounded much closer this time.

"Tell me you're not in that damn rhododendron bush? I thought I told you to steer clear of that crazy thing. You don't know where the hell it leads."

Galen resisted the impulse to laugh. *You don't know the half of it, bud.* "Trust me, I didn't plan this, but I'd sure like to get out of here. Any ideas?"

Without warning, a gnarled hand attached to a plaid-shirted arm extended through the shining disk, and waved about. "Take it, boy! I ain't got the energy to hold this open for long."

Galen dove for it, using some of his own energy to grasp Everett's spectral hand—and was yanked forward with astonishing speed. The orange mist of the featureless world was instantly left behind, but he wasn't in the backyard of Kerri's house. Instead, Galen found himself torn from his friend's grip and rocketed through a long corridor of bright light. No matter how hard he tried, he could neither slow down nor turn back. *Well damn, I must* really *be dead now. Head towards the light, right?*

This new disappointment threatened to crush him. He'd accepted being marooned in the strange orange world, until the billion-to-one event of finding Everett had given Galen a sudden huge dose of pure hope. Only to have that cruelly yanked away.

Can the pity party, McAllister. What happened to being satisfied that Kerri's safe? Well, he loved her like crazy and wanted to be with her, of course. But he also knew damn well that you couldn't always have everything you wanted. "Have a good life, Kerri," he whispered into the shining ether as he hurtled through it. "I hope you remember me, at least a little, but don't forget to move on." The words hurt like hell, but he meant every one of them.

As for the journey ahead, he supposed he should try to pay attention to the experience. *A person only gets to die once. Usually.* Galen fully expected things to get brighter as he approached whatever his final destination was. Moments later, he realized that the tunnel was narrowing. Was it his imagination or was the light getting dimmer?

"Just my luck to go the wrong direction. I wonder—"

Without any warning, he was left in total darkness. Worse, he couldn't breathe. Something was in the way, he couldn't get any damn air! Galen fought to get his hands to his throat, but his hands wouldn't obey him. He gagged hard. Christ, he was going to suffocate, he was—

"Galen! Galen, calm down! I'm right here, son."

The booming voice was familiar. *Fred?* He fought all the harder, determined to communicate. He had to have help before he…before he…

"Settle down, the air's there. I know it's plenty weird, like breathing through a garden hose, but I swear there's real air going into your lungs," said Fred, then switched tactics. "You're a firefighter, Galen. You've had some training on tanks, right? What happens when you panic?"

He *had* been trained in air management, and the answer was instinctive: a panicked firefighter used up his oxygen fast. *Okay, okay, not gonna suffocate here.* Galen talked to himself just as he'd coach a rookie. *Just dial down the alarm, and try to breathe normally.* Easier said than done, since he felt like a fish stranded on a shoal, but he tried his best. And discovered there actually *was* some oxygen being pushed into his lungs. As he began to relax a little, a new thought arose. *Wait a minute—since when do I need air?*

"Can you hear me, Mr. McAllister?" said another voice. A doctor. What was his name? "I want you to try opening your eyes."

Confused, Galen blinked—and discovered that his eyes had, indeed, been closed. Now he squinted into the overwhelming light even as his brain tried to process what was happening to him. *I'm in my* body. *Holy shit, I'm* inside *my body!*

Faces gradually swam into focus, faces he recognized from the hospital staff. Fred, bless him, was right there. Galen tried to lift his hand, but it was tied down! He yanked at whatever was holding his wrists, and tried to protest. Instead, he began gagging again.

"Easy, easy," said Fred. "Breathe with me now—in and out. In and out. Nice and slow. The air is there for you. Don't worry about the restraints, they're just temporary. We want that tube out of your throat as much as you do, but if you make a grab for it, you'll just injure yourself. Understand?" He spoke slowly and clearly, holding eye contact with Galen. "Let us do the work and take the breathing tube out properly. Then, I promise you, I'll personally undo your hands."

"He's right. We have to take this slow," said the doctor, and Galen recognized him now as Dr. Suri, the neurologist. "You trust this big guy, don't you?"

Their communication was a bit disjointed, like a badly dubbed movie. Galen heard their words, and a half-second later, comprehended them. But he got the message. He closed his eyes and let them do their work while he tried to wrap his head around his own personal miracle.

I have my body back!

Three hours, forty-two minutes, and fifty-five seconds later he was breathing on his own, and unrestrained. His throat felt like he'd swallowed a cactus, but he didn't care. To be able to feel anything at all was a frickin' privilege. It was a privilege, too, to have a friend like Fred. When the rest of the medical staff finally left the room, the big man lingered, even though his shift had ended long ago. He quickly filled Galen in on everything he'd been missing, things the other nurses and the doctors couldn't know.

Such as the fact that Galen had been MIA for more than *five months*. It hadn't felt like that long when he was trapped in the strange rust-colored world—unless you measured time in boredom instead of days. Small wonder that the doctors feared he'd regressed irretrievably, and had been discussing moving him to another care facility. Worse however, was that Fred, Libby, Everett, and most of all, Kerri, naturally believed Galen to be just plain *dead*, destroyed along with the Rabisu.

"K—" That was as far as he got before a coughing spasm nearly doubled him in half.

Immediately Fred raised his head for him, and coached him through the fit, then held the straw of his water bottle steady. Galen struggled just to get a few drops down. *Damn, you'd think little things like breathing and drinking would be like riding a bike...* The spell that had bound him had preserved his physical condition as if in suspended animation, but muscle tone wasn't everything. His body was completely out of practice when it came to following the simplest commands.

"And that's why Dr. Suri said *no talking*," said the big man. "Give it a couple of days, okay? Besides, I know darn well that it's *Kerri* you really wanted to ask about. She's okay, Galen. She went off on a camping trip in Utah until Thursday. Told her aunt she needed to look at the Milky Way for a while."

His eyes filled at that. He couldn't help it. *That's my girl!* She'd taken his bucket list seriously, and was getting on with the business of living.

"Gotta tell you, Libby and I were relieved to see it," continued Fred. "We all had a tough time when we thought you'd died, son. But Kerri took it hardest of all."

Galen closed his eyes. He would have given anything to have spared her that pain. But then, he'd thought himself a goner too. *Thursday... That's three, no,* four *days from now.* He turned an idea over in his head. Four days could be just enough time, especially if Fred and Libby helped him.

He motioned for a notepad, and began the laborious task of trying to hold a damn pencil.

* * * * *

As the sun set, Kerri followed the familiar highway that led into Spokane, and turned off on the road that would take her to her neighborhood. As much as she loved the outdoors, camping always gave her a renewed appreciation for her house. And for the first time in a long time, she'd be alone in it. It was going to be strange without Everett's TV blaring upstairs, and with no excited Waldo to greet her. But she'd been away a great deal over the past month or so, and her friends had naturally gravitated to spending time at her aunt's house.

Fred had been spending time there too. He got along great with Everett of course—*figures they'd like the same TV shows!* And if Kerri wasn't mistaken, there was more than friendship blossoming between Fred and Libby...

For herself, she was looking forward to a little alone time. She wanted to test herself, practice being in her home when the man she loved was no longer in it. Like a kid with a skinned knee, she was poking at the wound to see how deep it might still be.

How much it still bled.

It hurt, of course. It would probably always hurt some. But gazing into a flawless desert sky at night had started the healing. Her very first glimpse of the Milky Way had filled some of the emptiness in her even as it loosened some of the tight bands of pain that gripped her heart. The vast ribbon of stars had been a lifeline of sorts, just like all the other items on Galen's bucket list so far. It was still going to be hard to pick up the threads of everyday life and go on, but she would find a way. She'd promised Galen that much—

What the hell happened to my house?

She looked around wildly, thinking she'd made a wrong turn somewhere, but no, it was indeed her street, and her house. There were Christmas lights of every color outlining each eave and gable. Strings of sparkling lights framed every window and door—even the chimney!—and wrapped around the railings and pillars of the porch. On the ground, not a tree or bush was undecorated, and the entire fence was swagged with glittering garland.

As if that wasn't enough, a veritable *herd* of electronic reindeer, twinkling with hundreds of white bulbs, had taken over her front yard.

Kerri pulled over to the curb half a block away, and frowned as she studied her thoroughly illuminated property. Was this a joke? Some strange summertime prank? Who would do such a thing? Anyone who knew her well—even her fun-loving older brothers—would realize the sheer tactlessness of Yuletide décor right now; that season would never be quite the same for her again since losing Galen on Christmas Eve. And who *could* do such a thing? The old Victorian house was tall, just like its contemporaries up and down the street. It would take a lot of ladders plus many human hands to accomplish the job. Ghosts could have done it easily, of course, but Everett certainly wasn't responsible. Nor would he have permitted any of her clientele to take such liberties.

As she watched, new lights suddenly switched on to reveal a large and shining Christmas tree in her living room window! *Someone's inside…*

Feeling very much like one of the Three Bears discovering Goldilocks, Kerri slipped out of her car and marched down the sidewalk, determined to confront the intruder.

Once on the porch, she was surprised to find the entrance still magically warded. *No one should be able to get past that.* A wave of her hand caused the front door to swing open, and upbeat holiday music poured out like water through a sluice. It was hard to decide which was stranger, the fact that the serial decorator was not only still here but playing tunes, or how something that sounded so enjoyable in December could be so damn irritating in May. As a precaution, she mouthed one of Libby's more powerful spells, leaving off the very last word. If Kerri found herself in trouble, uttering that one word would activate the magic as surely as pulling a pin on a grenade would initiate an explosion.

But she sincerely hoped she got to sock the perpetrator first.

Her living room was a festival of lights, a warm golden ambience punctuated by vivid color. In the center of it stood an enormous tree—and at its base, a man knelt with his back to her, carefully prodding and rearranging stacks of gifts. She didn't recognize his clothing, something she always paid attention to since her otherworldly clients never changed theirs. She couldn't see through him either, even when she squinted. *Not a ghost.*

"Hey!" she shouted. "What are you doing in my—"

Her voice failed. Feeling blindly behind her, Kerri found the doorframe just in time and gripped it for support as her knees wobbled. *Galen McAllister* was standing tall in her living room, with his golden-brown eyes and irreverent grin. As if she'd only seen him a day ago, an hour ago, a heartbeat ago...

Galen! Her lips couldn't release the name her heart was screaming. She couldn't speak, couldn't move, could only stare at him with wide eyes. Unable to believe he was really there, yet terrified to break whatever spell had brought him back to her—or had sent her back in time to him.

Making calming motions with his hands, Galen was saying something to her as he took a step forward. But she couldn't hear a single word. Her brain was too busy processing dozens of little perceptions, like the fact that his hair was combed differently. His ubiquitous gray hoodie was gone, replaced with a shirt she'd never seen before. A jacket.

As the connections added up, the truth suddenly exploded across her senses like a lightning bolt. And she did the only thing she could do.

She tackled him.

They went down in a flurry of garland and gifts, knocking the tree over in a cascade of ornaments and still-twinkling lights, but Kerri hardly noticed. She was too busy holding, kissing, patting, grasping—even pinching—and exulting in the fact that Galen was not only back, but solid, tangible, physical, *real*.

"How?" was the only word she could manage as she brushed aside a string of tinsel to cover his face with frantic kisses.

"Long story short: I don't know. It was like a weird dream, and eventually I woke up inside my body."

"When?"

"While you were away camping. You did it, you know. You, and Libby, and Fred, and Everett too, even Waldo. You all did it. You made this possible."

"*You* did it. You killed the Rabisu." She framed his face with her hands. "But afterwards, nobody could find you. *I* couldn't find you and I thought you were *dead*." She'd thought she'd finished with crying, but fresh tears started in her eyes at the terrible word.

"Oh God, I'm so sorry. I tried to get back to you." He hugged her tightly to him with one arm. With the other, he brushed her hair from her face, and kissed her tears away with infinite tenderness. "It's okay now, it's all okay. I'm here. I'm right here, and damned if I'm going anywhere without you ever again."

He nuzzled gently over her forehead, her cheeks, the tip of her nose, her chin, the corners of her mouth. Soothing, comforting, sweet, a balm for all wounds. Kerri's heart eased, her spirit lightened as pain and sorrow released their hold completely. For the first time in what seemed like forever, she took a long, deep full breath. And another. Breathed in the sharp tang of the live tree, mingled with something else, something brand new: Galen's own warm, masculine scent.

"Are you *smelling* me?"

"You bet I am." She grabbed his lapels and buried her nose in his neck. He laughed until she kissed her way up to his mouth. She *loved* his mouth. Gone was the tingling buzz of energy he'd once substituted for it. Now Galen's lips were warm and firm. Real. And she couldn't get enough of them. Kerri moaned aloud as he deepened the kiss, as his tongue teased hers.

She pushed the jacket from his shoulders, pulled at his shirt, and he broke away to plant hot, moist kisses all the way down her throat. As he lingered at the little hollow there, he slid his hands beneath her thin sweater, then slid it up and away. Her bra followed quickly, but not fast enough to suit her. At the first brush of his fingertips on her bare skin, she was wet for him. Aching for him. Ready for him as he mouthed her nipple and sucked it hard.

"Now," Kerri insisted, as he allowed her to push him backwards. "I want you now, *right* now, dammit!"

She barely got his clothes out of the way before she was straddling him, rubbing herself up and down his very solid cock, slicking its velvety surface with her own need. The strength of her craving for him shook her, the overpowering imperative to be in one skin sang in her blood. *Now. Now, now, now…* She took him in, exulting as he stretched her, filled her, and somehow, all the little empty spots in her heart, her soul, were filled too.

He rolled with her then, and she wrapped her legs around him, ran her hands everywhere she could reach, drawing her nails lightly down his back and pinching his nipples hard. Galen rocked his hips, surged deeper, harder, as she urged him on. She needed this. She needed. She *was* need. And he was the answer to every question, the fulfillment of every want. His strong arms were tight around her, his lips over hers as he moved inside her. As he moved her.

They climbed together, pushing and pulling each other to an unseen brink. Then toppled from the cliff together like mated eagles, tumbling through bright layers of sky. Clasped. Merged.

One.

* * * * *

Galen opened one eye. His face was resting against Kerri's warm breast, his mouth within easy kissing distance of a delicate pink nipple. He opened the other eye, noted that he was sprawled with one leg thrown over both of hers. He had no idea how long they'd been lying like that, but it was definitely time to move. The glorious sensation of not knowing where one of them ended and the other began had finally given way to wondering just what *was* that thing jutting into his shoulder blade, and were they in any danger of being electrocuted since the tree lights were still on?

He stretched experimentally, discovered his hand still stroking over her body as if it couldn't bear to stop touching her. He couldn't blame it. Tops on his list of *things to do* was to catch up on a year's worth of doing exactly that— touching. Right up there with it was *being* touched. His throat tightened as he thought of how much it had meant to him to have Kerri's hands on him.

"Hey," she said, lifting her head to look at him. "How're you doing?"

"Hey yourself. I'm great—"

"And I know it," she grinned.

He laughed. "I'm thinking maybe we need a change of venue."

"I could get behind that idea. I've got a tree branch poking me in the butt."

The hapless tree rolled away from him as he rose, and more decorations bounced on the floor. "You're sure none of these are glass?"

"Only one is. And I can see it over there by the couch, so we're both safe. I think."

"More than I can say about the presents." He held up a squashed box.

It was her turn to laugh. "Who needs presents? I just got everything I ever wanted."

"Same here." He struggled to his feet, one leg still trapped in his jeans. Gave Kerri a hand up, then picked her sweater out of the debris, brushing some tinsel off the soft material before offering it to her. It didn't bother him a bit, of course, that she didn't put it on.

"I'm still wondering how you got all this Christmas stuff put up," she said. "And why?"

"The *how* was easy. I have friends with a fire truck."

"You didn't!"

"After Fred was satisfied I was okay—and I promised to come back for tests later—he busted me out of the hospital and drove me to the fire station. You missed one helluva party! Everyone who wasn't on shift showed up, plus guys from several other stations too. After the beer and pizza— dear God, I can't explain how incredible it was to taste pizza again!—I talked the guys who weren't on call into giving me a hand."

"And the truck" she asked.

"I admit, the truck was Brody's idea. It's an older one that's pretty much retired. It doesn't get used much, so it's not like we left anybody unequipped to deal with an emergency.

"By the way, before you ask, I cleared the whole decorating scheme with Everett first. Let me tell you, it's damn handy that he can answer the phone now! He helped a lot with the decorating too, although only Fred and I knew about that."

"I'll have to thank him. And all your friends."

"You can come with me and meet them when I give all this Christmas stuff back. I think everyone brought along every string of lights they owned. Although I'm thinking of keeping some of those reindeer…"

"We'll talk about the deer later. Tell me why we're having Christmas in May?"

"Because I wanted to pick up where we left off. It was our first Christmas together and I bailed—"

"Are you kidding me? You *saved* us. You saved everybody from the Rabisu by what you did."

"Okay, *saved us*, *bailed*, whatever. The point is, I wasn't there. And I wanted to be. And I still want to be. I want to be wherever you are, every day of my life. Period. I just figured maybe Christmas—Yule—was a good place to start. Kind of like going back in time so nothing between us gets lost."

She slid her arms around his waist so they were skin to skin. "Nothing was lost. You were in my heart all along."

He rested his cheek on her hair. "I know it. Same here. Which brings me to the other reason for all the holiday cheer. I had to set the stage for adding one more thing to my bucket list."

"What's that?"

"Marry Kerri Tollbrook."

"I could help you with that one." She looked up at him and grinned. "I've had a lot of practice lately in checking off the items on your list."

"Oh yeah? What about the mayonnaise jar?"

Crap. He *would* ask about that. "Um, didn't get that far."

"Good. We'll do it together. This afternoon at Riverside Park, right after you say *yes*."

"Yes to the mayo?" She feigned an innocent expression.

"Nice try." He pressed something small and cool into her hand. She looked and gasped in pleasure at the fiery opal in a silvery setting.

"I know diamonds are more traditional, but your Aunt Libby told me it's Beltane tonight. That it's a celebration of life. It sounded to me like the perfect beginning for us, and I wanted a stone associated with that. Naturally I had to draft your aunt into taking me shopping—but I picked this one out on my own."

"It's gorgeous. And meaningful. And *yes*."

He kissed her then, long and deep and slow. Finally, he scooped her up in his arms and headed for the stairs. A tinkling sound caused him to turn just in time to see another ornament rolling away from the ruins of the Christmas tree.

"That poor tree," said Kerri. "You know, it looked almost as good as our Yule tree did."

"Almost. I couldn't find one with two heads, though." His body was hollering at him to carry on to the bedroom, but the ruined tree bothered him. "Seems a shame to leave it in such bad shape, doesn't it?" He set her on her feet, kissed the top of her head, then turned towards the living room. It was tough to keep his expression neutral as he made tiny circling motions with his fingers and hands—and stole glances at Kerri's face.

Her expression was nothing short of priceless as the large tree suddenly floated up and righted itself in its stand. At

Galen's direction, strings of garland unwound and untangled in mid-air, then looped themselves in scalloped rows along the branches. A galaxy of ornaments spun around the tree like so many planets, until each of them found its perfect home and hooked itself in place. Ribboned packages leap-frogged over each other and stacked themselves neatly. Finally, Galen pointed at the star. Instantly it sprang from the floor and tumbled end over end until it came to rest on the treetop, glowing brightly.

There was a long, stunned silence. "Omigod," Kerri managed at last. "You can still—"

"Hey, I practiced every day for a whole year. It stands to reason I wouldn't forget how."

"Really? I wonder what else you remember..." She eyed Galen with speculation, her lips quirking. "You know, there's another holiday we missed out on. I've always wanted to ring in the New Year in the shower."

"What a coincidence. Me too," he said.

They raced each other up the stairs.

THE END

Thank you for reading *The Holiday Spirit*.

If you enjoyed this story (and I hope you did!), would you be kind enough to **leave a short review** on Amazon or Goodreads?

It only takes a couple of words to make a BIG difference.

Your reviews do more to bring my stories to the attention of new readers than any amount of advertising can ever achieve.

Thank you!

ACKNOWLEDGEMENTS

Huge hugs to Sharon Stogner at *Devil in the Details Editing* for her painstaking work on this story. Hopefully someday I WILL master quotation mark consistency, and perhaps even the troublesome *em dash*. (http://devilinthedetailsediting.com/)

Many thanks both to my beta readers and to my enthusiastic cheerleaders on this project: Katie Dalton, Ron Silvester, Samantha Grekul, Jaime Lovgren, Susan Grekul, Martina MacDonald, Dianne MacDonald, Erin Murphy, Nathanial Murphy, and Joy Smith. Some of you had to be extra patient with me as I tried to do too many things at once (as usual). Your kind understanding was appreciated more than you know.

Special appreciation goes to my agent, Stephany Evans of *Ayesha Pande Literary*, who generously donated her time to read the original short story for me. You rock!

Hats off to Fiona Jayde of *Fiona Jade Media* for the amazing cover she created for The Holiday Spirit. It's everything I hoped for. (http://fionajaydemedia.com/)

High-fives go out to each and every one of *Dani's Darklings*, my irrepressible and irreplaceable street team who turned into a wonderful posse of friends. Not only are you supportive, you've injected a great deal of fun into my writing life!

Last but never least, a round of MoonPies and Kool-Aid for the entire eclectic flock at the *I Smell Sheep* review blog and the *I Smell Sheep* clubhouse on Facebook. You guys always make me feel right at home. (http://www.ismellsheep.com/)

ALSO BY DANI HARPER

The Grim Series Novels

Storm Warrior

Storm Bound

Storm Warned

Storm Crossed

The Changeling Shapeshifter Series

Changeling Moon

Changeling Dream

Changeling Dawn

A Dark Wolf Novel

First Bite

The Haunted Holiday Series

The Holiday Spirit

ABOUT THE AUTHOR

Legend, lore, love, and magic. These are the hallmarks of Dani Harper's transformational tales of faeries, shapeshifters, ghosts, and more, for a mature audience.

A former newspaper editor, Dani's passion for all things supernatural led her to a second career writing fiction. There isn't anything she likes better than exploring myths and legends from many cultures, which serve to inspire her sizzling and suspenseful stories.

A longtime resident of the Canadian north and southeastern Alaska, she now lives in rural Washington with her retired mountain-man husband. Together they do battle with runaway garden gnomes, rampant fruit trees, and a roving herd of predatory chickens.

Harper's first foray into fiction began with a series of successful wolf-shifter novels: CHANGELING MOON (*a 2012 RITA finalist*), CHANGELING DREAM, and CHANGELING DAWN. A darker werewolf tale that brushes the edges of horror followed: FIRST BITE.

More recently she's been bringing ancient faery legends into modern-day America with The Grim Series: STORM WARRIOR (*a Top Ten Pick by Publishers Weekly*), STORM BOUND, STORM WARNED, and STORM CROSSED. A fifth book is in the works.

For those who love a ghostly love story: THE HOLIDAY SPIRIT, first in the Haunted Holiday Series.

You can see all Dani's books in one place on her Amazon Author Page at www.amazon.com/Dani-Harper/e/B004FD8RV2/, or check out her website at www.daniharper.com.

Keep up with the latest by subscribing to Dani's Official Newsletter at http://www.subscribepage.com/y1h2b9.

THE GRIM SERIES NOVELS

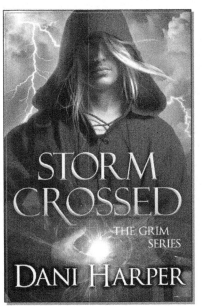

The fae are cunning, powerful and often cruel. The most beautiful among them are often the most deadly. Hidden far beneath the mortal world, the timeless faery realm plays by its own rules—and those rules can change on a whim. Now and again, the unpredictable residents of that mystical land cross the supernatural threshold...

In this enchanting romance series from Dani Harper, the ancient fae come face-to-face with modern-day humans and discover something far more potent than their strongest magic: love.

Turn the page to learn more about the latest standalone novel in this fantasy series...

STORM CROSSED

BOOK FOUR OF THE GRIM SERIES

A fae who doesn't believe in love.

A mortal who has no time for it.

And a desire that defies everything they know.

Heir to a noble fae house, Trahern is forced to watch helplessly as his twin brother is cruelly changed into a Grim—a death dog—as punishment for falling in love with the wrong person. Trahern doesn't believe love exists, but he will do anything to keep his brother alive—even join the Wild Hunt and ride the night skies of the human world.

Lissy Santiago-Callahan believes in love but has no time for it. She's busy juggling her career as an academic and her home life as a single mom to a young son with Asperger's. Her hectic life in sleepy Eastern Washington is made even more chaotic with the sudden arrival of a demanding fae and his unusual "dog."

Mortal and immortal have nothing in common, and the attraction between Lissy and Trahern surprises them both. But when their desire places Lissy and her child in the path of a deadly faery feud, will the connection last, or will their separate worlds prove too great a divide?

STORM CROSSED, and the other books in The Grim Series are available on Amazon in Kindle ebook, paperback, and MP3-CD.

Prefer an audiobook? You can find the entire series on Audible.com, narrated by actress Justine Eyre.

STORM CROSSED

UNEDITED EXCERPT

"What are you doing here?" demanded a new voice, a rich masculine voice, and every one of her friends fell silent.

Oh great, we've attracted a park ranger, thought Lissy as she turned to face this new issue. *How are we going to explain—*

It was no ranger. The first thing her eyes took in was a heavy black cloak, thrown back to reveal strange leather clothing. Ornately tooled and trimmed with silver, it hugged a lean frame.

No, some instinct decided, not lean but *lithe*. Lithe like a big cat, all coiled agility and snake-strike muscle in a deceptively relaxed package. She was forced to tilt her head to see the strong jaw that underscored the man's angular face—and the scar that ran diagonally across his throat.

Still, he could have been called handsome if it wasn't for a strange otherness to his perfect features that was impossible to describe. Human, yet decidedly not. And no human she knew boasted hair like that. Pulled into a thick braid that fell halfway down his back, it was white in the way that snow was white—not a single shade, but many.

She had to remind herself to breathe. This was no lost cosplay enthusiast or a Lord of the Rings extra, but an actual living, breathing member of the faery race. Somewhere in the back of her mind, a faint thought protested that such a thing was completely impossible. It wasn't very convincing, however, not with a flesh and blood dog the size of a goddamn Volkswagen already in front of her.

The man's pale hair glowed in the fire's light. A fistful of loose strands fell across his face, and beneath them his eyes were watchful, alert. A panther scanning for prey.

And he had found *her*.

The stranger's unnerving gaze lingered for only a moment before apparently dismissing her. "What are you doing here?" he asked again, and Lissy realized he spoke to the enormous canine behind her.

"Wait a sec. This is your dog? Yours?" All the shock and fear of the past few minutes transmuted into anger. She'd been prepared to die defending her child, and this man, this being, was totally responsible! It was as if a switch inside had been thrown. Normal-everyday-college-science-professor Lissy was abruptly replaced with I-will-savagely-tear-apart-ten-man-eating-lions-to-save-my-kid Lissy. She stepped directly into his line of sight. "What the hell were you thinking, letting this animal run around loose like that?" she demanded.

He merely looked around her, as if she was a tree or a bush or a goddamn rock, and that just ramped up her fury. "You! I'm talking to you!" Without thought but backed by a considerable amount of adrenaline, she shoved him with all her strength. The element of surprise gave her an extra advantage, and the tall man stumbled back a step.

Now she had his full attention.

Most nature documentaries she'd watched advised against locking stares with wild animals, yet Lissy stood her ground and met the stranger's riveting gaze boldly—despite her resentment at having to look up to do it. She all but bared her teeth as she stated her case: "You. Endangered. My. Son."

"There was no danger to your offspring. The hound does not devour mortals."

Was he mocking her with that imperious tone? "Yeah, well us mortals had no way of knowing that your monster dog doesn't snack on humans. You have no right to frighten people like that!"

"I require no rights from you. I ride with the Hunt."

Her gaze flicked to a faint ripple of movement at his side. The heavy cloak drew aside as if by its own volition, and the fae's hand casually rested on the handle of a large coil of plaited leather at his hip. Ghostly tongues of bluish light flickered continuously over the heavy whip, here then gone in an instant only to reappear in a different spot, as if they were living things.

Lissy could hear some gasps from her cluster of friends, and some hurried words between Morgan and Brooke. Though she'd never encountered the Wild Hunt herself, she knew that had to be what the stranger referred to. As a mere human, she should be utterly terrified.

Instead, she couldn't care less if he was a unicorn. "Well, I require a goddamn apology from you, Mister," she heard herself say, and folded her arms to wait.

All novels in The Grim Series are available on Amazon in

Kindle ebook, paperback, and MP3-CD.

You can also find the entire series on audiobook at Audible.com,

narrated by actress Justine Eyre.

Other Titles in The Grim Series

STORM WARNED

When Caris's unearthly musical talent attracts the attention of the Wild Hunt, the Welsh farm girl is stolen away to serve as a faery grim, a herald of death. Two centuries later, she's finally escaped back to the human world—and into the present-day life of a reclusive and heartbroken American musician.

Music was Liam's whole life—until a crushing betrayal left him desperate to flee the public eye. Yet long-dormant passions awaken within after a powerful storm strands a beautiful, strong-willed woman on his isolated farm. When a fae prince bent on ruling both human and faery realms threatens Caris's life, Liam must decide if he can finally believe in love again, not just for her sake—but for the sake of two worlds.

STORM BOUND

Kidnapped on his wedding day in the twelfth century and forced into a thousand years of servitude by a cold-hearted faery princess, rugged blacksmith Aidan dreams of nothing but revenge on his captor. Then the spell of a beautiful witch awakens him to the present day—and a passionate desire. But to build a future, he must first confront his past...

Modern witch and magic-shop owner Brooke doesn't think her life is missing anything, until a wayward enchantment lands a brooding medieval blacksmith in her spell room—and in her arms. Yet even after their passion proves to be truly magical, Aidan's first commitment is to vengeance. Now Brooke must team up with friends and ancient warriors alike—and push her own powers to their limits—to save her love from the wrath of an evil fae.

STORM WARRIOR

Enslaved for millennia by the masters of the Welsh faery realm, the fierce Celtic warrior Rhys is doomed to wander the earth forever. But when a brave beauty unwittingly breaks the enchantment, he is drawn into a strange new world...and an all-consuming desire.

Sensible Morgan doesn't believe in magic—until a mysterious being saves her from a fate worse than death, and life as she knows it changes forever. Now the man of her dreams has become flesh and blood, igniting a spark in Morgan's soul which science cannot explain. But even a love that transcends time may not be strong enough to withstand the power of an ancient curse.

Made in the USA
Monee, IL
21 February 2022

91588108R00157